The Princess of Dhagabad

The Princess of Dhagabad

BOOK I
THE SPIRITS OF THE ANCIENT SANDS

Anna Kashina

HERODIAS

NEW YORK LONDON

Published by HERODIAS, INC.
346 First Avenue, New York, NY 10009
HERODIAS, LTD. 24 Lacy Road, London, SW15 1NL
www.herodias.com

Manufactured in the United States of America
Design by Patty Harris
Illustration by Stephen Hickman

LIBRARY OF CONGRESS CATALOGING-IN-PUBLICATION DATA

Kashina, A.
    The princess of Dhagabad / Anna Kashina.-- 1st ed.
        p. cm. -- (The spirits of the ancient sands ; bk. 1)
    ISBN 1-928746-07-1
        1. Princesses--Fiction. I. Title.

PS3561.A6965 P7 2000
813'.54--dc21

                                                    00-024270

BRITISH LIBRARY CATALOGUING IN PUBLICATION DATA

A catalogue record of this book is available from the British Library

ISBN 1-928746-07-1

135798642

First edition

 # Contents

I
Mistress

II
Awakening

III
Ancient Bonds

I
Mistress

❋

WHITE ROBES

✿

*T*he rock in her hand shines and sparkles in the sun with all the colors of the rainbow. An ordinary piece of gravel, but the princess imagines it to be a priceless treasure that holds a mystery in its gray depths, a mystery that she as a mere mortal will never comprehend. Little specks of mica that cover the stone, brightly reflecting the beams of the sun, seem to her to be tiny windows into the unknown. Perhaps the rock traps someone's immortal soul? And each of its rough curves, so precisely fitting her palm, is really trying to tell her something....

The princess starts, hearing distant voices.

"Alamid told me the princess was playing in her favorite corner of the garden."

The voice belongs to Airagad, the youngest of the princess's nannies. She is always being sent on errands that involve fetching the princess from places that lie far away from the palace.

The princess recognizes the other deep and soft voice that answers Airagad.

"The sultaness wants to see her in half an hour."

Nimeth. A slave woman from the desert land Aeth. Her mother's best friend. According to rumors whispered in the palace—a witch...

"Over there, behind those bushes," Airagad says.

The princess hears the rustling of the footsteps on the gravel. Why can't they leave her alone? This is, after all, her free time. And she is already practically a grown-up! She will be twelve in a week, and they still seem to think she is a little girl. Why

1

would her mother send for her at this time? As far as she knows, the evening prayer is not due for a while.

Moving as noiselessly as she can, the princess crawls deep into the thick, sweetly smelling jasmine bushes that surround her favorite corner of the garden. Through the intertwining branches she can easily see the curve of the path running around a giant boulder, covered by the will of a skilled gardener with a gray-green pattern of succulent plants.

The two women emerge from behind the boulder and stop before an empty glade.

"I don't understand," Airagad says with dismay. Her round childish face frowns, and a little vertical line creases her forehead. "Alamid came back to the palace, and, just before, they were playing here together."

A barely visible smile appears on Nimeth's dark thin face. The princess knows this smile all too well. It means that Nimeth is very sure of herself and that nothing the princess can do will trick her.

"It seems that we will just have to leave," Nimeth says matter-of-factly.

"But..." Airagad turns her face to Nimeth and meets the look of her slanting dark eyes.

Nimeth runs her hands over her unusual outfit that the sultaness lets her wear in spite of Dhagabad's traditions—a long dark dress trimmed with silver along the neckline and the hem of the skirt. Her thin arm moves to straighten the hair that runs down her back in many thin braids, and her metal bracelet gleams in the sun. The metal bracelet—the sign of slavery. Airagad's arms, bare to the elbows, have no bracelets on them. Nannies are appointed not from the slave women but from the free servants.

"I am certain that the sultaness wouldn't mind going to the bazaar in the lower city without the princess," Nimeth says slowly and deliberately.

Bazaar! Lower city! Countless hours has the princess spent gazing at the barely visible colorful mass of the lower city from one of the higher balconies of the palace. Countless times she dreamed that a wizard from her favorite tale would appear beside her and with a mere wave of a hand transport her into this, as she thought, center of life, the focus of all miracles. She often begged her mother to take her along on one of her usual trips to the bazaar. And every one of those times she had to clench her fists to hold back the tears at the usual response: "You are too young for that." But today, finally, her dreams are coming true! It couldn't be any other way—she is almost twelve now, and no one, not even the sultaness herself, would dare to say that she is too young for such a trip.

Noisily tearing aside the jasmine branches, the princess pops out into the glade.

"Is it true, Nimeth? Is my mother really taking me to the bazaar?"

"Great gods! Princess! I didn't know you were here!" Nimeth's eyes narrow into slits. "Did you lose something in those bushes?"

"I…" The princess stops with an uneasy feeling that Nimeth sees right through all her tricks. "This rock," she says hopelessly, feeling that she is betraying a friend for the sake of a foolish lie. Witch or not, Nimeth is not easy to fool.

"A very valuable thing." Nimeth laughs, and the princess, hurt at this contempt toward her newly acquired treasure, blushes and hides the rock behind her back.

"I was hiding, Nimeth," she says, lowering her head. "I thought you and nanny wanted me to do something boring."

"Princess!" Airagad exclaims with reproach.

"I value your honesty, princess," Nimeth says in an icy voice, "but I will have to tell the sultaness of your doings, and I cannot guarantee that she will still want you to go with her to the bazaar."

The princess sighs and clenches the rock tighter in her hand.

With a sinking heart she follows Nimeth and Airagad down the winding garden path. To think that she was so close to fulfilling her wish to take a look at the mysterious world outside the palace and that her own foolishness may have robbed her of that wonderful chance!

The princess looks around at the garden, blooming wildly after the recent season of rains. Numerous paths, barely visible through the thick bushes, run everywhere like small streams of gravel to merge with one of the main alleys that run straight from the palace to the outside wall. The princess knows that the garden was designed as a halfcircle adjoining the back of the palace with three main alleys radiating from the three palace entrances like the beams that radiate from the rising sun. Or, with all those winding little paths connecting them, with all the lakes and ponds and hidden glades, the garden now looks more like a spiderweb, wild greenery sprouting out between its delicate silky threads. And, similar to a web, the princess feels the garden and the adjoining palace are now trapping her in their embrace like a little fly that sees the outside world from its silky prison but can never set itself free.

She looks at the domes and towers of the palace rising through the green cloud of trees. From the garden the palace looks completely different than it does from the front, where the central courtyard leads straight to the main gate and the palace plaza. From the front the palace looks like a single being, all harmony and flight, the big dome, which crowns the throne room and the main ceremonial hall, flowing smoothly into cascades of side galleries and towers that connect the central part of the palace to its four wings. But here, from the garden, the palace looks more like a random collection of small domed buildings that run in rounded steps up to the back of the central dome, barely visible through the forest of leaves and flowers. The princess's quarters, as well as her mother's, are located in the south wing and it is the south entrance to which Nimeth is now directing her firm steps, with Airagad and the princess in her wake. The princess sadly thinks how boring it is to go to her rooms now, leaving behind the greenery and heady aromas of the spring flowers that make her head swim with their rich sweetness. She clenches the little rock in her fist so hard that its rough edges, now warm and moist with the sweat of her palm, dig painfully into her skin.

The gaping doorway of the south wing brings a wave of cool air carrying smells of dust and stone and the barely perceptible aroma of bread baking in the kitchens. The princess steps after Nimeth into the cool shade of the hallway. After the bright sunlight of the garden she can barely see in the dim indoor light, and she nearly runs into Nimeth who suddenly stops right in front of her.

"I'll go tell the sultaness that the princess is on her way," Nimeth says. "Try not to take too long, princess. We have lost enough time already."

"But… " It is still unclear if the sultaness will want to take the princess along after her misbehavior. But if Nimeth is telling her not to take too long, it means… The princess fearfully looks up into Nimeth's slanting, impenetrable eyes.

"I'll see you soon, princess," Nimeth says gently, and her thin fingers lightly touch the princess's cheek. Blushing with joy, the princess turns and rushes along the corridor to catch up with the Nanny Airagad.

Why did you seek all this knowledge, why did you let unsolved problems make you restless, why did you spend years reading ancient books and marvel at learning another high truth if such is your reward? You shut your eyes, but your eyesight does not fail to see the endless dunes; you see the wind raising flamelike tongues of sand from their surface; you also see the intolerable crimson haze marking the spot where the sun should be. You praise your stars that this haze does not let you see the fiery disk, whose beams so mercilessly pierce your soul. And you ask yourself again and again: would you have followed this way to the end if you had known what this end would

be? Your mind is clinging to the tiniest straws: I did not know! If I had known, I would have stopped sooner! No one in his right mind would wish for such an end. And another thing: maybe this is not the end. Maybe somebody is trying to scare you to make you leave your uneven, slippery way of knowledge and turn to the simple and solid ways of the mortals…. And, along with a new blast of hot wind carrying another cloud of sand, along with the constant stream of sunbeams that never tire of piercing you, you realize in the depths of your tortured self that this is the end, the natural end, and if you had known it all beforehand, if you could have chosen even a thousand times, you would never have missed this eager search for the unknown, this marvel at learning the high truth, your growing wisdom and power, and the terrified admiration of the endless depths of eternity.

The thing that amazes the princess is *not* the big palace gate that opens for the first time for her, nor the palace plaza with its paving stones that run from the gate straight to al-Gulsulim mosque. Hitherto forbidden to her, the solemn grandeur of the gate and plaza seem like an extension of the palace itself, an enlarged version of the gates that open into the main ceremonial hall. While her litter is being carried across the plaza toward the left side of the mosque, she feels as if the whole procession is actually moving through the hall itself, its dome removed to reveal the clear blue of the cloudless sky. Only later, when the procession finally makes its way around the smoothly hewn walls of al-Gulsulim minarets into a real city street, do the princess's eyes open with wonder.

The *first* thing that amazes her is the blind emptiness of the walls.

From the mosque, the street runs down through the upper city of Dhagabad, where the palace is surrounded by the luxurious residences of rich and noble citizens, to the lower city, where the houses of merchants and commoners form a mesh-work of narrow curved streets and plazas. Further down, ships bring all kinds of goods up the River Hayyat el Bakr straight from the sea, and the busy port gradually merges with the Dhagabad bazaar.

From her lessons in local geography the princess knows that there are many streets that run eastward from the hills of the upper city to the lower areas of Dhagabad that surround the bazaar and the port. Only this main street runs more or less straight down into the heart of the bazaar itself, and it is used by everyone who needs to travel up to the palace or down to the port.

She always imagined the main street to be colorful, similar to the palace garden alleys in every way except for the crowds of richly dressed citizens, walking along in unhurried concen-tration or stopping to chat with their neighbors. She imagined every detail—down to the aroma of tobacco smoke rising from their pipes in thin wisps or near-perfect rings. Now all she finds is a wide cobbled road bordered by empty walls with no windows and a few tightly shut doors. Only by the slight changes in the shape and color of the walls can the princess see that there are indeed many houses or perhaps magnificent res-idences hiding behind the blindness. In some places she can catch a glimpse of a domed roof or the crown of a fruittree with pinkish-yellow, faintly aromatic blossoms. Sometimes a tightly clothed figure or two appear and press themselves against the wall, their heads lowered as they let the royal procession pass. Each appearance is preceded by the monotonous cry of Selim, the captain of the guard.

"Make way for the sultaness! Make way for the princess of Dhagabad!"

The farther down they go into the heart of the lower city, the more often the princess hears this cry, until it finally be-comes regular like the chant that muezzins sing from the tops of the minarets at the time of the evening prayer.

The procession crosses a bridge, allowing the princess a brief glance at the dark, turbid waters of Hayyat el Bakr. She knows that the river coils through Dhagabad like a snake, a quality that gave the river its name—Hayyat el Bakr, Serpent of the Sea. From the topmost balconies of the palace one can see it twist and bend through the city like a ribbon casually thrown on the ground. A ribbon that looks quite narrow where they are now passing—the official border between the upper and lower cities—and that widens considerably as it reaches the colorful turmoil of the port.

From her teachers the princess knows that Dhagabad is one of the biggest ports in existence, mainly because it is easily accessible by land from such places as Dimeshq, Megina, Halaby, and even the distant Avallahaim. The trade with these countries is one of the main reasons why Dhagabad is so powerful, but she also knows that it could be even more prosperous if Dhagabad had direct access to the sea. As it is, all the ships that travel up Hayyat el Bakr have to pay their passage fees to Veridue, a country that owns the lower reaches of the river all the way to the shores of the Southern Sea. She knows that there is some kind of trade agreement between Dhagabad and Veridue, enhanced by the great friendship between the two sultans of these countries, but that is part of the politics lesson she doesn't particularly like.

As they enter the lower city, the princess, used to the blind emptiness along the way, is amazed yet again. Instead of wide empty streets she suddenly finds herself surrounded by a lot of narrow side streets filled with people and boiling with action. Sitting straight on the pillows, rocking with the measured tread of the slaves carrying her litter, the princess looks around with wide-open eyes. Beyond her mother's litter ahead of her, the princess sees the first stalls with goods and the open doors of small shops. This part of town is occupied by the poorest merchants, placed at the lower levels of the hierarchy of the bazaar; but seeing the colorful variety of the rows of merchandise, the princess feels as if she has been suddenly transferred into the magical world of her favorite books. She thinks of herself as a beautiful maiden separated from her beloved or, perhaps, as a poor peasant girl suddenly finding herself surrounded by unimaginable wealth by the will of unknown powers. It seems to her that one of these bowing men should *definitely* be an evil sorcerer, that at any moment he will raise his head, and she will see his black beard and devilish grin. But no one they pass dares to raise his head for fear of seeing the faces of the slave women, wife, and daughter of the great sultan of Dhagabad. By law, anyone who sees them must be blinded on the spot, even though the faces of all women, including the princess, are covered with veils up to the eyes. Luckily, the princess thinks, this law does not apply to the inhabitants of the palace. It would have been so uncomfortable to have to always wear a veil that sticks to your nostrils every time you inhale and makes your face feel hot whenever you exhale! Wouldn't it be wonderful to be able to go to the lower city without a veil!

At this terribly indecent thought the princess throws an uneasy glance at nannies Airagad and Zulfia walking on either side of her litter, afraid that they may somehow hear her. Her eyes move over the tall, full figure of Zulfia on her right, over the double row of guards, toward the string of people standing against the walls, letting her see only their long robes and the very tops of the turbans on their bowed heads. Funny, she thinks, that when all these people bow their heads to avoid seeing her face, they at the same time make it impossible for her to see any faces of the inhabitants of the bazaar....

The guards reorganize from a double, sparse chain into a single, dense one. The street crowded with people has become so narrow the procession cannot possibly fit in a wide formation. All the space, as far as the eye can see, is now occupied by a colorful mass of people and goods. The princess cannot see any action, because all the action stops at their approach, but the variety of clothes, shapes, and objects makes her hold her breath in admiration. She sees merchants, buyers, money changers, onlookers, singers and dancers, thieves and respectable citizens—young and old, rich and poor—mixed to form a crowd, magnificent in its colorful disorder. She is trying to imagine herself in this crowd as one of the merchants, a part of this wonderful act, remembering all the books she read and fleshing out her knowledge with new substance. She inhales the odor of the bazaar—a mixed aroma of incense; jasmine and lavender oils; baked sesame seeds and roast lamb; the smell of horses, familiar to her from the palace stables; and the hitherto unknown smell of road dust. In the distance, in the widening side streets and plazas, in the crowd unaffected by the passage of the royal train, she sees fakirs and street dancers; baskets of fruits floating above heads that upon a closer look reveal eager young errand boys; and blind beggars, secretly eyeing handfuls of coins in their pockets from under their black eye patches. In some places she can see a heated argument between a merchant and a customer, sometimes even a fight between two claimants of the same rare object. The princess twists and turns on her pillows, trying not to miss a single detail.

The procession suddenly stops, her mother's litter is smoothly lowered to the ground, and the slave women who walk on both sides carefully help the sultaness up from the pillows. The princess's litter is also lowered, and she sees a door to a shop covered with a curtain and a tall thin man in a robe and a turban, bowing before them.

I hope he doesn't raise his head, the princess thinks. She sees the man's hands tremble slightly and imagines the horror of the idea that he can be cruelly punished any minute for a single upward glance.

The man raises his head and looks straight at the princess.

Her eyes immediately fill with tears. She wants to say something, but all she can produce is a sob. Overwhelmed by all the sights and emotions of the last hour, she suddenly feels completely incapable of behaving appropriately to her station.

"What happened, princess?" the sultaness asks with alarm.

The princess raises her eyes to the sultaness, trying very hard to gain control of her trembling lips.

"Will they blind him, mother?" she whispers.

"Of course not, princess!" The princess can sense in her mother's voice a smile hidden by the veil. "This is Mustafa, the cloth merchant. We came to see his goods."

Nanny Airagad gently puts her arm around the princess and gives her a handkerchief. Wiping her eyes and shivering, the princess clings to Airagad and follows the sultaness through the curtain into Mustafa's realm.

The big room they step into has no windows, and the princess, in spite of the abundance of artificial light, feels as if she has stepped right into the middle of the night. Several women, identifiable by the richness of their clothes as Mustafa's wives and daughters, bring out trays with tea and sweets. A smell of clove and cinnamon fills the air, and the princess, who hasn't eaten since lunch, feels her stomach growl. She throws a fearful glance at Airagad before picking from a tray a piece of freshly baked *pahlava*, sweet walnut paste wrapped in thin layer of crispy dough, still warm and moist from the oven. She knows she is not supposed to eat sweets before dinner, but today seems special.

True enough, Airagad doesn't seem to mind. Like everybody else in the room she seems preoccupied with something more important than tea, and the princess, carefully sipping from her cup, joins her in watching.

Mustafa and the two older women, probably his eldest wives, respectfully hold out rolls of beautiful cloth. Silk streams to the floor in purple waves; heavy folds of velvet shimmer in the uneven light of the lanterns.

The sultaness unfolds a white cloth with fine silver embroidery.

"How do you like it?" she asks the princess.

"Very much..." the princess says with uncertainty, not completely recovered from her unexpected tears.

"How much do we need, Zulbagad?" the sultaness asks.

One of the slave women, a strongly built middle-aged woman, separates herself from the suite and runs her deft, confident fingers along the cloth. The princess knows Zulbagad very well. A very skillful seamstress, she was bought from the caliph of Megina for the unthinkable price of three measures of gold. In spite of her being a slave, everyone in the palace, including the free servants, treats her with extreme respect. The sultaness, the same age as Zulbagad, is very fond of her and uses every opportunity to praise her amazing skills.

"Six cubits, your majesty," Zulbagad says with certainty.

The sultaness nods, and Mustafa takes the cloth into the depths of the room, making strange passes over it. The sultaness meanwhile whispers something to Zulbagad and Nimeth, throwing glances in the direction of the princess. The women serving them disappear for a minute and solemnly emerge carrying the most unusual cloth the princess has ever seen. Zulbagad runs her hand over the cloth, and the airy, cloudlike folds fall about in soft waves.

"This should be saved for the wedding," Nimeth says, shaking her head.

"For the wedding we'll find something else," the sultaness says with finality.

She turns and beckons the princess with her hand.

"Look at this cloth, princess."

The princess carefully holds out her hand and touches the airy folds. She feels a blow of warmth and light tingling. It feels as if she is finally fulfilling her wish to touch a cloud, a childhood wish before she learned that clouds are actually made of tiny droplets of water and that by touching a cloud one can only become wet and cold. Her wish coexists in her mind with this knowledge, useless like many other facts she learned. And now, finally, shaming the sages and scientists, human hands have created something so close to the cloud of her dreams.

"What beautiful cloth, mother," she whispers.

"For your twelfth birthday Zulbagad will make you a head shawl out of it," the sultaness says.

"For me?"

"You will wear it with an outfit she will make for you out of the silver-embroidered cloth we just selected."

"For me, mother? White robes?"

"You are a grown-up now, princess. You can start wearing white like all other young girls."

The princess sighs, not daring to believe her happiness. She always liked white, perhaps because none of her clothes had a single white spot on them. By Dhagabad tradition a person is only allowed to wear white upon reaching the age of adolescence. The reason for this tradition is undoubtedly very practical—what kind of a child would be able to wear white clothes for more than a few minutes without making them dirty? But at the same time, like any restriction, it arouses in little girls an unbearable desire, if not to wear, at least to try on, a white outfit.

"Five cubits," Zulbagad tells Mustafa.

The princess, filled with happiness, looks at the pile of packages in front of them. What a wonderful age—twelve, when she can go to the bazaar with her mother and wear a white outfit! How much she had wanted her twelfth birthday to come! A day when so many of her wishes will come true, including her most sacred one...

THE BRONZE BOTTLE

�֍

*I*t is not yet bedtime, but the palace is already absorbed in that dreamy twilight state of one who puts his head on the pillow, closes his eyes, and waits for sleep to come. Slowly sinking into restful slumber, the palace prepares for the big day of the celebration.

Escaping the watchful eyes of the nannies, busy with the preparations, the princess and Alamid are creeping noiselessly along the long corridor that leads from the South wing of the palace to the central chamber.

"What are you going to wear tomorrow?" Alamid asks, straightening her white head shawl. The friend of the young princess, Alamid is ten months older, having proudly donned her first white robe the summer before. This has been the subject of the princess's secret envy and of Alamid's open boast. And now, at this casual question of her older friend, the princess hurries to answer, swelling with pride:

"I will wear the white outfit Zulbagad made for me."

"Be careful not to stain it too much at the feast," Alamid says, not wanting to give the princess too much triumph. She doesn't like the way everybody fusses over the princess just because her father happens to be the sultan, and she never misses a chance to point out that she is older and more experienced.

The mention of the feast makes the princess's mouth water. They are now approaching the central chamber, and the smells from the kitchens are getting stronger by the minute. By the sweet aromas hanging in the air as they approach the door to the service area, the princess recognizes her favorite dish—roast quail served with a sour paste of sesame seeds, mint leaves, garlic, and vinegar.

"Let's go to the kitchen to see Naina," the princess suggests; and Alamid, forgetting her authoritative behavior, happily nods and hurries along to the service door.

The first thing they see as they enter the kitchen is a giant cauldron of *plov*—rice cooked with lamb, raisins, figs, and lots of other tasty things, yellow with saffron and oil, exuding a thick aroma of herbs and spices that momentarily enfolds them in its heady waves. *Plov* is the specialty of the master chef, without which no official feast is ever complete.

The milky steam from the cauldron half hides the cooks and their helpers, who are hurrying around in constant motion. The palace might be settling down to sleep, but here, in the kitchens, there can be no rest. In fact, everyone is so busy that for a while nobody notices the two girls standing by the door.

They see a large woman emerge from the misty depths of the room. Her hair is completely covered with a tight head shawl. Her round, kind face is red and little beads of sweat glisten on her forehead as she smiles, approaching them and wiping her hands on her apron.

"My goodness!" the woman exclaims in a deep voice. "Look who is here! It seems to be none other than the birthday girl herself!"

"Hello, Naina," Alamid says, stepping forward.

"Are we interrupting?" the princess asks quickly, feeling slightly uneasy at the sight of all the action.

"Of course not!" Naina exclaims. "I am always glad to see my little girls! Come in, have some *sankajat!*"

At the mention of her favorite sweet the princess's mouth waters more. Exchanging quick glances, the girls follow Naina through the kitchen, passing by the piles of freshly baked onion bread, sugared dates and tangerines, honey-stewed walnuts, almond cakes, and other dishes that make the princess hungry for a bedtime snack.

They enter a small pantry, where the smell of vinegar and spices hangs in the air, overwhelming all the rest. In the dim light of a single lantern they see rows of barrels with tightly sealed lids.

"Now, girls, you remember the rule," Naina says. "Only one each, otherwise your nannies are going to be really angry at me for giving you too many sweets."

"Which one will you have?" Alamid asks the princess, quickly stepping into the room.

Each barrel has a small label. The princess slowly moves along the row, craving the contents of each barrel and yet careful not to be too hasty in her choice. She enjoys reading the labels themselves, feeling like the queen of her small treasure trove of tastes. SOUR PLUM, SPICY PEACH, DRY TANGERINE, DRY OLIVE, SPICY OLIVE, SWEET AND SOUR OLIVE... Yes, that's what she feels like now—sweet and sour olive!

A new wave of vinegar smell hits her as she carefully lifts the lid and picks out a hard, slightly moist ball. She rubs the olive on her tongue, feeling the strong taste of vinegar, sugar, and cinnamon fill her mouth. *Sankajat* represents to her a whole world of sensations that she craves. She puts the olive in her cheek, carefully biting through its crispy flesh down to the stone to release more juice, sucking it slowly to make it last as long as possible. She watches Alamid, usually slower and more methodical in her choice, pull out of another barrel the brownish ball of a dried spicy apricot and put it into her mouth.

"There you go!" Naina smiles, patting both girls on their heads. "Now run along before your nannies come here looking for you!"

"Thank you, Naina," the princess says, forcing the words through the sweet-and-sour juice that fills her mouth. Normally they would have stayed to talk to their cookfriend, but today the kitchen is too busy, so they think they better leave.

Each absorbed in savoring their treats, the two girls slowly wander back to the central chamber.

"We should probably go back now," the princess says. "It is getting late."

"Come on," Alamid insists. "Let's go just a little bit further! Let's see the big ceremonial hall!"

Torn between her sense of duty and insatiable curiosity, the princess follows her friend further down the passage. In front of the ceremonial hall they run straight into armed guards, standing motionlessly on both sides of the big doors.

"Guards?" Alamid exclaims in surprise. "Why? What happened?"

"I don't know," the princess mutters, fearfully eyeing the big, motionless men. She never saw the guards so close-up before, and the sight of them somehow disturbs her. It seems that one of the guards, a muscular giant with long hair and a golden ring in his left ear, gives her a slight wink, and she hastily steps back, blushing.

"They are from the sultan's personal guard," Alamid observes. "Maybe the sultan is inside. Do you think they will be here all night?"

"I don't know," the princess whispers again, throwing another cautious glance at the long-haired guard. His handsome square-jawed face is now motionless; his eyes look straight ahead, as appropriate for a guard on duty.

"Princess! Here you are!"

She turns quickly to see Nanny Zulfia, tall and full figured, rushing out of the side passage with a reproachful look on her face.

"Nanny! I—"

"Where have you been? Went to see Naina again? I have been looking all over for you! It's your bedtime!" Words pour out of Zulfia like grains of rice out of a broken sack. She hastily leads the girls back into the passage; and the princess sees her full, rosy cheeks flush as she throws a glance at the longhaired guard.

"Why are there guards, nanny?" she asks.

"They are only getting ready for tomorrow," Zulfia explains. "They won't stand watch all night."

"But why do they have to be here at all? Why tomorrow?"

"You know what is going to happen here tomorrow," Zulfia says, looking away.

"What?" both girls ask simultaneously.

"You know, the ceremony." Zulfia's voice sounds reluctant, and realization slowly dawns upon the princess.

"You mean, because...," she half whispers.

"Yes, princess," Zulfia says firmly. "No one knows what is going to happen. And it is only right that his majesty take some precautions."

You are a spirit; you are all-powerful and nothing can possibly have any command over you. Why then does this merciless sun haunt you with its deadly beams? Why do the blowing sands pierce you with their endless grains? Why do these unbearable walls press upon you, making it impossible for you to break into the outside world but not preventing the outside world from torturing your all-powerful, helpless, eternal mind? And you, pressed in this tight space, again vainly call upon the highest powers that you could never comprehend in all your wisdom. And, being all-powerful and wise, you know that you have been imprisoned here because such is the order of things; you know that your prayers will not be heard, and that even the happiest savior called death cannot reach you here in this desert, beyond the world that you studied and understood all your life until you finally learned everything there was to know about it. And all that is left to you is your eternal mind; and all you can do is lose this mind, give it up, and then, maybe then... No, you will not be free from your imprisonment, but you could return to that world as a

slave and resume your existence in the place you know so well,
where the fiery sun and the piercing sands cannot penetrate the
bronze walls and where the suffering of the body and the suffer-
ing of the mind are kept apart.

"Bring me the bottle, nanny. I want to wish it good night."

"But, princess," Airagad says helplessly.

"Go ahead, bring it," the oldest nanny, Zeinab, grumbles. Zeinab used to look after the newborn sultan, the princess's father, and everyone in the palace respects her. "You know our girl. She will never settle down until she touches her bottle."

"Tell me about my grandmother, Nanny Zeinab."

Zeinab settles herself into an armchair near the princess's bed, crossing her wrinkled arms on her chest. Her white hair makes her dark skin look almost brown, resembling the bark of an ancient oak.

"Your grandmother, princess, was very old and very wise. She studied magic and everyone in the palace feared her. But in her heart she was kind, and she cared a great deal for the well-being of her subjects."

"How did she get the bottle, nanny?"

"I don't know, princess. It was before I came to the palace."

"Didn't you ever see what was inside?"

"The sultaness never opened the bottle in my presence. And, to my knowledge, in no one else's presence, either."

"Are you telling about her grandmother again?" Airagad asks, entering the room.

"The usual bedtime stories," Zeinab explains with good humor.

The princess, holding her breath, looks at the bottle in Airagad's hands. The old bronze softly glistens with age-darkened patterns in the weak light of the night lamps. Walking slowly and carefully, Airagad sets the bottle on a little table near the head of the bed.

The princess lightly touches the rough surface of the wax sealing the cork. The wax bears the imprint of the royal seal of Dhagabad—a coiled snake and an olive branch, except in the pattern pressed into the wax both the snake and the branch are depicted as a number of thin wavy lines.

"Before she died, your grandmother ordered the servants to bring her the bottle and some wax," Zeinab says. "She sealed the cork herself and pressed her royal signet ring to it. All the court was gathered beside her. Your mother and father were standing closest of all, right in front of her. And you were there, too, princess, although you were only a year old and Nanny Zulfia was holding you in her arms. Your grandmother turned to the whole court and said: 'I wish to leave this bottle to my granddaughter, the princess of Dhagabad. Let the princess open it on the day she turns twelve. And let no one touch the cork until that very day.' Your grandmother moved her hand over the cork and it seemed to all of us that we heard a soft and sad sigh. But no one dared to say anything. It was so quiet in the room, princess, that even a mouse's footsteps would have been heard."

"How many times have you told this story to the princess, Zeinab?" Airagad asks with the impatience of youth.

"I don't remember." Zeinab slowly shakes her head. "Children like to listen to the same stories again and again."

Enchanted, the princess runs her hand down the cold, smooth bronze, feeling with her fingers every turn of the unusual carving. She is terribly curious to know what's inside. All through her conscious life this bottle has been the most mysterious and the most desired object in the entire palace, but she never thought of disobeying her grandmother. If she wished for the princess to open the bottle on the day she turns twelve, let it be so. Especially because that day is so close! Finally this unbearable expectation will come to an end! The princess's heart beats faster, scaring away sleepiness.

"Tell me how my grandmother talked to the bottle, Nanny Zeinab."

"I only saw it once, princess," Zeinab says obediently. "Your father was being naughty, and when he was like that no one except your grandmother could bring him to order. Because of that, I had to go to her at an unusual hour. I knocked, but no one answered. Then I decided to look inside...."

"And what did you see?" the princess asks, completely absorbed in the nanny's story and forgetting that she has already heard it at least a hundred times.

"The bottle was standing on the table in the middle of the room. It was open, and the cork was lying beside it, but I couldn't see anything except the completely dark opening of the bottle neck. I heard the sultaness mutter something, but either I couldn't make out the words, or the words themselves were impossible to understand, as if spoken in another language. She spoke for a long time, not noticing my presence. Then she fell silent and bent her head to the side, as if waiting for an answer. And at that moment I heard a whisper coming from the bottle, or so it seemed to me at the time."

"A whisper?" The princess's eyes are shining; she is hanging on every word.

"The bottle was answering her." Nanny Zeinab seems to be completely absorbed in the story herself. "And I still couldn't make out the words. I wanted to come closer, and in my excitement I bumped into the sofa and dropped a pillow, a single pillow...." The nanny stops, seemingly overwhelmed by her own story.

"What happened next?"

"Your grandmother jumped up, as if stung by something. Her expression was so horrible that I couldn't even move. She beckoned me with her finger, but my knees trembled so much that I couldn't obey. And then she asked me what I was doing in her quarters. I said that her son, the sultan, was being naughty again and that we couldn't put him to bed. I was expecting all kinds of terrible punishments to fall on me right there and then... but your grandmother just promised that she would be along soon and sent me away. And never again did she mention that episode."

The princess looks at the bottle again. How unbearable it sometimes is to wait! How much she wants to learn immediately what's hidden inside!

"You had your story, princess. Now, off to sleep!" Airagad says mercilessly.

"Alamid told me she goes to bed a whole hour later than me!" The princess, like a drowning man, is grabbing at straws. But it is useless to argue with Nanny Airagad.

"Alamid is almost a whole year older than you are, princess. And she has her own parents. If her father, the master of ceremonies, had ordered her nanny to put her to bed an hour earlier, that's the way it would have been. You are not a boy, despite what his majesty the sultan may think."

"She is too young to understand," Zeinab grumbles, tucking the princess in. "What do fathers know about children?"

"Can the bottle stay with me tonight?" the princess asks.

"Be patient, princess, just a little while longer. After your birthday you will be in complete command of your bottle."

"Everything is ready for the ceremony tomorrow, your majesty."

Nimeth noiselessly appears by the door in the royal quarters. Her dark dress and skin are almost invisible against the dark outline of the doorway, and only the silver around her neck and at the hem of her skirt shimmers in the light of the lanterns.

"I am so worried about the princess, Nimeth," the sultaness says, impatiently standing up. Her long nightdress and loose hair, slightly touched by early gray, cling to her rounding figure. "She is almost twelve, and she still plays mostly by herself. And her toys are so strange—flowers and rocks…"

"Most parents would be proud of such a well-learned daughter, your majesty."

"I am very proud of her, Nimeth." The sultaness sits down again, throwing back from her forehead a stiff black curl.

Nimeth looks affectionately at her mistress and friend, at

her fresh rosy cheeks, at the black curls with scarcely shimmering silver strands, at the roundness of her figure, more revealed than hidden by her light nightdress.

"She rarely laughs, Nimeth," the sultaness continues. "And she worries about others so much! Remember how she was crying at the bazaar when she thought that Mustafa broke the law?"

"The princess is a rare creature, your majesty. Do you know the palace rumors that she is related to the peri?"

"I have heard it said, Nimeth. She is so thin, so fragile. And her white skin makes her look almost transparent. I know she will grow up to be a rare beauty, Nimeth! Blue eyes and black hair is such an unusual combination. Only it won't be easy for her, she is such a reserved person."

"She often plays with Alamid, the daughter of the master of ceremonies."

"Not so often, the nannies tell me. Alamid is a completely different girl. I am so worried for the princess, Nimeth. Why does the sultan think she can be treated like a boy? Why does she have to be raised in such freedom? All those history lessons, lonely walks in the garden, equal conversations with men in the palace. I was told the sultan even plans to teach her horse riding! I think it is completely unnatural." The sultaness drops her hands in frustration.

"You know how hard the sultan takes the fact that he cannot have a son, your majesty." Nimeth's voice wavers and dies, leaving the room in stiff silence.

They both remember all too well how, a long time ago, the sultaness nearly lost her life giving birth to a stillborn baby boy. How, a year later, she finally bore a son who died in two days, leaving her barren and her husband, the sultan, completely heartbroken. The princess, their firstborn, was three at the time, and she remembers nothing of these futile attempts to obtain a brother for her and a male heir to the throne of Dhagabad. Ever since that day the sultan insisted on giving the princess almost as much freedom and exactly as much education as he would give a crown prince, thus unofficially naming her the heiress to the throne. Perhaps things could have been different if one of the sultan's concubines had borne him a son. Perhaps, he could even forsake the law and make a lucky concubine his new sultaness. But all his sons by his concubines were born dead, leaving him surrounded by numerous daughters, making him lose his hopes, making him bitterly disappointed in his own abilities as a man.

"I almost wish somebody else would give him a son, Nimeth," the sultaness says softly. "The princess is too fragile for such responsibility."

"She is a very rare creature, your majesty," Nimeth says again. "She will be perfect for the part. You'll see. After all, it is not she but her husband who will rule. And even if it were entirely up to her, she would not be the first woman ruler in this palace."

"You mean... the sultan's mother?"

"Yes. How do you think she became the sultaness? Her father did not have any sons. It is obviously a curse on their whole dynasty. Why do you think she wished for the princess to inherit her favorite bottle? Why didn't she leave it to the sultan's heir in general, for instance?"

"There was no heir at the time."

"And nothing has changed since then. I am wondering if she had reasons to think there never would be a son. She was, after all, said to be a witch...."

"And this is precisely why I worry about the princess so much, Nimeth! Tomorrow she will open this strange bottle. There could be *anything* hidden inside! I never trusted the sultan's mother. Have you ever heard what people in the palace say?"

"Don't believe the gossips, your majesty."

"I don't know what to believe, Nimeth. I know that the sultan is putting extra guards in the ceremonial hall. And I heard the slave women whisper among themselves that there was a curse on the bottle. As if the guards could do anything against a curse!"

"Surely you don't think that a grandmother would place a curse on her own granddaughter, your majesty?"

"I simply don't know, Nimeth. I even heard the rumors that the old sultaness stole the princess's soul when she was born, and concealed the stolen soul in the bottle. And you know, Nimeth—when I see how the princess never laughs and always plays alone, I begin to believe it."

"Nonsense, your majesty. Why would you care about silly rumors?"

"In any case, if after opening the bottle the princess starts to laugh more often, I will be ready to believe that she simply got her soul back."

"But why would the old sultaness want to steal the princess's soul?"

"You remember what a horrible woman she was, Nimeth! Sometimes it looked as if she simply enjoyed harming people. And at other times she seemed to regret it. Perhaps she could not resist the pleasure of harming even her little granddaughter but, feeling guilty about it, was decent enough to leave behind the means of correcting the damage. Or even worse, what if the bottle hides the spirit of the old woman herself? What if this spirit will possess the princess as soon as she removes the cork?"

"The only thing I can say, your majesty, is that I am not at all surprised that the princess has such a wild imagination. I know precisely where she got it from!"

"It is so hard to have children and keep your sanity, Nimeth!"

"It will be all right, your majesty. Try to get some sleep."

The princess often has the same dream. And tonight, on the eve of her twelfth birthday, the dream seems to be more real than before. She is walking in a desert, wavy dunes run beyond the horizon, and the low sun is concealed by a hot crimson haze; but her feet do not sink into the sand, and the heat cannot touch her. She hears the tinkling of water and the singing of birds; she smells sweet aromas, as if she is walking not in a desert but in a beautiful garden.

She knows she has to meet someone here, but as she is looking around searchingly, she can see only the dunes; there is no one there. And then she sees the temple. Dark ancient stones compose its walls. Giant domes run in cascades toward a row of columns surrounding the temple. A chilling cold comes from inside the semidarkness of the columnar gallery.

She has to go there. She has to enter the temple, and she walks toward it along the invisible path. She comes closer and closer. She can see the entrance and she knows that inside the temple there is something she needs, something she cannot live without. She can see giant rough steps covered with small cracks, but she is not able to set foot on them...and suddenly she wakes up in frustrated despair, not knowing what is hidden inside the temple but realizing that she must enter it at any cost.

JUNIPER SMOKE

✿

The great ceremonial hall comprises in large part the central palace and has enough windows to be illuminated entirely by natural light. But today, on the princess's twelfth birthday, the hall is filled with so many lanterns and torches that their light seems to brighten the day itself—as if another sun had risen in the upper city, lighting the garden and the palace plaza with special holiday glow.

The ceremony is scheduled to begin at noon, but the main doors to the hall were opened at ten to accommodate the courtiers and noblemen of Dhagabad, dressed in their best holiday finery. A row of low tables with pillows extends along the periphery of the hall, prepared for the hundreds of guests invited to the birthday feast. At the end of the hall the royal canopy, shining with golden embroidery, awaits the sultan whenever he chooses to make his appearance. The arrangement leaves the center of the hall empty for everyone to stand around and chat, filling the air with the low buzz of a beehive.

Servants are scurrying around with dishes of fruit and *sankajat*, and trays of sour rye cakes and sweets, offering them to the guests. Musicians in the corner are playing a slow tune and seven Ghullian dancing girls move sensuously around the room, twisting and bending to the rhythm of an exotic dance. Their dark, smooth bodies, glistening with aromatic oils, are barely covered, raising in the guests desires of a different order than the delicious aromas wafting in from the kitchens.

Only one thing disturbs the celebratory mood—the presence of fully armed guards standing motionless, around a marble table at the center of the hall. The courtiers and other guests circling around the room instinctively keep their distance. It is the table, the guards, as well as the mysterious ceremony itself that occupies their minds and conversations, leaving no room for usual subjects like the feast, the dancing girls, or the beauty of the princess.

Noon draws near, and the rumors and gossip that started here early in the morning are inevitably approaching their highest pitch. The most fearful are starting to doubt whether they should be present at all. Is it really so important to know what is hidden inside the cursed bottle? Would the sultan really notice their absence at the royal celebration? After all, they *could* lock themselves in the safety of their quarters and wait for an account of the event! But so far nobody is leaving.

The princess is standing in front of the mirror in her quarters, trembling with joy at the sight of her new white outfit. The blouse and pants made by the skillful Zulbagad from Mustafa's cloth shine with silver embroidery. The slave women are fixing the white cloudlike shawl with a sparkling diamond hairpin in her black hair, wrapped in braids around her head. The princess watches the misty waves of cloth flow down to her feet, shod in light silver sandals, enhancing the transparent fragility of her small figure. She imagines herself to be a fairy of the magic tales, a peri, capable of gliding on the smooth surface of a mountain lake as if it were solid ground.

She tries to imagine what is now happening in the ceremonial hall. Before opening her gifts and sharing her birthday feast, she is finally, after so many years of waiting, going to open her mysterious bottle. She doesn't share in the fearful mood filling the great hall; she doesn't care about why her father, the sultan, has put armed guards at the center of her celebration. For years she wondered what was hidden inside the bottle, and today she doesn't want to think of her guesses anymore. Today she will cast them all aside and see the contents of the bottle with her own eyes. *What if something totally uninteresting is in there?* she thinks. *What if the bottle is empty? What if...? No, if any of those were the case, why would my grandmother make such a point of keeping the bottle closed?* No, she knows that there is something very exciting inside the bottle, and today she is finally going to learn what it is! She shivers with expectation, pulling her shawl around her, overwhelmed by anxiety matching the mood that now rules the great ceremonial hall.

In the hall, the bright sound of fanfare breaks the unbearable tension. The doors at the end swing open to reveal a long corridor. And at the very end of the corridor two figures appear from a great distance, clad in shining holiday robes: the sultan and the sultaness of Dhagabad. The sultan—tall with his bushy black beard sticking straight out from his dark face, a curved saber at his belt, and a giant ruby shining in the folds of his turban—is terrifying like a proper warrior and ruler. And the sultaness—full figured and majestic in her white-and-gold robes, with a diadem of pearls and rubies crowning her shawl-covered hair—is beautiful like a houri from heaven, like a proper queen and mother.

They slowly and solemnly enter the hall, replying with nods to the low bows of the courtiers. Through the parted crowd that holds absolutely still they walk to the rise at the end of the hall, where under the royal canopy many pillows are piled on the floor. While they walk through the hall to take their places on the pillows and the crowd rearranges itself for a ceremonial greeting, the most careful observers see the truth: the sultan and the sultaness are just as nervous as everyone else.

Amid the general tension the usual formula of greeting acquires the two-dimensional solemnity of a slow court dance.

"Chamar Ali, the great sultan of Dhagabad, greets his subjects!"

Backs are bent for a moment, and then, as if obeying an invisible signal, straighten up into the next movement. Arms slowly move to point forward and up, toward the canopy, and the hall freezes in a new figure of the dance.

"May he live forever!"

And again everything starts to move. The courtiers resume their conversations, throwing side glances at the canopy, and the tension grows and grows. As the sultan finally gives the long-awaited signal, as the Ghullian slaves with knots of muscle rippling under their black skin carry the marble table closer to the royal canopy and place a gold-embroidered pillow upon it, as the slave women carefully set on the pillow the mysterious bronze bottle, the silence of the hall becomes almost palpable. A barely noticeable sigh of relief accompanies the long-expected words that sound clearly in the giant hall:

"The princess of Dhagabad!"

The tiny figure clad in shining white robes solemnly walks into the hall. She is barely twelve, but no one doubts that long before she comes of age she will surpass all the legendary beauties Dhagabad has ever known. Her movements bring to mind the awkward purity and pointed alertness of a purebred foal. Her fine features, somewhat exaggerated in a girl, add to the anticipation of her grown-up beauty—her thin oval face; her crown of black hair; her smooth skin, unusually white for the hot desert climate; and her huge dark-blue eyes that both a poet and a simple shopkeeper could compare only to the deep luster of precious sapphires. On top of it all, the princess has the vivid sparkle of sharp intelligence that gives her classic features a special inner glow, making it clear beyond any doubt that the princess of Dhagabad has no match. And today in her birthday robes she is shining in the palace ceremonial hall like a beautiful jewel. Watching in transfixed admiration the movements of their young mistress—how she first approaches her parents to accept their blessing, and finally turns to the marble table—the spectators forget their anxiety for a while.

The nannies and the slave women of the princess's suite stop a few paces short of the marble table, allowing the princess alone to walk inside the ring of guards. The princess slowly approaches the bottle. Her heart is beating so fast she can barely gather enough strength to touch her treasure. She looks at the mysterious carving on the ancient bronze, the sealing wax with its signet imprint, and the notch where the snake's curves touch the leaves of the olive branch. As if in a dream she reaches out to the bottle, feeling the familiar cold metal under her fingers. Her hand runs up the smooth surface of the bronze to stop right at the sealed opening of the bottleneck.

The princess throws a glance at the marble table, noticing a golden dagger prudently set here, the dagger of the kind used to cut paper and open letters. She tries to interrupt the smooth movement of her fingers up the bottle, to break contact with the ancient mysterious object, to take up the golden dagger so conveniently prepared for her. But some strange force keeps her hand sliding up the metal, in spite of her certainty that her thin fingers will slip off the bottle without disturbing her grandmother's seal.

The cork pops out with the ease of a silk shawl pulled through a smooth golden ring. The empty bottle neck now looks like a black hole, an expectant opening into unknown depths. And from inside this black abyss, slowly and lazily twisting and curling into rings, rise wisps of white smoke. The smoke pours out of the bottle, filling the center of the hall, flooding it with a heady juniper smell. White clouds circle around, enfolding the princess, creating a curtain that for a while separates the marble table and the space surrounding it from the crowd of courtiers, frozen in terrified stillness.

Suddenly the clouds disappear without a trace, as if blown away by an immaterial wind.

The crowd gasps.

A man kneels before the princess!

His dark handsome face, strong muscular figure, the feline grace of his courteous bow, and his white shirt and dark pants of silk could easily belong to a nobleman or a traveling prince. But there are no signs of distinction on his simple garments. His thick dark hair is cut much shorter than is customary for the sons of noble families. His feet are bare, which sharply contradicts the refinement of his clothes. A whisper comes across the hall, and the courtiers stretch their necks trying to have a better look at the mysterious stranger. And then the stranger raises his arms, and everyone immediately sees the sign of distinction they searched for. A fatal sign. The wrists of the newcomer are clad in iron. The foreign prince is a slave.

The stranger speaks, dismissing all doubts, easily covering the murmur rising in the hall with his rich deep voice.

"I am your slave, mistress."

"Who are you?" the princess whispers in bewilderment.

"My name is Hasan, mistress. I am a djinn."

You are all-powerful and the law of nature forbids an all-powerful one to belong to himself. It would be too dangerous for the world. Submitting to the forces that protect the world from danger, you are doomed to become a slave at the very moment you become all-powerful. You become a slave of a tiny container, whose size and shape are determined the same way your looks were determined at your birth. You die in the physical sense but your spirit becomes immortal. And, for all the knowledge that was granted to you in your life, you, imprisoned in your container, are now doomed to bear the suffering, the joint suffering of body and mind. This suffering gives birth to a new spirit, a spirit that puts its ultimate power at peace with its imprisonment, a spirit that belongs entirely to the container, just as the container can entirely belong to anyone who is somehow able to take possession of it.

The container that imprisons your spirit was created in a desert that lies beyond the known world, the endless desert that does not know time or space, where only the hot sands under the rise and fall of the eternal sun form mountainous dunes under the blasts of the merciless wind. You are doomed to remain here, endlessly enduring your transformation and submitting, infinitely submitting.... Only when you submit and surrender completely may you return to the world you know, this time not as a powerful wizard or as a mortal fool, but as an immortal spirit, a slave of a container, able to create any miracle at the order of any mortal, but not of your own will.

And when, among the blasts of wind and sand, the burning needles that pierce you through, you are picked up by the strong hand of a woman with a commanding posture—a woman that appeared god knows how in this empty cruel desert—when she wraps your container in a rough cloth, finally shielding you from your tormentors, when she brings you to a cool room, with tinkling fountains and giant, magnificently thick leaves rustling outside the window, and removes the deeply set cork, so that in a moment you are able to become one with the cool air and to unravel all the giant power of your spirit, you fall to your knees at the feet of this strange woman and, not wanting to notice the wicked lines around her mouth, the greedy sparks in her dark impenetrable eyes, you exclaim:

"I am your slave, mistress!"

In bewilderment the princess studies the man kneeling before her. Of course, she knows about djinns. Many of her favorite books tell of those mighty slaves imprisoned in tiny containers and destined to grant wishes to unfair and demanding masters. She always wished that these mysterious creatures existed in real life. But she never thought that she would become the owner of one of them! And now, looking at the man in front of her—who doesn't really differ in looks from any other palace slave except, perhaps, in the simple elegance of his clothes and in some special inner dignity—she doesn't really know what to do.

"Rise, Hasan," she whispers.

The djinn springs lightly up from the floor and stands before her.

His movement breaks the enchanted stillness of the courtiers. The crowd starts to move; the guards place hands on their weapons, searching for a sign from their captain who stands close to the royal canopy; nannies step forward protectively surrounding their ward. The sultaness starts to say something hotly to the sultan, backed by the increasing rumble of the courtiers. And the princess, motionless amid all the bustle around her, has no strength to draw her eyes from the face of her new slave.

The direct gaze of his quiet gray eyes, along with the regular features of his face, could belong to any young man she has ever seen; but something in them sends shivers through her whole body. She feels herself sinking into his eyes, as if falling into an abyss, confronting depths of time she cannot comprehend in her naïveté. She feels a wisdom many thousands of times greater than she could ever comprehend. She shudders at the thought that this perfect creature was forced to endure the imprisonment in the bronze bottle, shaking from her memory of how stupidly she behaved when he could most likely see and hear everything that happened. At the same time, she feels in the depths of her heart some disturbingly strange pleasure in knowing that someone so perfect and wise belongs to her completely and she can do anything she wants with him....

The last thought makes her blush with shame. How can she think of commanding this ancient wizard, even in his youthful shape? How dare she, looking into his eyes, overwhelmed by their depth, think of her own wishes? How can she, standing near a source of such power, even remember her own life? She knows nothing about this creature that books describe as a spirit, an element, a demon burdened by his slavery and thinking only of destroying the world. But sinking with all her being, losing herself in his eyes, she cannot find in them any evil thought or any desire for destruction. Nor can she find any other feelings in them similar to those usually called human emotions. Sinking deeper and deeper into his eyes she sees nothing familiar, since her young mind has not yet faced eternal wisdom and eternal pain.

You look into her dark-blue eyes, trying to learn more about your new mistress, feeling with all your being every one of her feelings, absorbing them, so that none of her wishes will ever be surprising to you. Many times have you seen her through the bronze of your container and you know everything there is to know about her. And yet you have never looked her straight in the eyes, never felt her shiver before your might, never seen the sweetness of her realization that she can rule you as she pleases and her burden of shame that this realization bears sweetness for her....

But at the same time you feel surprised, searching and not finding in her that feeling, which for her grandmother, your previous mistress, was the sole reason for owning a djinn. She doesn't see you as the source of her own power; you cannot find in her any indication of the desire to use you for her own glory. She almost regrets that you are a slave in spite of all your knowledge, in spite of your ancient wisdom and ancient pain....

You feel her tremble like a captured bird, losing herself in the bonds of your eyes, and, coming to your senses, reminding yourself of her weakness and of the enormous difference in your strength, with a regret that you cannot completely understand, you break the contact.

The princess suddenly comes to her senses, realizing where she is. Her hands are shaking; she feels tired and empty; tears stand as a lump in her throat and fill her eyes. She feels as if she has just missed something very important and again looks search-ingly into the eyes of the djinn standing in front of her. But his eyes are now totally impenetrable; his face bears a look of in-difference, like that of an ordinary slave waiting for orders from his mistress. She starts at the sound of nannies and courtiers; she sees the master of ceremonies hurrying to them through the hall, and Nimeth following in his wake.

The master of ceremonies stops right in front of them. He directs his words not to the princess but to the djinn.

"The great sultan wishes for you to return to your bottle and to await further orders."

The djinn does not move, and it seems to the princess that a smile runs across his impassive face which at the same time re-mains totally still.

"Are you *deaf*?" the master of ceremonies yells, losing his presence of mind and at the same time releasing the tension that has risen in the hall. The courtiers, seeing a disobedi-ent djinn and hearing inappropriate shouting, start to back up. The most fearful ones regret with all their hearts that they failed to listen to the voice of reason and had come in-stead to the accursed ceremony. Even the guards step back in indecision, reluctant to draw their weapons in the face of an unknown power. But the princess, in spite of it all, can-not possibly feel any fear of her new slave and asks quietly:

"Why aren't you doing what he said, Hasan?"

"The sultan cannot give me orders, princess. I obey only *your* commands."

At this very moment Nimeth, delayed by the crowd, finally reaches the princess and whispers in her ear, holding her by the shoulder, "The sultaness is asking you to lock him in his bottle for now, princess. He is dangerous and before you can really let him out, you have to discuss with your parents what to do with him."

The princess turns to Hasan and opens her mouth to repeat this order. She cannot possibly disobey Nimeth relaying her mother's wish.

"Hasan...," the princess begins. Suddenly she feels the painful sting of the memory of his eyes, of the ancient abyss, of the eternal wisdom and pain that she cannot comprehend— she can still feel their distant echo. No! Such a creature has no place in a bronze bottle! Never, never can she order him to go back to his prison!

"Hasan will take his place in my suite," she says to Nimeth with finality. "Take the bottle away," she says, raising her voice and turning to the hall.

For a moment the hall freezes in complete silence. Nimeth stares at her with an open mouth; the nannies stand still in terror; and the master of ceremonies, in conversation with the courtiers around him, stops with his hands in midair. But the princess firmly holds Nimeth's gaze and then, turning away, nods to her slave women. Suddenly the hall comes to life again, resuming its usual hum of voices, just as the singing of birds resumes in a field when a thunderstorm passes. The slave women, bowing, take away the bottle, the cork, and the embroidered pillow. Nimeth and the master of ceremonies walk off in the direction of the royal canopy, while Hasan, following the princess's gesture, joins the group of her bodyguards who back off, looking at him with fearful curiosity.

The princess, trying to stop shivering and waving aside thoughts of what kind of punishment will follow her disobedience, feels at the same time that today has brought the most significant change of her life, a change too big for her to understand.

A WORD OF POWER

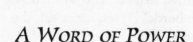

"**D**idn't mother tell you anything, Nanny Zeinab? What was she going to talk to me about?"

With sinking heart the princess is trying to slow her hurried steps to the shuffling steps of old Zeinab. The rest of her birthday was relatively uneventful and now, knowing that the time has come to pay for her disobedience, the princess is trying without much success to find out how great her mother's anger is.

"It isn't difficult to guess," Zeinab grumbles, throwing side glances at the princess's scared face.

"What, nanny? What?" the princess exclaims.

"I think you'll find out for yourself soon enough." The nanny stops in front of the sultaness's quarters and, lifting the heavy curtain, lets the princess through the half-opened door.

The sultaness is sitting on the pillows in the middle of the room and two slave girls are combing her long hair. Nimeth, dark and silent as a statue, is standing one step behind, her arms crossed.

"Mother," the princess says, but her trembling lips keep her from finishing the thought.

"I am waiting, princess, for you to explain your behavior." Her voice is so stern that the princess's heart stands still with fright.

"I..." The princess clenches her fists hard, forcing her lips to fold into words. "He is so old and wise, mother," she says hurriedly, fearing that the ability to talk might fail her at any minute. "I know he looks just like an ordinary man, but if you look into his eyes, you can see that he is a mighty wizard who has survived much pain. I thought of how hard it was for him to languish in his bottle.... I simply couldn't force him to return there."

"Do you realize how dangerous he is, princess? Your grandmother never let him out in front of the court."

"He is not dangerous to me, mother. He is going to do whatever I tell him."

"You should understand, princess," Nimeth says, "he is so much older and more powerful than you are that he can easily trick you and do something terrible."

"But he—he will never do me any harm."

"How do you know, princess?"

"I—I looked into his eyes." The princess lowers her head, unable to hold back the tears any more.

"Enough!" the sultaness says. She jumps up from her seat and, stepping forward, presses the princess tightly against her chest. "It is not her fault! That sorcerer has already tricked her into disobeying her parents. Call him in here, princess. I want to talk to him."

The princess clings more tightly to her mother, then rubs her eyes with both hands.

"Hasan," she says in a voice hoarse with tears, "I want you to appear here."

The djinn appears in the middle of the room without a sound, without a sign or movement of air. Zeinab and the slave women jump aside, covering their heads with their arms, as if this gesture could somehow protect them from terrible magic.

"What is your wish, princess?" Hasan's voice sounds gentle, almost tender.

"My mother wants to talk to you."

"Your majesty?"

His impeccable manners and easy friendliness make the women relax a little bit. How can such a pleasant young man possibly be dangerous? But then, if you think about it, how can they see a djinn as a pleasant young man without the help of magic?

"I am worried about the princess, Hasan," the sultaness begins, not quite knowing how to carry on this conversation. There are so many questions in her head that she seems to be unable to choose, or to phrase, any one of them. "We know very little about djinns," she says finally. "We heard that they are mighty wizards destined to slavery. We weren't even certain that djinns really existed. Tell us about yourself."

"All your information is absolutely correct," he says without emotion.

"But…" The sultaness spreads her hands in a gesture of helplessness. In spite of all her efforts the conversation has made a loop and returned to its beginning. With a sigh, she makes another attempt.

"How did the mother of our sultan come to possess you?"

"The sultaness of Dhagabad, like myself at one time, chose the way of eternal knowledge. But she decided not to follow this way to its end, choosing instead to get herself a djinn, an all-powerful slave."

"You are all-powerful??"

"At the princess's orders I can do anything."

The sultaness feels the floor start to float away from under her feet and presses her daughter more tightly against herself.

"So, how did the princess's grandmother acquire you?"

"She managed to find a way into the desert where the djinns are created. Unfortunately, I can tell you very little about it. The desert, and the forces that rule it, are beyond my power."

"Why didn't she give you to the sultan? A ruler of a country could surely put an all-powerful slave to a good use!"

"Obviously, she thought that I could be of more use to the princess than to her father."

Hasan meets her eyes, and she suddenly has an uneasy feeling that the djinn completely understands all her doubts and difficulties and that he is purposely making no effort to help her.

"How do you see your place in the palace, Hasan?" she asks, overwhelmed by a new wave of helplessness.

"Similar to any other slave's, your majesty. Only…" A barely visible smile moves over Hasan's lips. "I think I can do much more good."

"Or harm."

"If such is the princess's wish," the djinn says calmly.

Why does the sultaness get the feeling that she has surrendered her daughter into the hands of unknown forces—as if this impassive, devilishly attractive sorcerer were not a slave, but her own master?

"She is just a child!" the sultaness exclaims. "How can she possibly command an all-powerful creature?"

"As any other slave, the purpose of my existence is to make the princess's life better. I regret that it causes you trouble."

The sultaness doesn't see any regret on his quiet, impassive face. But it seems that the sultan's old mother left her no choice. The damned witch! No wonder everyone in the palace feared her evil tricks so much! It would have been better if one of the palace rumors had come true! It would have been better if there really had been a curse in the bottle!

"What would have happened if the princess never opened the bottle?"

"I would have remained inside forever."

"Hasan…" the princess says suddenly.

"Princess?"

"I will never make you return to the bottle! Never!"

"But…" The sultaness tries to interfere, feeling her total helplessness in this uncontrollable situation.

"You are kind, princess," Hasan says, "but my bottle cannot harm me. It is like my body, only I have a way to leave it from time to time."

A wild hope springs up in the sultaness's heart.

"You see, princess…" she starts. But her daughter isn't listening to her.

"I like the body you have now, Hasan."

This is it! Her innocent daughter, brought up in decency, is saying such words to a man! Let her be damned forever—the heedless old sultaness! How could she have done such harm to an innocent child?

Hasan's answer, however, somewhat eases her fears or, rather, offers her an excuse to calm herself a little.

"It is only an illusion, princess. I am not a man. I am a spirit."

❈

Chamar Ali. Chamar the Blessed.

Blessed with everything a man could wish for, except that which is most important to any man. A son and heir.

Striding along the gallery of the north wing toward the elegant white building of the harem connected to the palace, the sultan is patiently listening to the grand vizier, hurriedly following one step behind.

"Surely, your majesty knows that this creature, the djinn, is all-powerful."

"Yes, Shamil, I heard," the sultan replies impatiently, sliding his glance over a bald spot on the top of the grand vizier's head, that glistens with sweat in the bright afternoon sun. Shamil, a man in his later years, can never understand the impatience of someone who was forced by the palace festivities to spend almost a week away from his women. Chamar feels his body ache for a gentle woman's touch, a longing enhanced so much by the desire to have any one of his concubines bear him a son. He needs a son who will live. He cannot possibly waste his time talking to his vizier.

Shamil, however, is not about to give up.

"If I may be so bold, your majesty, I believe that your majesty should feel worried about having this creature loose in the palace. Perhaps your majesty should call the princess to order and have her contain this... thing in the bottle where he belongs."

"I don't think you should worry so much, Shamil," Chamar says, shielding his eyes from the sun to look directly into Shamil's eyes. Sensing the sultan's impatience, the older man becomes even more nervous. His whole face is now glistening with tiny beads of sweat, standing in the wrinkles on his forehead and sparkling in his bushy gray beard.

Realizing how nervous his vizier is, the sultan softens to the point of slowing down.

"The djinn cannot do anything the princess doesn't order him to do," he says, summoning to his aid whatever is left of his patience. "Because of that he is as harmless as a child."

"But, your majesty!" Shamil, encouraged by what he mistakes for the sultan's sudden attention to his words, rushes into a new attack. "This creature, as I heard, is an ancient wizard. I also was informed that the princess spends a great deal of time with him. He can put ideas into her head that could threaten your rule in unimaginable ways."

Chamar sighs, measuring with his eyes the last ten paces that separate him from the elegantly carved door, eunuch guards standing still on both sides of it.

The princess was told to use the djinn only for her games," Chamar says, suddenly feeling like a little boy, impatient to run off to play, forced to recite the lesson to a tedious teacher. "Besides, she is never alone with him. And she is a very obedient child. Just think, Shamil, what harm can possibly come from the djinn when he spends all his time with the women?"

"Your majesty," Shamil begins again. But the sultan's patience has finally come to an end.

"I have no time for this, Shamil," he says. "Later, perhaps."

He covers the ten paces to the desired door and waits for the eunuch on the left to open it for him. Not wide, in the presence of another man so close, just enough for the sultan to go through.

"Good-bye, Shamil!" Chamar says, feeling like a mischievous child who found a trick to escape his teacher, and he slides through the opening of the door.

✣

"Your move, Hasan."

Hasan throws a careless glance at the chessboard. The black queen floats up and sweeps in an arc into the very center of the white defenses. A white rook, displaced by the queen, falls to the side and stops in midair, as if held by an invisible hand. Rocking for a second in this off-balance, impossible position, the rook drifts into the air and lands in the princess's palm. The princess frowns.

"In how many moves were you supposed to win this game, Hasan?"

"In twelve, princess."

The princess raises her head and meets his indifferent gaze. Since the day Hasan appeared before her for the first time, she has never again seen even a glimpse of the look they exchanged. As if she had merely dreamed the incredible pain and wisdom going back into the unknown depths of countless centuries and millennia. As if he really is similar to all other palace slaves in everything but his magical abilities. The princess feels an unbearable longing to see once more at least a small part of this gaze, but Hasan's gray eyes look at her with polite indifference, as if closed off from the whole world by tiny iron shutters.

The princess shakes off her thoughts and takes another look at the chessboard.

"Twelve moves?" she says thoughtfully, frowning in calculation. Suddenly her face lights up. "You lost, Hasan!" she exclaims. "You just made your twelfth move, didn't you? But to take my king you will need to make another, thirteenth, move!"

Hasan glances at her, and in his eyes the princess for a moment sees something human, a merry surprise similar to that of a child caught at his favorite game. But Hasan's eyes quickly become impenetrable again.

Sighing, the princess looks around the room. Nannies Zeinab and Fatima are embroidering near the window, talking to each other in low voices and, from time to time, throwing suspicious glances at Hasan. Everyone in the palace is afraid of the djinn, and although nobody argues the princess's right to spend time with her new slave, she is strictly forbidden to be alone with him. She is also forbidden to use his magic for anything but small tricks. Being an obedient daughter, the princess doesn't dare to order Hasan to do anything more complicated than, for instance, moving the chess pieces with his gaze.

The princess lets out another sigh. What is the use of owning a djinn if she cannot order him to do anything interesting? What is the use of the constant presence of this wizard and mage if he closes himself off from her, and from the rest of the world, with iron shutters? Who knows, for that matter, what is really on his mind? Perhaps even now, sitting across from her with the indifferent face, he is thinking up something evil. Perhaps he really hates her and wishes something bad for her, just as her mother and Nimeth say. But no! she couldn't have dreamt that look that passed between them! The look, which she saw for a brief moment in the depths of his eyes, couldn't go along with evil! It is just that the pain of his soul is so great that he has no choice but to close his mind to the outside world and look at it with indifference.

"Princess! Princess!"

Airagad, panting, runs into the room and stops, trying to catch her breath. Her round, childish face is flushed; loose strands of hair are scattered over her face and neck. She straightens out her shawl, trying to catch enough breath to talk.

The princess jumps to her feet.

"What happened, nanny?"

"There—" Airagad takes several deep breaths. "The sultan of Veridue sent your father an Arabian stallion—I never thought there could be such a beautiful horse. It is all black like a raven, but its forehead is white like a star, bright as fire. Let's go look!"

"Come on, Hasan!" the princess shouts, rushing to the door. It is not every day that a beautiful Veriduan stallion arrives at the palace! And, judging by Nanny Airagad's excitement, this stallion is more beautiful than any other horse in the royal stable, which the princess often admires from a balcony as they are exercised in their morning rides.

"Is my father already there?" the princess asks, running.

"Your father is in the harem," Airagad replies, "but I know they sent for him already."

In the harem. The princess throws a glance from the gallery, along which they are now running, toward the elegant white stone building adjacent to the north wing of the palace where the sultan's quarters are located. She doesn't really understand what a harem is, but her mother explained to her that by law the sultan, unlike other citizens of Dhagabad, is allowed to have not four but only one wife from a noble family. To compensate the sultan for the hardships of such abstinence he is allowed to have as many women at his disposal as he wants. These women are called by a strange name, concubines, and they live in a building called a harem. The princess knows that they are not allowed to leave this building, must always cover their faces in the presence of strangers, and dwell in their beautiful garden like exotic birds, seeing only one another and their master, the sultan. The princess also knows that from seeing the sultan these women have children who are not considered to be of royal blood. They are called *Chamari* and *Chamarat*, sons and daughters of Chamar, and as they grow up they join the lower ranks of the palace courtiers. By Dhagabad law only the sultaness's children are called princes and princesses, and the elder of them is considered to be heir to the throne. The princess knows that the heir is supposed to be a boy, but since she has no brothers, it is her place for now to take this role upon herself. She was told that this means a lot of responsibility for her, but she knows that so far this role only allows her to enjoy freedom unheard of for any other girl in the palace, princess or not. It seems to make her mother displeased, but this is something the princess doesn't understand.

Trying to keep up with Airagad, the princess looks back to make sure that Hasan is following her. The djinn's face is still emotionless; he is walking lightly and noiselessly over the stone floor of the gallery, effortlessly keeping three paces behind the princess, who is running with all her might. The princess admires the frightening ease of his grace, like that of a panther chasing its victim. Distracted, she almost bumps into Airagad who suddenly stops in front of her.

"If we go down these stairs, we'll find ourselves right in the courtyard where the horse is being walked, waiting for the sultan to come," Airagad whispers confidingly, throwing a cautious glance at Hasan. The princess nods, and all three of them rush down the narrow winding stairs in one of the side towers of the palace. In the dark the princess carefully feels her way over the narrow, slippery steps that are covered with smooth dips and bowls, worn in the stone by the numerous feet walking those stairs during the past centuries. In one place the princess stumbles and, to avoid falling, grabs an arm offered to her. She pays no attention to the hardness of the muscle under the silk sleeve or to the cold of the metal encasing the wrist. Only when she finally pops out from under the stone vault into the sunlit yard, does she notice that Airagad is walking ahead and that all this time she was holding the arm of Hasan, smoothly walking beside her. The princess looks at him with uncertainty and carefully releases her grasp.

"Princess!" The sultaness shouts from a low gallery across the yard. "What are you doing here?"

"I wanted to see the stallion, mother!" the princess says, shielding her eyes from the blinding sun with her hand.

She suddenly hears a neigh and a snort beside her. Turning, the princess finds herself face-to-face with the most beautiful creature she has ever seen. Its shining raven-black coat sparkles like a rainbow in the bright sunlight. Slender legs, fluffy mane, arched neck—all these features, which to the experts merely mean the unmistakable signs of a thoroughbred, create for the princess a feeling of magic and wonder about this beautiful creature. Its large brown eyes are looking straight at the princess, as if studying her face. The stallion prances playfully, moving his eyes and blowing out his nostrils. Two huge Veriduan grooms are barely able to control the mighty horse.

The princess turns, looking for someone to share her excitement with, and sees Hasan, three steps behind, standing still with an expression that she could never imagine to be possible for an impassive djinn. Or, rather, his face is still impassive, but his eyes shine with admiration exactly matching the princess's own feelings.

"Princess!" the sultaness shouts again. "Don't get too close to the horse! Come here!"

The princess regretfully takes her eyes off the stallion who, guided by the two grooms, was turned around right before her and is now being led diagonally across the yard to its opposite corner. Holding her shawl, the princess starts running across the yard to share her excitement with her mother.

Everything happens very quickly. A sudden gust of wind tears the shawl off the princess's head at the very moment she passes the horse. The shawl sweeps up and, clinging for a moment to the horse's neck, slides off its black coat and flies away in the wind like a white flame. The frightened horse jumps aside, breaking free of the grooms, bumping into them with its mighty body to send them flying helplessly to the stone walls of the yard. The stallion rears and starts to rush about the yard.

Left alone in the middle of the yard with a raging horse, the princess freezes with fear. She cannot even move. She doesn't hear the terrible cries of the sultaness and her slave women, the wild neighs of the horse, and the beating of his hooves, every time sweeping closer and closer to her.

The princess feels strong arms close around her, holding and supporting her in a protective ring. She sees the shine of metal in front of her eyes and hears a voice by her ear, saying a word or, rather, a combination of sounds, since it doesn't seem like any human language she has ever heard. She can still see the shining black belly and the silvery sparkling horseshoes when the stallion rises on its hind legs right in front of her. She can still hear the neigh that sinks and dies in the echoes of the word spoken near her ear by the unknown but somehow familiar voice. The silence that follows this combination of sounds seems to last forever. Or maybe it lasts for just a few seconds, allowing the princess to come to her senses, to feel on her cheek a slight touch of the suddenly quiet breeze, to inhale the smell of juniper, to see the pale-faced sultaness, surrounded by slave women, rushing downstairs from the gallery, and the perfectly calm black stallion quietly letting the Veriduan grooms, scared to death, get hold of him again. She feels the strain that encased her body slowly release its grasp, giving way to deadly fatigue. She feels the unknown arms support her, keeping her from sinking limply to the stone floor of the yard. She raises her head and sees Hasan's face, still calm but not impassive anymore.

"What did you say to the horse, Hasan?" she whispers.

"I ordered it to calm down, princess."

"With one word? Why did it listen to you?"

"This word belongs to the language of the highest order, princess."

The princess feels a chill, remembering the strange sounds of the unknown word, the crazy horse suddenly standing still, the suddenly quieted breeze. She sees the pale face of the sultaness who finally reaches them and is saying something to Hasan, but the princess cannot make out the words anymore. She feels Hasan's arms release their supporting grasp, letting her fall semiconscious into the arms of the sobbing sultaness. She feels Nanny Airagad and the slave women fussing around her, holding her from all sides, helping her up and guiding her through the first uncertain steps, as if she has just learned to walk. And, through all this noise and bustle, she watches the face of Hasan who, pushed away from her by the crowd, excluded from all this activity, returns to his usual indifference.

❊

"Drink it, princess."

The princess, not yet recovered from her trance, takes a cup of hot steaming drink from the hands of Nanny Fatima. A sip, filled with aromas of herbs and flowers, fills her body with pleasant warmth. Somebody wraps a blanket around her, someone's hands slip a pillow under her back, and she, leaning back in relief, looks around.

An unusual excitement fills her chambers. The slave women crowded around her are talking all at once, somebody is patting the princess on the head, and she sees the sultaness sitting in front of her and the dark shape of Nimeth at her back.

"What's the matter with her, Hasan?" the sultaness asks worriedly.

"The princess will recover at any moment," Hasan says softly. "She came under the spell of my word."

"You put a spell on her with your magic!"

"This word wasn't magic. It was just a part of my knowledge. I cannot use my magic without the princess's orders."

The princess feels her strength returning to her and sits up on the pillows.

"Mother, Hasan saved me! You saw it, didn't you?"

The sultaness sighs in relief, seeing the princess's blue eyes shining again, seeing the whiteness of her cheeks give way to their usual pale pink. She holds out her hand to pat the princess on the head.

"You scared me to death, princess! How could you jump in front of a wild horse like that!"

"It is not the princess's fault, your majesty," Nimeth says, interfering. "It was just an accident."

"It was all my fault!" Airagad moans. "Why did I have to drag the princess out into the yard!"

"It is nobody's fault," Nimeth says peacefully. "Luckily, Hasan was near."

"Now you can see that Hasan is not dangerous, can't you, mother?" the princess demands. "He saved me even though I never ordered him to!"

The sultaness slowly raises her eyes to look at the djinn.

"I have to apologize, Hasan," she says reluctantly. "I never believed that you wished the princess well."

"The only purpose of my existence is to serve the princess" he says quietly.

Do you really believe the words you just said? Do you really know what is, or ever was, the purpose of your existence? Are you aware of the power that made you rush to her rescue, when she, frozen with fright, didn't even remember that you existed? Or of the power that allowed you to speak of your own will the word of the language of the highest order, mastered only by the most learned mages? Perhaps you heard her silent plea that she was unable to say aloud. Or perhaps the purpose of your existence really is to serve your mortal mistress, to whom you belong entirely by the will of the unknown powers that rule your destiny.

You watch how she, still shivering with the terror she lived through, is slowly regaining her senses after the word you threw by her ear, just as the Arabian stallion is now regaining his senses in the hands of the Veriduan grooms, and as the wind you quieted is now slowly resuming its careful gusts. And you think of how little you know about your destiny and about the fate of djinns, belonging entirely to their containers and thus to any mortal creature who, one way or another, came to possess them.

THE ESSENCE OF A STONE

✾

Y*ou never thought much about the fate of the djinns. Starting out on your way to absolute power you never believed that your knowledge about the world could have a limit, that your marvelous existence among books, talks with wise people, mysteries gradually opening to your widening vision would suddenly come to an end. The old formula that everyone had been taught since childhood kept its place somewhere in your mind, constantly reminding you, in an inner voice resembling the voice of your childhood teacher, that the world is endless and unknowable, that absolute knowledge is unattainable, and that absolute power belongs only to the gods. Even the smoldering scroll that caught your eye in a dusty corner of the Dimeshqian library didn't alert you—at least not at first.*

Trying with difficulty to make out on the age-darkened parchment the faded hieroglyphs of the dead language Agrit, you were reading with amazement an ancient warning to someone who wished to learn everything about the world. The scroll said that such a man was doomed to eternal suffering. You learned that the gods—the same gods that exist in great numbers for some people and are united into the one protector in heaven for others; the gods that you considered to be a fantasy of those who needed to depend on and worship something superior to themselves; the gods that symbolize for people everything incomprehensible and unknown and whose existence somehow explains for people their very inability to know and comprehend certain things—these gods never forgive one who achieves absolute power, being unrelenting to those trying to discover their secrets.

Not believing a single word of the ancient scroll, at the same time you had to acknowledge its inner logic. If the gods, or some forces symbolizing them, really existed, having no power to prevent a man from learning, they should be able to appoint a punishment for obtaining absolute knowledge, a punishment so terrible that no one would ever wish to discover these highest secrets.

Straightening out the folds of the ancient parchment, you eagerly consumed the information about a man close to absolute power. The spare phrases told about the already familiar satisfaction of learning, of the infinite mysteries and the joy of discovering them... and the burden of wisdom, lying on one's shoulders heavier than a mountain. The man who many centuries ago wrote those intricate hieroglyphs on the piece of parchment achieved great wisdom but lost his peace and, feeling that his end was near, left a warning to those who could insanely wish to follow the same path....

You were reading the ancient lines with wonder and mistrust. You, who had just overcome time itself, you, who were rapidly walking along a path that seemed in your euphoria to be endless and victorious, you, who along with hard work felt great joy in every step along this path—you simply couldn't believe that the author of the scroll, who obviously was ahead of you on the same path, could possibly feel such pain. Maybe, you thought, the unknown sage had chosen the wrong path; for no pain, no burden of knowledge, no fear of the dark mysteries could possibly overcome the joyous thrill of the awareness that the world around you was becoming more and more dimensional, further and further opening to your vision its distant secret corners....

The Agritian scroll stopped in mid-sentence. You never learned the fate of this man and whether he was able to reach absolute knowledge. Later you returned to the parchment again and again, and even translated it into another language, one of those more familiar to you, before the scroll completely deteriorated. From this scroll you learned for the first time the strange word—djinn…

The jasmine smell, floating in waves from behind the boulder covered with plants, mixes with the tinkling sounds of slowly running water, with the rustling of the giant magnolia leaves, and with the fleeting warmth of the patches of sunlight moving over her face. The princess's heart is racing with joy at the thought of how they would soon walk around the boulder to find themselves in her favorite glade. She glances at Hasan walking beside her, looking forward to sharing one of her most precious secrets with him, a secret nobody in the palace understands but which, she is somehow sure, the djinn will understand very well. Maybe she would even have time to catch on his face one of those fleeting expressions that break from time to time his impassiveness. She even dreams that today will be the day when the djinn will smile at her and not at his inner thoughts—smile, meeting her eyes, and let her steal a single look through the defenses of the iron shutters.

The encounter with the Veriduan stallion completely changed everyone's attitude toward Hasan. Of course, he is still feared for what a djinn is capable of, even without being able to command his own magic. But now he is no longer looked upon as a terrifying sorcerer of old tales, burdened by his slavery and angered by his ages of imprisonment. By rushing to the princess's rescue he did the same thing any caring human being would have done in his place, and this makes Hasan to some extent more understandable to the inhabitants of the palace. The princess is now allowed to be alone with him, and even to take walks with him in the garden, including its very distant corners; and now the princess is eagerly looking forward to showing Hasan her favorite place.

The princess and Hasan walk around the boulder and stop in front of the glade. The princess proudly looks at her realm: thick silky grass, the even semicircle of the creek running through its far end, the wall of jasmine bushes, and two giant magnolias whose branches and wide leaves create a ceiling over this place, letting through only the finest web of delicate sunbeams. The princess, as usual, feels as if she just walked into the castle of the queen of the fairies that mere mortals can see only as a garden glade. She cannot help asking herself whether the djinn can see the real face of this glade and what he can see now, standing beside her at the border of her realm.

"I want to show you something in the creek," the princess says, taking a decisive step into the glade.

The grass ends close to the edge of the water, leaving a yellow streak of sand between the silky greenery and the tickling water. The water is carefully finding its way among the rocks scattered in its bed, from time to time creating tiny waterfalls and deep calm pools. The princess likes to sit on the bank of this stream, imagining herself reduced to a size whereby the grass looks like a forest and the deep pool with its sandy banks and the tiny waterfall like a giant lake. At those moments she dreams that there are peri living on the lake—the spirits of air and water, mysterious phantom beauties—and that if she makes just a tiny effort, she could for a while become one of them, a part of the lake and the waterfalls.

The princess carefully puts her hand into the water and brings out a piece of gravel, shining in the sun.

"Look at it, Hasan," she murmurs.

She wants to tell him how the curves of the stone fit her little hand, trying to tell her the mystery concealed in its depth. Failing to find the right words, she holds out the stone to him and carefully puts it into his palm. In Hasan's large hand the stone looks much smaller, but its wet surface still shines mysteriously in the sun.

"There is a secret hidden in this stone," the princess says, "but it can only talk to your hand. Can you feel it?"

She hesitantly looks into Hasan's face, and her heart beats with joy. She sees in his eyes a reflection of her own enchantment, of the same concentration she always feels watching closely something as ordinary and as amazing as a piece of gravel.

"Every stone hides something, princess," Hasan says softly. "Only this stone is able to tell of it better than others."

The princess feels her heart leap and quiver with excitement. She brought Hasan here to share a game with him. Never, even in her wildest fantasy, had she dreamed that he, by far the oldest and the wisest creature she has ever known, would tell her that her favorite game was—real.

"What does the stone tell you, Hasan?" she asks quietly.

"I'll show you, princess. Look closer."

The princess carefully looks at the stone. The effort makes her eyes fill with tears and slowly lose their focus; the tiny specks of mica fuse into a single golden glow. And then she sees, enclosed by the contour of the stone, an amazing creature—like a tiny lizard, curled to repeat the curves of the stone that so precisely fits her hand. The creature sleeps, emanating a golden glow, silent like the gravel that conceals it.

The fiery lizard loses its shape, dissolving in the golden sparkle of mica in the bright afternoon sun.

"I saw an amazing creature inside the stone, Hasan," the princess whispers.

"It is one of the ways to see the essence of the stone, princess," Hasan says softly.

One of your first lessons in magic was to see the essence of a stone. Only you had to do it by yourself, without the help of a mighty wizard, ready to share a part of his vision with you, as you shared your vision with the princess. You vaguely recall those times when you, a youth barely older than she is now, were studying the basics of magic with your first teacher, not knowing even of such simple things as overcoming time.

You can barely remember the name of your teacher, who, even during the times of your mortality, was already a venerable old man and who died, never learning the secret of becoming immortal—before you lived your first century in this world. You need several seconds to recall that name you uttered once with such respect—Haannan. And the sound of this name rings in your mind, bringing you back into his large airy room in a house that was only a small distance from your Dimeshqian home.

The sage Haannan is trying to teach you a lesson of concentration, but you, young and careless, cannot manage to focus on his words.

"Hasan," patiently speaks the sage sitting on the pillows across from you, "the first step of learning magic is being able to concentrate. You cannot possibly succeed in doing the simplest task without concentrating on it completely."

You sigh, looking at a pile of smooth pebbles lying in front of you on the floor.

"Focus on these stones, Hasan," the teacher says. "Forget everything that is going on around you now."

For some time you try your best to fix your eyes on the stones. A shadow of a palm leaf, which swings outside in the blasts of the hot midday wind, runs over the floor next to you; and, almost against your will, your gaze moves to follow.

"Look at me, Hasan," the teacher says suddenly.

You raise your head and meet the stare of his tranquil blue eyes.

"Forget the seriousness of the task, Hasan," the teacher says, and merry sparkles dance in his eyes. "This is a game. Let's pretend that you can see the inner glow of these stones."

"The inner glow, teacher?"

"I am telling you that every one of these stones is shining with its own inner light. Let's see if you can name the colors of these lights."

"But how?"

"You are too tense, Hasan. Concentration has nothing to do with tension. Try to relax."

You lower your eyes again to stare at the accursed pile of stones that in spite of all your effort still remains for you just a handful of plain river pebbles.

"Don't pay any attention to their shape, Hasan. Try to focus on the essence of the stones and not on their looks."

You feel a wave of fatigue slowly sweeping over you. You don't care anymore whether you will ever be able to see the inner glow of the stones or lift them with your gaze, which was the initial purpose of today's lesson. You are not looking at the stones now, letting your tired eyes stare through them to follow the white lines woven in the carpet, guessing the shapes of those lines in the places concealed by the gray pile of pebbles. But you cannot see clearly anymore. All the shapes are diffusing before your unfocused gaze. You don't see anything defined in its outline. All you see is a dark mass that was a pile of stones just a moment ago, the dim and unclear shapes of the white ornaments on the old worn carpet, a fuzzy, many-colored spot that shimmers with different shades of the seven spectral colors…a colored spot?

You jump to your feet, forgetting your tiredness.

"I saw the colors!" You feel so overwhelmed you can barely breathe. "Many colors! Every stone has its own color!"

The teacher laughs at your excitement.

"Very good, Hasan," he says quietly. "You were able to concentrate and see the essence of the stones. Now, sit down."

Still trembling, you slowly settle back into your place.

"Now you should find no difficulty in moving, even lifting, one of these stones," the teacher says distinctly.

"But how?" You still cannot forget the vision of the transparent rainbow that just now shone before your eyes in the place of a lifeless gray pile.

"You must manage to see the glow again, Hasan. But do not stop this time. You must become familiar with this glow, define for yourself the color of the glow originating from each individual stone. Only then will you be able to do what you want with them."

You relax, searching for the now-familiar state of mind, making the white lines on the carpet diffuse before your eyes, making the pile of pebbles become a single gray mass. This time you manage to catch the moment when the stones in front of you start to shine. At first you cannot determine which light comes from which individual stone. Then you suddenly notice that the pebble lying on top, the one shaped almost like a disk, is spreading yellow light around it, and that the yellow on one side seems green because of the overlapping blue glow coming from the elongated stone closest to it, the one that bears a dimple on its smooth side.

"Can you see it, Hasan?" the teacher asks.

"Yes," you whisper, afraid to move, afraid to scare off this unbelievable sight. You feel as if you are peering at something sacred, some quality of these simple stones, carefully hidden from human eyes, which you now regard as something almost alive.

"Try to separate the glow of one stone from the others, Hasan," the teacher says.

"Separate—how?" you ask, keeping all your attention on the colorful radiance in front of you.

"Choose one stone and look at its glow separately. Don't let the glow of other stones interfere with it. Make its color look pure to your eye."

You choose the elongated stone with the dimple, carefully separating its blue light from the surrounding yellows, reds, and greens. Gradually you start to feel that the chosen stone is floating in a basket woven of blue light that doesn't let it touch other stones in the pile.

"Now lift it, Hasan," the teacher says.

You suddenly realize that the teacher's request doesn't raise any questions in your mind. You somehow know that by simply pulling at the blue basket with your gaze you will be able to make the stone float up from the pile and rise to any height within this large room. Almost without thinking, completely absorbed in your new perception, you gently pull the stone out of the pile of others, so similar in looks and so different in their essences, and make it float through the air straight to your teacher, lowering the dim blue shape into his open hand. Tears of wonder come to your eyes, washing away the colorful glow, bringing you back to the familiar airy room covered with a worn carpet, where the specks of dust circle and dance in the slanting beams of sunlight coming through the narrow windows. Relieved, you lean back against the wall, looking with a smile at Haannan.

"You are very talented, Hasan," the sage says. "If you study hard, you will achieve a lot."

"I never knew inanimate objects could glow."

"There are many ways to make the objects float. The glow is just a game meant to explain to you these ways."

"*A game, teacher?*"

"*We just played that the stones can glow, Hasan. And that game helped you lift a stone with your gaze.*"

"*A game? But I saw them glowing with my own eyes, teacher!*"

"*Maybe if I had offered you another game, you would have seen something different.*"

Back then you didn't understand him. But you forever remembered the joy of seeing the many-colored spot in the place of a pile of gray river pebbles, of making a simple rock float up like a bubble of soap and easily fly into the teacher's outstretched hand. And from that day on, the basics of learning magic were forever linked in your mind with the word "game." Playing games, you studied under the guidance of the sage Haannan, easily learning things that seemed impossible to his other pupils. Perhaps the feeling of constantly playing games, sometimes difficult but always fascinating, was the thing that set you on your way, leading you from those games to the state of wisdom unknown to your teacher, leading you through all the stages of knowledge straight to your terrible end.

EYES OF DESIRE

❁

*T*rying to walk as noiselessly as she can on the smooth marble floor, Alamid, daughter of the master of ceremonies, carefully lifts the heavy curtain over the entrance to the princess's bedroom. She knows that the princess and Hasan are in there by themselves, and all her being is filled with a sweetly shameful desire to catch them doing something forbidden. During the past month, after the episode with that stupid horse, the princess seems to spend too much time alone with her new slave. She seems to pay too much attention to this mysterious creature in his attractive human form, forgetting her other activities, forgetting Alamid, who up to now was considered in the palace to be the princess's best friend. Alamid wants to learn more about the person who has deprived her of her most cherished privilege.

She pulls the edge of the curtain further back, finally opening it enough to be able to see the whole room from her velvet hideout. She sees the princess cuddled in her bed. The flame of the lantern quivering in the gentle, barely perceptible movements of the night air, lights up in orange and yellow patches her profile, her half-opened mouth, the deep curve connecting her forehead and her nose, which seems to Alamid to look too smug in the wavering, uneven light. The dancing patches of light make the princess's cheek look unnaturally red; and her black hair, loosely arranged for the night, blends with the shadow, merging into the darkness of the unlit wall, making the princess's head look almost like a part of the pattern on the tapestry behind her. The princess seems to be completely absorbed in something; her attention is directed toward someone concealed from Alamid by the heavy tassel decorating the curtain, hanging right in front of her face. Holding her breath, Alamid carefully extends her head a little bit farther out from behind the heavy velvet, finally seeing the object of her curiosity.

Like other inhabitants of the palace Alamid had seen the djinn many times. As the princess's good friend she even saw him at close range and heard the short phrases he exchanged with his mistress. But never had Alamid seen what the princess and Hasan do when they are alone, and her wild thirteen-year-old imagination draws the most incredible pictures in her mind.

Sitting at the head of the princess's bed, Hasan is turned almost directly toward Alamid, and the light of the lantern falls straight on him, giving her a good view of his face and figure. Lazily quivering shadows, thrown by the uneven light, make his slender body and his dark face look almost devilish. Unwittingly admiring the graceful ease of his pose, Alamid feels at the same time some hidden force emanating from him. Almost against her will she finds herself giving in to this force which, she believes, must seem irresistible to any living being. And at the same time she sees something in his features that she feels is capable of making any living being trust this force as something unconditionally good. Or, perhaps, *good* is not the word. Rather, looking at him, one doesn't care anymore whether he is good or bad, whether he wishes for your happiness or your sorrow; but all other feelings fall away before the overwhelming desire to belong to him entirely.

Alamid shakes her head. Without doubt, all this is just an illusion created by the unsteady flame of the lantern. The real question is, what are they doing over there, in the dark, at such a late hour? It seems that the djinn has something in his hands, something he is looking at all the time, something that draws his attention more than the princess at his side.

Looking closer, Alamid sees his lips move, as if he is talking —or telling something. Their poses do not change. The scene is totally static. *Looks like there is nothing really happening here,* Alamid thinks. *Honestly, this princess is such a baby! As if she never notices how handsome her new slave is, as if she really sees him only as an immortal spirit, all-powerful sorcerer, and wizard. As if she doesn't realize that this unusual freedom, granted only to her, could allow her to...* Alamid flushes from the daring of her thought and, moving the curtain completely aside, steps into the room.

She stops at the edge of the dim circle of lantern light, not hiding herself anymore but wanting to see as much as she can before her presence is noticed. Hasan's steady voice that up to now sounded like nothing more than a monotonous hum, finally shapes itself into words.

> "In great anger the supreme god Garran left the temple of his mother, the goddess Aygelle, and was about to strike down Avallahaim and its surroundings, but his hand froze in midair. So fair were the lands of Avallahaim that even his great anger could not drive him to strike down all this beauty."

Now Alamid can make out the object in the djinn's hands—a book with a heavy carved cover and pages brown with age. Straining her eyes, Alamid sees that the pages are covered not with letters and words but with some strange elaborate signs. She seems to recall that Avallahaim is a land that lies very far from Dhagabad, at least a month's travel. She also remembers that the Avallahaim sages coming to Dhagabad talk to each other in a strange tongue in which all the sounds seem to be pronounced entirely without the help of the vocal cords, as if squeezed out through the teeth. In must be, Alamid guesses, that this book is written in the language of Avallahaim and no one except the djinn is able to read it. Alamid feels another sting of jealousy, remembering how quickly and easily Hasan has come to occupy a central place in the life of her royal friend, and, unable to stand aside anymore, she makes the final step into the circle of light.

"Alamid?" the princess asks, surprised.

The djinn looks up from the book, and for a moment it seems to Alamid that the uneven shadows shifting across his face shape it into a sarcastic smile. Alamid has the unpleasant feeling that Hasan not only knew of her presence from the very minute she lifted the corner of the heavy curtain but that he also knows precisely all her jealous thoughts. She forces herself to look away from his face, covered in shadows, and absent-mindedly smiles at the princess.

"I—I came to say good night, princess."

"Come, sit, Alamid," the princess says invitingly, pulling up her legs to make room in an absent, needless gesture, since her bed is really big enough to fit at least a dozen thirteen-year-olds, even ones as tall and shapely as Alamid.

Alamid carefully lowers herself onto a corner of the princess's bed, trying to convince herself that her presence, her participation in this bedtime reading, is perfectly natural and wanted by everyone in the room.

"Hasan was reading me the Avallahaim myth of the dragon," the princess explains. "I found this book in the library, but I could never read it without Hasan."

"How interesting," Alamid says with indifference. She is much more interested in the djinn, who, as she now notices, is not sitting on the pillows at all but floating in the air about a cubit above the floor. He looks calmly into space, waiting for the signal to resume his reading; but it seems to Alamid that his eyes, though not directed to her, are piercing her through, making her every shameful thought, her every little lie, echo in her heart with an unpleasant sting.

"Go on, Hasan," the princess says sleepily, curling into her blanket. The djinn readily resumes reading.

"The goddess Aygelle wanted to distract her son, the great Garran, and to avert the danger to fair Avallahaim. She created a vision, both beautiful and terrifying, a vision of a creature with the body of a snake, the claws of an eagle, the wings of a bat, and the head of a lizard. The phantom creature floated in the air, breathing fire, blowing its fiery breath over the angered Garran. Garran, admiring the vision, tore off a giant piece of rock and carved from it a body for the fiery creature. Thus a being was born that all the later myths call a dragon, and this dragon loved Garran, its creator, with a great love. This love and the creature that embodied it became symbols of life and prosperity in fair Avallahaim...."

Hasan's voice dies away; his eyes rise from the book and move over the princess curled in her bed. Her breath is even, her eyes are closed, she is—asleep?

Panicked, Alamid looks around the room. She never expected the princess to fall asleep leaving her alone with the djinn. She never realized that the princess's presence created complete protection for her from this strange creature, who really, in spite of his handsome looks, is a horrible sorcerer, the limits of whose power Alamid cannot even imagine. She suppresses her urge to wake the princess, unable to avoid the terrifying allure of being alone with Hasan. Or, maybe, she is not afraid of *him*, but of the fact that he knows all the truth about her. Alamid shuts her eyes in a wild hope that the djinn will disappear, evaporate into thin air, since it must be impossible for him to exist when his mistress, to whom he belongs so completely, is asleep. Carefully opening her eyes again, she freezes, meeting Hasan's impenetrable gaze in which she seems to detect something suspiciously close to sarcasm.

"You don't have to be afraid of me, Alamid," he says. Alamid with her active imagination seems to hear a chuckle in his quiet voice.

Alamid opens her mouth to say something, but no words come to mind. Most of all she wants to jump up and run away. But at the same time a part of her feels a strange longing to stay and perhaps even to step forward and touch his relaxed arm resting on his bent knee, an arm whose strong muscles are clearly outlined under the fine silk of the sleeve. These two wishes intertwine, overwhelming her to the extent that she is unable to speak at all, and only a barely audible sigh escapes her lips.

All clear thoughts have left Alamid's confused mind, replacing her favorite verbal deductions with visual images. How horrible is this sarcastic smile that haunts her, these calm impenetrable eyes, this devilish, devilishly attractive look. What if he purposely put the princess to sleep with his magic in order to be alone with Alamid? What does he want with her? A sweet feeling of helplessness overwhelms Alamid and, closing her eyes and shivering from the feelings she is unable to hold back, she reaches out with her hand to the place where the djinn is floating in the air in front of her, and where his muscular arm is resting on his knee, open to her touch.

You look at this girl in front of you, amazed at how different she is from your mistress, the princess of Dhagabad. But it is not the physical difference between the tall, dark, and wide-faced Alamid and the fragile white-skinned princess that strikes you, nor is it the difference in emotions overwhelming each of them, emotions that fill Alamid with a desire to command people, whereas the princess dreams only of being transported into the world of her favorite books. This unlikeness that amazes you comes from the difference in the ability of these two girls to face the truth. You feel with all your being the emotions of Alamid, who, closing her eyes and giving in completely to the flow of her desires, is stretching out an uncertain

hand toward you. But the dissonance within her true self, and of her complete inability to face this truth, rings inside you like a false chord. You see how this inability makes her so vulnerable in your presence, for your immortal eyes are able to see right through her, perceiving every one of the feelings that arise in her soul. You see how this fear to find herself face-to-face with her true being fights in her with the destructive desire to test herself by reaching out her hand toward you in spite of the complete inequality of your strength, in spite of her full realization of the possible consequences of such a careless action. Curiosity is still alive in her heart, but this curiosity itself only makes more obvious her dissimilarity to your young mistress, whose thoughts, heard by you even through her semislumber, completely lack any fear of her own wishes and are filled only with an unquenchable desire to learn something new about the outside world. Suddenly you realize that her childlike desire for knowledge is similar to the feeling that guided you at the very beginning of your own journey. And, feeling this strange closeness to the sleeping girl and the understandable awareness of the wakeful one, ready to meet the touch of her outstretched hand and knowing that this scene cannot end peacefully, you remove the substance from your body, making it ghostly as is appropriate for an immortal spirit.

Alamid's fingers move forward without any resistance. Her tension, finding no release in this outpouring of emotion, making it impossible to bear the uncertainty, forces her to carefully open one eye.

The djinn is still floating in the air right in front of her. The sarcastic smile has left his face, which now bears an impassive expression. Alamid's hand should have touched him long ago and, meeting no resistance, has moved right through his body, which now seems airy like juniper smoke and through which she can make out a dark outline of the window covered with a light drape. Terrified, Alamid pulls back her hand, half expecting that the movement of air created by that gesture will mix up the image of Hasan in front of her, turning his human form into a shapeless cloud of smoke. Covering her face with her hands, scared to death by this new evidence of the strange qualities of this mysterious creature, overwhelmed by the unexpected strength and shamefulness of her desires, Alamid produces a wild, inhuman scream.

"What really did happen, Alamid?" the princess asks insistently.

She is sitting on her bed beside the helplessly sobbing Alamid, the nannies fussing around them. The sultaness, who ran in after hearing the noise, accompanied by the dark and silent Nimeth, is holding the princess by the hand, glancing cautiously at Hasan, who is standing motionlessly against the wall, removed from all the fuss.

"I... he..." Alamid sobs, pointing at Hasan.

"What did you do to her, Hasan?" the princess asks.

"Nothing, princess."

"Will you finally tell us what's the matter, Alamid!" the sultaness exclaims, unable to bear the uncertainty anymore. She grabs the sobbing girl by the shoulders and shakes her, trying to look her in the eyes.

Alamid takes several deep convulsive breaths, raising her eyes to the sultaness. Her stiff black hair is scattered around her back; her wide dark face is swollen with tears and looks completely childish. Her lips tremble and twist, getting ready for the new outburst of tears. But the despair in the sultaness's eyes unexpectedly makes her come to her senses. Two huge tears roll down her cheeks, painlessly releasing the coming outpouring. Her lips open up, letting out, instead of screams and tears, ordinary human words.

"The princess fell asleep, and I was left alone with Hasan, and he—" Alamid stops, meeting the impenetrable eyes of the djinn.

"He—what? What?" The sultaness urges her on. "What did he do to you?"

"He..." Alamid suddenly feels an uprush of devilish joy. Now she knows how she will get back at this sorcerer for the way he laughed at her, causing her so much shame! She will show him who is the master here and who is the slave! Alamid takes a deep breath and says distinctly:

"He purposely put the princess to sleep, and then he ordered me to come closer and grabbed me by the hand— He was trying to take me somewhere, and he put a spell on me so that I was unable to move— I don't know what he wanted to do to me, but at the last moment I managed to scream." A new flood of tears overtakes Alamid, who now feels like an actress on the stage after a performance well done. Realizing instinctively that tears, not words, are more efficient right now, Alamid covers her face with her hands again, completely giving in to the outburst of sobs, and listens with pleasure to the results of the scandal she has started.

"Hasan!" the sultaness exclaims.

"Wait a minute, mother!" the princess says with sudden energy. "Is it true, Hasan?"

"No, princess." The djinn's voice startles Alamid. Not only can she not hear any fear or repentance in his voice, she seems to hear in it again the light undertone of sarcasm.

"You see, mother," the princess says with relief.

"He is lying to you, princess!" the sultaness exclaims. "You don't think he will confess so easily, do you?"

"But why would Hasan do such a thing, mother?"

"You are still too innocent, princess. Alamid is older, and she knows better about these things."

"Mother, I trust Hasan! He has no reason to lie!"

"Don't try to interfere in things you don't understand, princess. A djinn is not a joking matter. Next time he might do something like that to you."

"Hasan could never order me to do anything, mother! I am the one who orders him!"

The princess is flushed with anger, her eyes shining. She stands on her bed, looking like a little angry cloud in her wide nightdress.

"Let me tell you this!" the princess exclaims, daring, in the heat of the argument, to throw forth the worst of all accusations. "I trust Hasan more than I trust Alamid! I do!"

"Princess!" Nanny Airagad says with reproach.

"Let me ask her myself. Look at me, Alamid!" The princess takes several steps toward her crying friend and sits down, unable to keep her balance on the soft bed.

Almost against her will, Alamid raises her head and meets the angry gaze of a pair of dark-blue eyes.

"Tell me what happened!" the princess commands.

"You fell asleep," Alamid whispers and falls silent, unable to continue.

"And what did Hasan do?"

"Nothing— He told me I didn't have to be afraid of him— He was just sitting there."

"And...?"

"And I wanted very much to touch his arm." Alamid's whisper becomes barely audible. Blood rushes up to her head, making her face and neck crimson with shame.

"Go on!"

"My fingers went right through him," says Alamid with difficulty. "I was frightened, and I screamed."

"Enough of that," the sultaness exclaims. "You may go, Alamid. As for you, princess..."

"What, mother?" the princess asks, suddenly quiet.

"Be careful with Hasan. Don't forget that he is a djinn."

Signaling for Nimeth to follow, the sultaness collects her nightdress about her and follows Alamid out of the princess's quarters.

You are grateful to the daughter of the master of ceremonies, the princess's friend Alamid, for helping you to learn more about your mistress. Being an all-powerful spirit, you can see everything that goes on in the princess's mind, but no kind of vision is equal to the knowledge that small actions reveal. In some sense knowing the thoughts and feelings of a person only clouds the reality, since no one can ever act in complete accordance with his inner urges, and in this sense your absolute power never helped you to know more about people. The passion with which the princess fought to prove your innocence, allowing her to drag the truth out of Alamid, revealed something in her that made you feel much closer to your young mistress. You suddenly saw in her the echo of the same joyful curiosity that accompanied you through your physical existence. In some sense your transformation into a djinn meant giving up this childlike enthusiasm, the loss of the ability so cherished by you to learn one by one the highest truths, the oldest mysteries, and the wisest thoughts. Now you feel in some strange way that the presence of this child, her hunger for knowledge, and her endless ability to wonder somehow return you to your favorite state of mind when you are able again, if not to learn yourself, at least to share with another being something so dear to you, something that used to be the sole reason and purpose of your existence, and something that you had to give up forever. And, feeling this new bond with the princess, you suddenly realize that in spite of your apparent opacity you are ready to put your whole heart into her games, enjoying them no less than she does, enjoying beyond measure the joy and interest on her face, and your ability to call forth this joy and interest with your almighty power.

BEYOND THE NORTH WING

❖

*F*or sultan Chamar Ali, the most exquisite distinction that in his mind separates a married woman from a concubine is a name. Hearing a woman's name—her name alone, without a title in front or instead—always makes Chamar's blood boil with tiny bubbles of unexplored possibility. He knows that the sultaness used to have a name before she was given to him as his bride, but he always called her "princess," and after their wedding he called her "madam," or "your majesty," or, rarely, "*Sitt* Chamar," an official title which in reality means nothing more than Chamar's wife. As for his daughter the princess he never even learned her given name, although he assumes she has one, as any of his daughters would. For him, as for everyone else in the palace, she is forever to be called by her title, which in his mind symbolizes, among other things, his unfulfilled hope for a more appropriate heir.

It isn't that the sultan is incapacitated as a man. He is proud that he never wastes time in his harem, unlike other rulers who often have many concubines just to show off, making everyone believe they can handle so many women when, in fact, their ability to enjoy women is long lost. Chamar Ali is not and never was like that.

He enjoys women as others enjoy the beauty of rare jewels, and he collects women as others collect gems. In his harem he feels as if he is admiring his treasure, where he can pick any beautiful piece he wants and play with it for as long as he pleases. And then, every once in a while, he receives a precious prize for his games, a new baby that may—or may not—be a boy. That is a pleasure no collector of gems could ever experience—holding the fruit of his sport, a tiny creature from his own loins that is part of him blended with the features of its beautiful mother. For Chamar Ali does not keep any concubines he doesn't consider beautiful.

Unlike other rulers who think that their unlimited supply of women makes it unnecessary for them to pay attention to their looks, Chamar enjoys keeping himself attractive—the better to consort with his beautiful concubines. Reaching his fortieth year, he takes special pride in the fitness of his dark, slim body and the thickness of his hair that bears virtually no trace of gray. A passionate fire keeps alit his dark eyes, giving his handsome face a terrifying look appropriate to a mighty ruler. When he walks in the harem in his bright silk robe, opening up the front just enough to reveal his smooth hairless chest, his unruly beard sticking out straight from his face, he feels the admiration in the eyes of his concubines, making worthwhile his every effort to keep himself in top form.

He likes going to the harem casually, without anything particular in mind, to sit around with his women and children, watching them go about their usual activities. He listens to the older slave women tell stories while the concubines are engaged in their handicrafts, watching the children play around, splashing in the fountains and running about the gardens of the seven harem courtyards. He sits there, waiting for the bubbles of excitement to rise in him in response to anything at all—a seductive movement, a slender curve of a body, a smile, the sound of a voice. He never knows on whose cushion he will end up. He likes to be spontaneous and care-free, just the opposite of what he has to be on the other side of the door, in the palace, in that other world that is so demanding, so cruel, so quick to judge.

Today, as he enters the first and the largest courtyard, Chamar stops to admire a peaceful sight. Ten of his women are sitting on the grass with their needlework, watching a flock of little girls running in circles around the marble fountain shaped like a giant lotus flower, water flowing down its numerous petals into a basin of carved lotus leaves. Every once in a while the girls end up in the water and the yard fills with their happy screams.

Noticing him, the women rise to their feet. One of them, a tall girl with long flowing hair, tries to round up the children, but it is impossible—like trying to catch a flock of playful birds. She glances at the sultan, and he gestures for her to stop.

"Greetings, master," the eldest concubine begins.

"How fare you, my beauties?" Chamar asks, settling down among them and motioning for them to sit down.

"Sad, without the sunlight of your presence, master," she continues, smiling at Chamar.

"I am sorry I was away so long, Ana'id," Chamar says, regarding her through half-closed eyelids. Ana'id has seniority in the harem, approaching her thirtieth year, but she is still as beautiful as ever, perhaps more so—with ten years and two daughters to her credit and a mature beauty that Chamar finds very appealing. The other concubines treat her as their older sister, the one to whom they can bring their problems.

"I hope your majesty fares well," Ana'id says, bending her head to the side, a strand of her dark hair falling over the thin oval of her face. Her eyes, in the soft light of the setting sun, are the color of dark honey. Chamar has almost no hope for a son from her, but she is still enormously attractive to him.

"Some affairs of state have kept me away," he says. "Is everything here well?"

"Zarema!" the girl who was trying to catch the children suddenly says and stops, blushing, as the sultan turns to look at her. This one, named Leila, is new. She was brought into the harem a few weeks ago from Megina, and she is still shy of her new master. Chamar likes her for being unusually tall and thin, almost his height, with very white skin and straight black hair, reaching almost down to her ankles. He feels a strong desire awaken in him, but he doesn't want to rush it.

"What *about* Zarema, my pretty Leila?" he asks, making her blush even more.

"She wants to say that Zarema is about to have a baby," Ana'id explains. "Anytime now. The midwife is with her."

Another baby. Maybe, finally, a son? The sultan's heart beats faster. He had forgotten Zarema's baby was due so soon. He stopped seeing her several months ago, when her belly became too big for his taste. And now he is about to see another fruit of his sport, his pleasure, his game. Chamar raises his face into the reddish stream of the waning sunlight and makes a silent prayer to the gods, the only ones who have the power to give him what he wants.

Something heavy lands in his lap; and he looks down to see a girl of about five, her dark eyes shining with mischief, fluffy hair all messed up from running around. One of the women hurries toward them and stops, seeing Chamar smile at the child.

"What is your name, little one?" Chamar asks.

"Chamarat Ida," the girl proudly says, stumbling through the syllables of the difficult word "Chamarat."

"Ida? What a beautiful name!" Chamar absently pats the girl on the head and, lifting her, hands her to her mother. He has so many daughters. Why not sons? *Why not just one son?*

"Will it be your pleasure to eat something, master?" Ana'id says.

Looking up, Chamar suddenly feels the longing for her mature calmness, for her comforting touch. She has been his for ten years. She knows exactly what he likes.

"Why don't you have dinner served in your chamber, Ana'id?" Chamar says.

"With pleasure, master." Ana'id rises from her seat. "I will make the arrangements."

Chamar watches her walk away, her back straight, her hips gently rocking with her steps.

He looks at Leila, bent over her needlework, a few paces away from him. Not much more than a child herself, she looks tender and fragile, as warm patches of orange sunlight pour through the palm leaves onto her face, the sharp angles of her narrow shoulders, and down her long thin arms. On impulse Chamar moves closer, reaching over and touching her milky skin, just above the elbow.

She trembles slightly but doesn't draw away as Chamar runs his fingers up her bare arm, over her shoulder, along her neck to stop at her cheek. He gently strokes her face, drawing her closer and closer, feeling her hesitate without any real reluctance to submit to his caresses. Extremely young and bashful, she has remained a virgin much longer than the others, and even now Chamar is trying to hold off his passion, to take it slowly, to be very patient with her. At the same time he feels that today she is finally ready for him.

"Come with me," he whispers, holding her at half arm's length, looking straight into her cherry-black eyes.

"My lord," she whispers back, not struggling and yet not coming any closer of her own will.

"Come. Don't be afraid. We'll just eat together." He gets up from the ground and pulls her with him, drawing her after him in the direction Ana'id had disappeared. Gently but firmly Chamar takes Leila to the second courtyard, the third door on the left.

Inside, the light is dim. The low table is set with food and cushions are carefully placed around it. Cushions for more than two. Ana'id knows all his tricks and fancies even better than he does himself. The air in her chamber is warm and lightly perfumed.

"Come in." Ana'id beckons them, bowing to the sultan. She had decorated herself, putting on a robe of green silk and a heavy diadem of gold, with crystal droplets hanging down over her forehead. She helps the sultan down to his pillow, the silk flowing seductively over the curves of her body, and gently pats Leila on the shoulder, placing her on Chamar's left and sitting down herself opposite him. At Chamar's sign, the slave women serving at the table leave, closing the curtain behind them.

A simple meal of *dalma*—stewed lamb in marinated grape leaves—garlic chicken, and hot bread, seems especially delicious to Chamar. He eats his food slowly, knowing what is to follow and not wanting to rush it, to waste any moment of his wonderful anticipation. He looks admiringly at Leila, who blushes and looks down. From time to time he reaches out to touch her arm or shoulder or cheek, and her shivers fill him with renewed desire.

Ana'id pours three cups of sweet garnet-colored wine and rises to serve it to Chamar and Leila. She kneels on the floor between them and puts her arm around Leila's shoulders, holding a cup to the girl's lips and urging her to drink. Watching them, Chamar sips his own wine, feeling light-headed, a pleasant warmth flowing through his body. He picks up a handful of grapes, glistening in the light of a single lantern like long oval pieces of amber, and eats them one by one, their bursts of fresh sweetness in his mouth adding to the taste of wine, rising up in bubbles straight to his head. Unfastening the belt of his silk robe he lets it slide half off, baring his torso to the warmth of the fragrant air, and to the closeness of the two women that makes the muscles in his body tense up as if in preparation for battle.

He watches Ana'id pour another cup of wine for Leila, the two of them now sitting close together on the floor. Their faces begin to move slowly toward each other, their arms touching; Ana'id looks deeply in the girl's eyes and plants a light kiss on her mouth, brushing her lips back and forth against Leila's lips as the girl's breathing begins to quicken. Unable to contain his mounting desire, Chamar leans forward, drawing Ana'id closer as he presses her lips in a passionate kiss. He reaches beyond her toward Leila and finds her hands respond to his touch with an awkward caress that suddenly makes him feel every hair in his body rise in excitement.

Wine is the nectar of desire. Leila's eyes sparkle as she puts down her empty cup, her usually pale face aflame. As Chamar draws her toward him, he senses none of her usual reluctance.

She comes to him willingly, without hesitation, submitting to his kisses and to Ana'id's caresses. Chamar barely remembers undressing them, the cool smoothness of the sheets, silk robes sliding off to reveal the softness of skin to his eager touch. He submerges into their caresses as if diving into warm tingling water; two pairs of unhurried, supple hands gently stroke his arms, his neck, and the insides of his thighs, as he feels moist silky hair and hard breasts rise and sweep again and again across his chest, his face, and burning fingertips. He hears the low moans of Leila's now aching desire.

Excitement fills him like a vessel sailing the waves of a now endless sea of arms, breasts, hair, kisses, each of them telling a tale, guiding him, surer and surer, to his uncharted goal. As the three of them merge into a single creature of passion, he grows stronger and stronger, to the point of being unbearable—and beyond, over the peak, into a deep ocean of relaxation, of bliss, where the caresses are soothing, calming him down after the moment—the eternity—of ultimate happiness. And then, deeply satisfied, he sleeps.

Chamar wakes up, feeling the body against him stir. Moonlight streaking in through the window falls on the floor near the bed, on the table with the remains of yesterday's meal, on the pillows, scattered around the floor. In the dim glow of reflected moonlight Chamar sees a slender naked body at his side, long hair flowing loosely, covering him like a silky blanket. Leila is sleeping beside him like a baby, all her fears of last night gone, her head on his shoulder, her arm thrown boldly across his chest.

Chamar smiles at the sleeping girl, slowly awakening to the realization that Ana'id is not in the room with them and that the light outside is coming not only from the moon but from blazing torches as well, their yellow patches wavering against an even silver sheen. He also hears voices in the courtyard and realizes that perhaps what actually awoke him was some noise from the outside, a noise that also causes Leila to stir.

What could the fuss be about at this hour of the night? Chamar wonders sleepily. *Where is Ana'id? What is going on?*

He carefully removes Leila's arm from his chest and places it on the curve of her thigh. The girl mumbles something in her sleep and curls up, pulling her knees up to her chest.

She must be cold, Chamar thinks, pulling up a sheet to cover her and noticing, his eyes adjusted to the dim light, that the sheet is stained with blood.

She was a virgin last night, he remembers. And now she is carrying his seed inside. Maybe she will be the chosen one, the mother of his son and heir?

He takes another sheet and covers the sleeping girl, then puts on his robe and carefully finds his way to the door.

Several women with torches are standing in the courtyard, talking in lowered voices. As he moves toward them, one of the women separates from the group and runs straight to him. The sultan recognizes Ana'id, her hair in disorder, her nightdress flowing loosely in the breeze.

"Your majesty!" she exclaims, her eyes shining with excitement. "Zarema gave birth to a son!"

At first Chamar feels as if his heart had suddenly fallen into an abyss and, instead of recovering its regular beat, keeps falling down, leaving his chest hollow and himself breathless and weak. He raises his head, fighting against that hollow place, focusing all his feelings in a silent prayer of thanks. Thanks to the gods who heard his wish. Thanks to these women who were by him through all his misery. Thanks to Zarema, the new mother of his hope.

"Where is she?" he asks as soon as he gets his breath back. "Where is my son? I want to go to them!"

"This way, your majesty," Ana'id takes him by the hand and leads him, almost senseless, to the fourth courtyard, where the crowd is the largest, all gathered around Zarema's open door.

"Make way for the sultan!" Ana'id exclaims in the manner of a captain of the guard escorting a royal procession. Women back off—their faces a mixture of joy and fear. Joy at the birth of a son; fear, because this son is not the first to be born to the sultan. It is not enough for the son to be born. The newborn has to live.

The sultan knows the reason for the fear, but he pushes it aside in a wave of excitement as the old midwife hands him a tiny bundle of cloth, a wrinkled head, no larger than Chamar's fist, buried deep in its folds.

Chamar had held many of his babies soon after they were born and he never ceases to marvel at the eyes of these tiny creatures, not quite human in appearance but bearing that bright look of ancient wisdom, as if they had come from a world more perfect than the one they have been just brought into. Later, after several weeks, this expression disappears completely, replaced by the more familiar, cute, senseless, and curious look of a little baby. But with the newborns Chamar always feels inferior, as if beholding a higher truth.

"Is he well?" Chamar asks the midwife, his lips slightly trembling with emotion. He feels like crying. But nobody has ever seen him cry, and he, the ruler of a great empire and the master of this palace, will not cry.

"So far he is fine, your majesty," the midwife answers. She has delivered almost all of the sultan's children and she knows the stakes better than anyone. She is not about to disillusion the sultan in any case, and her calm confidence soothes him. He holds the child as a priceless treasure, watching the moonlight stream upon his wrinkled face, the huge eyes, blue like all babies' eyes are. He watches the boy stir in his wrappings, opening and closing his toothless mouth.

"Why doesn't he cry?" Chamar asks in alarm.

"He is a good boy, your majesty," the midwife says. "He doesn't need to cry. His mother will feed him anyway."

She takes the child from the sultan with firm hands and carries him back into the house. Chamar, standing in the middle of the courtyard, suddenly feels completely lost.

"Come, master," Ana'id says from behind, gently putting an arm around his shoulders, as if he himself were a child. "Come back to bed. Zarema and the baby need rest. We'll visit them again in the morning."

Unwittingly, Chamar lets her lead him away, undress him, and make him lie down beside Leila, who is fast asleep, curled in her blanket at the farthest corner of the bed. Ana'id takes off her robe and lies next to him, covering them both with a single blanket. She puts Chamar's head on her shoulder and caresses him, and he feels more and more like a child cuddled against his mother. He feels like crying again and swallows a lump in his throat, burying his face in Ana'id's breasts, letting her soothe him to sleep just like a mother would. Just like his new-born son, now asleep at his mother's breast.

The first sunbeams shine into the window. Overwhelmed by a sense of urgency, Chamar gets out of the bed, trying not to awaken the two women sleeping at his side. He puts on his robes and goes straight to the fourth courtyard.

The crowd of women in front of Zarema's door is gone. The door itself is open and, feeling his heart beat faster, the sultan walks inside.

Zarema is lying in her bed, asleep, her face pale and drawn, her hair in disorder, her swollen breasts bare over a sheet that covers the rest of her body. The midwife, sitting at the side of the bed, is dozing off, her head rhythmically nodding forward and jerking back in an unconscious reflex to stay awake. Two slave women in the corner, putting away the bloodstained sheets, throw fearful looks at Chamar and move further away into the depth of the room.

At first Chamar cannot see the baby, but then he notices a bundle on the bed, by Zarema's left arm, a tiny wrinkled face close to her breast.

"Wake up!" Chamar exclaims, striding into the room and shaking the midwife. "How can you sleep?"

The old woman sits up, yawning. It takes her several moments to awaken completely and hurry over to the child.

"It wasn't an easy delivery, you know," she mutters. "Let the poor girl sleep. We'll take care of the baby."

As she reaches over to pick up the child, the mother stirs too. Seeing the sultan, she tries to sit up, but she is still too weak.

The sultan gives her a gentle nod of appreciation. But his attention is devoted to the child.

"How is he?" Chamar asks the midwife. Seeing the concern on the old woman's face he rushes toward her, watching her slowly unwrap the tiny body, unlike other newborns, barely moving its tiny arms and legs. Alas, he has seen it all too often.

"I'll fetch the doctor!" he exclaims. "By the gods, he needs a doctor!"

"Your majesty! A man?" The old woman rolls her eyes.

"I don't care!" Chamar runs out, calling for the eunuch guards.

"Have all the concubines stay in their rooms!" he orders. "And fetch me Doctor Rashid! Hurry!"

The wait for the doctor seems like an eternity. Chamar sits on the edge of the bed, watching his tiny son struggle, watching the women try in vain to offer a breast. The lump in his throat just won't go away. When finally the eunuchs open the curtain to let in the doctor, Chamar feels the relief of exhaustion. He is glad, more than anything, to place his problem on somebody else's shoulders.

Rashid, a deft middle-aged man, is probably the best doctor in the whole of Dhagabad. He does not specialize in childbirth, leaving it to the midwives, but in case of serious problems Chamar trusts him above all. And now, even as Rashid walks in and opens his bag of instruments and medicines, Chamar feels easier.

In strained silence he watches Rashid examine the baby, using some strange tools that include a metal tube with two widened ends, resembling a trumpet of sorts. Rashid puts one end against his ear and the other against the baby's tiny chest, listens, and then consults with the midwife in a low voice. The frown on their faces makes Chamar's heart sink.

Finally they approach the sultan, their faces grim.

"Alas, your majesty," the doctor says, "there is nothing we can do."

"Do you mean—" Chamar pauses to collect himself. "Will my son die?"

"I am afraid so," Rashid says, bowing his head. "I am very sorry, your majesty."

Chamar clenches his teeth, once again addressing the gods in his silent prayer, this time stained with bitterness. Why do they give something to him only to take it back? *Why do all my sons have to die?*

He sees the little body in the midwife's arms stir less and less, finally ceasing his struggle. Unable to watch anymore, Chamar strides out into the now sunlit courtyard, sinks down onto its cobbled stones, buries his face in his hands, and weeps.

THE WILL OF THE GODS

❁

*T*he princess is absently watching the sage Haib al-Mutassim move a long wooden pointer over the old maps covering the walls. The sage is saying something, but the princess finds herself unable to focus on his words. She is much more aware of Alamid sitting next to her.

She hasn't spoken to her friend since the incident with Hasan, more than a week ago, and she is torn between her hurt feelings and a natural desire to be on good terms with the outside world and all its inhabitants. More than that, in the very depths of her soul, she somehow understands her friend's desire to touch Hasan's arm, forgetting herself completely in the face of his overwhelming charm. This understanding itself disturbs her, and although she is trying to cover it up with her anger at Alamid for lying, it doesn't allow her to feel righteously offended.

From time to time she glances sidelong at Alamid, who appears to be fully absorbed in the history lesson. But when the princess looks away it seems to her that Alamid also steals occasional glances in her direction, making the princess more and more certain that her older friend also wishes for peace between them.

"Princess!"

The sage's stern voice makes her jump. She realizes with terror that the teacher has been addressing her, and that she, absorbed in her thoughts, doesn't have the slightest idea what the lesson is about.

She stands up, eyeing the sage with fear. He is probably the wisest and the most well-read man in the whole palace, and he takes it upon himself to teach the princess those disciplines that are necessary for her difficult role as the sultan's heiress. She takes lessons with him three times a week, with Alamid as her companion, and she knows very well what it means not to pay attention to the lesson.

The sage's long wrinkled face, his skin looking even darker because of the whiteness of his hair and beard, is not smiling.

"Repeat what I just said, princess," the sage says with terrifying calmness.

"You—you called me, teacher," the princess says desperately, knowing how useless it is to try to stall her teacher like this.

"Before that."

"I—I wasn't listening, teacher." She lowers her head, feeling blood rush up to her face and make her ears burn.

"Very well," the sage says. "Today's lesson, for your information"—he frowns and she feels her heart sink—"was on the Ghullo-Aethian War. Since your highness did not consider the subject worthy enough to pay attention to, I expect you to study it on your own and to tell me about it tomorrow."

The princess knows well what it means when the sage calls her "your highness," and she lowers her head even more. She respects the sage Haib al-Mutassim greatly, and she always struggles to win his approval. When she fails to do it, like today, she feels completely defeated.

"Yes, teacher," she manages.

"I will see you tomorrow at noon then," the sage says. "The lesson is over."

As the princess and Alamid find themselves again outside the classroom, all the concerns arise in her with new force. This is definitely not one of her best days.

"Alamid," she begins, willing to take the first step.

"Well," Alamid bursts out. "You shouldn't worry about that lesson, should you? Just tell your new slave to punish the old man!"

"Punish?" The princess suddenly feels lost.

"You should use your djinn for *something*, don't you think?" Alamid exclaims with sarcasm.

"What do you mean?" the princess asks.

"Well..." Alamid rolls her eyes. "I know you are beyond such things, but he is a man, you know. And a handsome one, too."

"He is a spirit," the princess corrects her.

"That is what he told you. But it is enough to take one look at him to realize he is a man. I mean, he is a sorcerer, and he knows all their tricks, but in the end it is just the same. And you can order him to do anything you want, right?"

"Right," the princess says, still uncertain.

"Well," Alamid says impatiently, "you are not the saint you are trying to look like. And it is time for you to grow up, just a little bit! All I am trying to say is that you can put him to many uses."

"Like what?"

The conversation is not going the way she expects, and the princess is trying very hard to catch her friend's meaning.

"Like—not having to learn lessons. Like—making people do what you want. Like—*enjoying* him, you know!"

"I think I do, Alamid," the princess says quietly. She suddenly realizes that Alamid is completely missing the point. To her, Hasan is merely a slave, a tool to serve her pleasures and to achieve her goals. That was why she behaved as she did, the princess suddenly understands. And that is why they are so different. In fact, they are so different that they may never understand each other.

"I'll see you at tomorrow's class, Alamid," the princess says. Turning, she walks away.

"Your majesty," Shamil repeats with monotonous patience, "as a vizier I must counsel your majesty to the best of my knowledge. Everything I know about the djinns—and I took the liberty of consulting the sage Haib al-Mutassim about them—everything tells me it is extremely dangerous to use them. Take the sultan of Veridue, for instance."

"I know the old Veriduan tale about their great-grandfather or something," Chamar interrupts impatiently. "He just didn't use the djinn properly, that's all. It takes nothing to create rumors of how dangerous the djinns are. In reality, one just has to be wise dealing with them."

"The sultan of Veridue died because of his mistake, your majesty. I respect your wisdom greatly, but don't you think the stakes are a bit too high?"

"I am not asking for myself, Shamil," Chamar insists. "I merely want to have a son who lives. All my sons are dead anyway, remember? My last son died yesterday. Things cannot possibly be any worse."

"You never know, your majesty," Shamil says with a sigh, realizing the uselessness of arguing in this matter, where the sultan's overwhelming desire to get what he wants overpowers all the rest. *And perhaps the sultan is right*, Shamil thinks. *Perhaps there is nothing worse than having your sons die at birth.* He himself has two sons and they are a great support to him in his old age. He has only one daughter and she is more of a burden than a joy, given the necessity of marrying her off with honor and profit.

"Come on, Shamil," Chamar says, sensing the end of the argument. "I think it would be best if you go to the princess yourself and ask her to make the djinn available for conversation. Have him come to the audience chamber. And also—the sage Haib al-Mutassim. Since he knows so much about djinns, I want him to be present."

"Your majesty—"

"I will see you in the audience chamber, Shamil," Chamar says and strides out of the room.

The princess closes the heavy library door behind her and stops, looking around the room. There are more books here than she could possibly read in several lifetimes; and although she often comes here to read or to pick out a book to take back to her quarters, she still can't figure out how to actually *find* the exact books she wants.

She walks between the rows of shelves that run from floor to ceiling, enclosing her in a long narrow space she somehow finds comforting. The books seem to absorb sound and movement, creating a feeling of soft stillness that seems to scare away time itself. In some places the even rows are interrupted by long boxes containing, as she knows, the old scrolls people used before bookbinding was invented.

She knows that books here are organized by subject, and she finds the history section easily, having been there before. But where should she go next? Books within subject sections are arranged alphabetically by author's name or, in the absence of author, by title. But who would write about the Ghullo-Aethian War? What would be the title of such a book?

The library is the realm of the sage Haib al-Mutassim. He is the one who, with the help of several young scholars, keeps the books organized and properly accounted for. Of course, she could simply go to her teacher and ask him, but she doesn't even want to think about how humiliating that would be. She has to prove to him she is capable of doing her homework without his help, however impossible it may seem.

She stops again, feeling lost. There is no way to find the right book and learn it by tomorrow! Maybe she could ask one of the sage's scholars? But they would surely tell Haib.

The princess walks along the shelves of the history section, running her eyes randomly over the titles. *The Prosperity of Megina, Dimeshqian Caravans, Baskary of Old, The Customs of Stikts...* She moves to *G—Ghull. The Great River, Ghullian Traditions...* nothing on war. Maybe *W* for *war?*

She searches briefly through the *W* section. *Willful Rulers, The Wonders of Dimeshq...* She stops in frustration. Some books don't even have titles on their bindings. She has to take them off the shelves and look inside. This is taking too long. Even if she does find the right book in the end, she will have no time to read it. What can she do?

The answer suddenly pops into her head; and she smiles in relief, amazed that she didn't think of it before.

"Hasan!" she calls out softly, watching his figure materialize right in front of her even before the sound of her voice dies down. She sighs happily, relaxing after her strain, feeling like a child who was lost in a strange place and suddenly wanders right into his mother's arms.

"Princess?" Hasan says with a flicker in his eyes that tells her he knows exactly what she needs.

"I need to learn about the Ghullo-Aethian War by tomorrow," she says, knowing by now that she has to spell out her wish to enable him to fulfill it. "Can you help me find the right book?"

"There are a hundred and thirty-seven books here on that subject, princess, and many more that have at least some mention of the war. But I think the most useful for you would be this one."

Hasan moves to the shelf in a single graceful movement and, without any hesitation, pulls out a small book in a thick leather binding. Even from where she stands the princess can see that there are no words or markings on the smooth leather cover, no indication on the outside of what the book may be about. She takes it from Hasan's hands and carefully opens it not to disturb the thin parchment pages inside. The title reads: *The Most Accurate Account of the Conflict Between the Two Kingdoms on the Shores of the Great River*. Such a long title. No mention of Aeth and Ghull whatsoever. Of course she should know that these two kingdoms are on the shores of the Great River, but in her rush she would have missed it for sure.

"I would never have found it by myself, Hasan," she says slowly, realizing how helpless she is in this library without guidance. "I wonder, how does the sage Haib al-Mutassim do it?"

"Actually, princess," Hasan says, "there are index volumes over there."

He points to the corner of the room, where three huge books are lying open on stands nearly as tall as she is.

"Each of these books has cross-references that point to the numbers on the shelves."

"Can you teach me how to use it, Hasan?" the princess asks hopefully.

"Certainly, princess."

The library door creaks, and the princess looks up sharply, afraid to be caught by her teacher. But the newcomer is not lean and longhaired, like the sage. He is bald, and, although somewhat younger, he moves with the difficulty of a man who pays little attention to his physical fitness. It takes a few moments for the princess to place a name to the bald man with a bushy gray beard who unhurriedly walks toward her and respectfully stops a few paces short.

Shamil. Her father's grand vizier.

This man belongs to the world to which the princess has no access—to the special world of the north wing of the palace, to her father's dwelling, to the world she associates with the ruling power of the country. Seeing the vizier close up fills her with a mixture of uneasiness and curiosity. It must certainly be something very important that made the old man seek her out in the library and stand before her now, with his head bowed.

"Princess," Shamil begins, glancing uneasily at Hasan beside her. "I apologize for disturbing you. The sage Haib al- Mutassim suggested you might be found in the library."

The sage. Does he know everything?

"The sultan wishes to speak with your slave," Shamil continues.

It takes the princess several moments to realize he must mean Hasan. During the past months Hasan has become so much more than a slave to her that it sounds strange and unpleasant when somebody refers to him as such.

"You mean—Hasan?" she asks, not showing her displeasure,

and yet trying in her own quiet way to point out the mistake to the vizier.

"Yes, princess," the old man says calmly, raising a finger in Hasan's direction. "The djinn."

"What does my father want with Hasan?" the princess wonders, half to herself.

"His majesty's higher purposes are beyond my knowledge, princess." Shamil bows his head in a gesture of respect. Also, the princess knows, this bow is in a way intended to show the princess her place, and Shamil's intention to keep silent—because after her father's will is spoken there is nothing more to say.

"Hasan," the princess says, turning, "will you go with Shamil and talk to my father?"

"If such is your wish, princess," Hasan replies.

Her wish. Of course, she wishes for Hasan to stay with her in the library. But, like everyone in Dhagabad, she is one of her father's subjects and cannot possibly disobey him. Besides, it must be something important if her father sent Shamil to ask her for the djinn. After all, what does she, a girl, know of the affairs of state?

"It is my wish, Hasan," she says quietly.

As she watches the two men walk toward the library door, another thought occurs to her.

"Hasan," she calls out, "when you are finished, please come back here. I will be reading."

"Your wish is my command, princess," Hasan replies, and before he turns to walk away she catches a merry sparkle in his eyes.

The audience chamber, in the heart of the north wing, has none of the glamour of the great ceremonial hall, but it has something else instead—a feeling of the ancient power of the royal dynasty of Dhagabad emanating from its walls. It is the oldest part of the palace, and the gloominess of its small windows and dark vaulted ceiling immediately overpowers anyone who walks in from the sunlit front gallery.

The sultan always liked this place. To him, unlike anyone else, it feels that it is *his* power and *his* glory that these stone walls project, and that its depressing massiveness is designed to diminish anyone before *him*. He often uses this hall to receive ambassadors, watching with some pleasure these haughty men lose more and more of their self-importance with every step they take into the chamber.

Chamar doesn't know why he chose this place to speak to the djinn, passing up the more casual comfort of his own quarters. Does he want to acknowledge in this way the importance of the subject? Or, perhaps, he wants to diminish this ancient wizard the way he diminishes the ambassadors that come to court? Is he trying to somehow compensate for the fact that he has to *ask* something of his daughter's *slave*?

He slowly walks around the hall, talking to the sage Haib al-Mutassim, their voices hollow under the vault of the ceiling.

"The princess is a very talented student, your majesty," the sage is saying. "I have rarely seen anyone progress as fast in their studies. I think, where learning is concerned, she is equal to a man, even better than some of them, if I may be so bold."

The sultan listens to the teacher's praise with a mixture of pride and bitterness. If his *daughter* is so good at learning, one can only imagine how good his *son* would be. Everyone knows women are less capable of learning simply because they are women. His bloodlines must be exceptionally good to produce such a talented daughter. Why is he accursed in this horrible way?

These thoughts direct him more toward matters at hand, and he interrupts the sage's praise.

"Tell me more about the djinn, Haib," he says. "What can we expect from him?"

"Nothing magical, without the princess around," Haib says. "But he is very old and wise. Don't let your majesty be deceived by his youthful appearance. He is much wiser than anyone your majesty has ever met. Whatever advice he gives may be tricky."

It is not advice that I seek, Chamar thinks. *But I will not tell that to Haib.*

He hears the clanking sound of the door, and a streak of sunlight for a moment slides into the dark hall and disappears again. Two figures enter and stop several paces into the room. The one on the left is Shamil. As for the one on the right…

Since his daughter's birthday ceremony, the sultan hasn't seen the djinn at all, and even then he didn't pay much attention to the looks of this strange creature, overwhelmed by the general chaos that surrounded his appearance. And now, facing the djinn, the first thing he feels is disappointment.

An ordinary young man, no better looking than some of his guards, is standing before him with an impassive expression on his face. Chamar suddenly feels awkward seeking help from him, just as if he were seeking help from a common guard in the palace.

"Are you—the djinn?" he asks with uncertainty.

"Yes, your majesty."

There *is* something different about him, Chamar notes. None of his guards would address him with the calmness of an equal. No man who ever stood in this chamber looked so unaffected by its ancient grandeur, by the majesty of the sultans of Dhagabad.

"And your name is—" The sultan tries to remember, feeling that it would be somehow right to address this creature properly.

"Hasan, your majesty."

"Well, Hasan, there is something I wish to ask you."

The djinn silently meets his eyes, and the sultan feels startled by the absence of the usual responses—"It is my honor to serve your majesty," or "Anything you wish, your majesty," or something else like that, something that any one of his subjects would say. No, this creature is definitely different from anything he has seen before.

Taken aback, the sultan feels at the same time somehow

more comfortable that he is dealing with someone out of the ordinary and that this time his request may reach a capable ear.

He also feels something else. He absolutely cannot continue this conversation, feeling vulnerable, with his usual servants around.

"Leave us," he says, turning to Shamil and Haib.

"But, your majesty," Shamil says weakly.

"I wish to speak to Hasan alone."

Hearing the finality in his voice, the two old men bow and leave the room. Chamar watches them close the door behind them, then shifts his eyes to the djinn whose expression doesn't seem to change a bit. His gray eyes are completely impenetrable, and yet something in his face tells Chamar that Hasan knows what the sultan wishes to ask him, and he is not going to make it any easier.

"Why is it that I don't have any sons?" Chamar asks on impulse.

"Is this what you wished to ask me, your majesty?"

A shadow moves over Hasan's face as he looks straight into the sultan's eyes—a shadow of something that resembles both a frown and a smile.

"No," Chamar says, swallowing a lump in his throat. "But first I wish to know the answer to this question."

"It is a quality, a—condition—that makes it highly improbable for your sons to survive, your majesty," Hasan says. "While your chances of conceiving a son are just the same as any man's, your sons are destined to die before, or just after, they are born."

"But why?"

"Such is your inheritance, your majesty," Hasan says. "In your mother's dynasty all men suffered the same condition."

"You call it a condition, Hasan," the sultan says with a sinking heart. "Is that an illness?"

"Not really, your majesty. You yourself are in perfect health. It affects only your sons."

Chamar clenches his teeth. He cannot, will not, give up!

"Can I ever have a son, Hasan?" he asks.

"There is a chance, your majesty," Hasan says, "but it is very small."

Chamar takes a deep breath and rushes straight forward.

"I wish for you to make it possible for me to have a son," he says, "just one. I need an heir to the throne."

He slowly raises his eyes, half expecting to see devilish scorn on the djinn's face. But what he sees startles him even more. The expression on Hasan's face is gentle. Chamar even seems to see something close to compassion in his features.

"By your mother's will I belong to the princess, your majesty," Hasan says. "I cannot obey anyone else's wishes."

"Does it mean"—Chamar's heart races in wild hope—"if she wished for it, you could do it?"

"Yes, your majesty," Hasan says, "but it must be her whole-hearted wish. She has to have her own reasons to want me to do it."

"She is a nice child," Chamar says. "She never disobeyed me. She will do it for me."

"I believe she will not disobey you, your majesty," Hasan says, "but to make it a genuine wish she has to go beyond simple obedience. Your majesty does realize that she is your heiress now, and I believe she graces her station quite well. Being an heiress she is already involved in this problem more than anyone else. Does your majesty really want her to get even more involved? Do you want the princess to wholeheartedly wish for another heir to the throne?"

Startled, the sultan takes another look at the djinn and catches a glimpse of something that escaped him before, something that he believes most people in the palace must be missing. There is something human in this ancient creature. Chamar senses genuine concern in his speech that goes somewhat beyond the indifferent responses of a slave. He suddenly sees something he thought impossible before. The djinn, this spirit of an all-powerful wizard, enslaved by a force nobody knows anything about, seems to care for his young daughter. Perhaps there is really something in all this that the sultan doesn't understand. Perhaps there is a higher purpose in his having no sons, so that his firstborn daughter with her extraordinary scholarly abilities can be ruler of Dhagabad. Perhaps married to the right man and with the help of her all-powerful slave she could serve Dhagabad better than any of Chamar's sons would.

Chamar suddenly feels small and inadequate in the face of higher powers and purposes. Does he really want to forcefully change his destiny, the will of the gods, knowing nothing of their motives and goals? And does he really want to get his daughter, his heiress and commander of a mighty wizard, involved in his problems even more than she already is? It must be not easy for her. A great burden already lies on her shoulders. Does Chamar really want to make her his tool in changing the will of the gods?

"I don't want to get her involved, Hasan," Chamar says finally, bowing his head.

BAZAAR

❈

"You know, Hasan, I read a tale about a caliph who, together with his grand vizier walked on the city streets disguised as merchants. It sounded so wonderful! Let's turn into merchants and go to the Dhagabad bazaar!"

The princess says this, trying with all her might to make it sound like something insignificant, but her effort fills every word with anxiety, blown completely out of proportion. Trying to counterbalance this impression, the princess glances sidelong at Hasan, making her face look as easygoing as possible. She is dying to fulfill her wish to go to the bazaar in the lower city as one of the ordinary citizens, and she is very proud of the way she thought to suggest it. At the same time, remembering how long the bazaar has been forbidden to her, and not wanting to do anything against the better judgment of her new friend, she is mortally afraid of being refused, forgetting that Hasan has no power to deny her any of her wishes.

She sees a smile pass through Hasan's eyes—a smile that, as usual, fleetingly changes his face, showing her better than words that he sees all her complicated feelings, all her tricks and schemes. But his reply, as always, is calm and impassive.

"It is not safe this time of the year, princess."

The princess sighs, ready to submit to the inevitable and forget her new idea. But instantly pictures start floating up in her mind's eye, colorful scenes she saw in the side streets and plazas of the bazaar, where people somehow feel no obligation to bow their heads at the passage of the royal train. The longing that she used to feel as she stood on the palace balcony, peering into the distant network of narrow streets, overwhelms her, replacing her childish wish to play a new game with the unreasonable stubbornness of an adolescent whim.

"But you can protect us from anything, Hasan!" she insists.

"Unfortunately, I cannot protect you from bad experiences, princess."

What bad experience can one possibly have at the bazaar? the princess thinks, still remembering the brightness of the colors, the mixture of strange sounds and smells, and the joyous bustle of the seething crowd.

"I wish to go to the bazaar, Hasan!" she exclaims.

"Your wish is my command, princess," the djinn replies with a slight bow.

In a moment his looks change completely. The simple elegance of his loose white shirt and pants of dark silk is transformed to the rich brightness of a typical merchant's clothes: colorful wide robe, crimson pants, and gold-embroidered shoes. His short dark hair is now hidden by a turban, with a piece of cloth coming out of it like a scarf, lying on his shoulders and covering the top of his chest. The princess sees nothing but a young merchant in front of her, indistinguishable in appearance from any other Dhagabad merchant. Only the quiet look of the gray eyes and the face, half familiar in its new frame, remind her that this new acquaintance is her djinn.

Excited, the princess forgets all her stubbornness.

"You make such a funny merchant, Hasan!" she exclaims. "I have never seen you in a robe and turban."

"Wait until you look in the mirror, princess!" he says with a barely perceptible smile.

The princess throws an uninterested look at the mirror, where she sees a venerable old man in a bright pink robe, blue pants, and a gold-embroidered turban. And then she is suddenly startled—*an old man—in the mirror?*

"Do you mean to say that the old man in the mirror is me?"

"Why old, princess?" Hasan grins. "About fifty—quite a respectable age."

"Respectable? What about you? Couldn't you at least wear a beard?"

"I don't need a beard, princess. I will pretend to be your son. What could be more natural at the bazaar than to protect your venerable old father from the roughness of the throng?"

"Just you wait, Hasan! You will regret this!" The princess shakes her fist at him in mock anger.

Hasan glances briefly at the princess, and she sees indecision in his eyes.

"Is something wrong, Hasan?" she asks, hurriedly looking over her new appearance. It is strange to see her new body, which reminds her of the grand vizier, Shamil. Physically she doesn't feel any different, but seeing herself move her big hand with its short fat fingers, seeing her sagging belly partly obscure her large feet, shod in elaborate pointed slippers, makes her feel completely detached from reality. Yet nothing seems to be wrong with her. Her new appearance, while not exactly attractive, seems fitting for the occasion.

"Let me create a magical defense around you, princess," Hasan says unexpectedly. "We could be separated in the crowd and I may not be able to come to your aid at once."

"You speak as if we are going into a battle," the princess says impatiently. She knows about battles from history books and the lessons of the sage Haib al-Mutassim, and she is certain she knows best. "No merchant needs a magical defense around him to go to the bazaar! I want to feel exactly like a common Dhagabad merchant!"

"As you wish, princess."

The princess barely has time to blink as a wave of half-familiar smells, deeply imprinted into her memory, hits her in the face, and she suddenly feels as if she is diving headfirst into whirling water. The quietness that surrounded her in the palace suddenly bursts with sound—loud wails of the merchants praising their goods, horses neighing, the disorderly music of the street bands, and the shrill cry of a peacock coming from somewhere nearby. Looking around, she finds herself and Hasan standing on a curved narrow street running straight into the Dhagabad bazaar.

The princess's breath catches with excitement. Forgoing all stubbornness, she happily hurries after the djinn. Harking back to that unimaginable time when she was still under twelve, she vaguely remembers the whirlpool of colors and sounds of the bazaar that she passed in her litter as a part of her mother's suite. The thought that she will soon enter the very heart of this magical place—the center of her dreams and desires—makes her want to scream with excitement. The way to the bazaar is no less wondrous than her wildest expectations. Clinging to Hasan's arm and fighting her way along the rows of merchandise, she tries not to miss anything. She watches a fakir playing a monotonous tune on his flute while a fat sleepy cobra lazily swings to the music. She sees a rug merchant wearing slippers with enormously long curled toes—his mustache carefully hidden in a special sheath—jumping up and down before a comely respectable old man accompanied by four captious wives. A handsome emir, surrounded by dark-skinned Ghullian bodyguards, swings a black Dimeshqian blade back and forth, carefully listening to the whizzing sound produced by the noble weapon; and the owner of the weapons shop fusses around, trying to please a rich customer. Everything here is strange and unusual to the princess. But the strangest thing of all is that everybody is calling her "father."

"Buy some silk, father! The sultan himself has never seen such a fine silk!"

"Spices, father, buy some spices! Spices from distant Megina!"

"My fruit is the best in all Dhagabad—ask anyone, father! I know a secret to growing persimmon—it just melts in your mouth! And these figs are pure honey!"

Someone shoves the princess hard from behind. She stumbles and, trying to regain her balance, releases Hasan's arm.

The crowd immediately sweeps her aside, and, struggling against the powerful stream, the princess is forced into an alley adjoining the main street of the bazaar.

"Hasan!" she yells, but her voice is completely drowned by the street noise.

"Quiet, father," an evil voice whispers behind her. A hand covers her mouth, and she feels the cold of steel at her throat.

"Come with us," the voice says. "And don't even think of trying to escape."

Feeling a chill inside her, the princess lets unknown hands lead her through a gate into a small courtyard. Her terror is made worse by her feelings of guilt—like a child who grabs a lit candle in spite of its being strictly forbidden, burning himself. Hasan had warned her they could become separated in the crowd and she might need a magical defense. Behaving like a spoiled child and insisting on having her way, she deserves every possible punishment, she chides herself. After all, everything happened just as Hasan said it would, and now he'll never help her because she is not worth it! Besides, he doesn't have to help her every time she gets into trouble without her direct order. He saved her from the Veriduan horse out of kindness; but now, when she no doubt hurt his feelings by stupidly refusing to follow his advice, why would he ever want to save her again? The princess shuts her eyes as burning tears run down her cheeks. Will she really die so needlessly at the hands of these people who don't even know who she really is?

"Give us your money, father," whispers the evil voice. She hears at least three men talking behind her, but she can't make out the words.

"I don't have any money," she answers. "Let me go."

"Search the old man," another voice says. "If you are lying to us, merchant, we will cut out your tongue!"

"Let him go!" A distinct voice resounds at the end of the courtyard.

Hasan!

The princess makes a movement to free herself, but the razor-sharp steel presses hard against her throat.

"Now, now! Here is the sonny boy!" the first voice says. "Listen, boy, run home on the double and get us three hundred dinars. That is, of course, if you don't want us to cut your daddy's throat."

The princess is turned around to face the courtyard entrance and she sees Hasan. He has thrown away the merchant's robe and turban and is moving with soft catlike steps along the wall, eyeing the two huge cutthroats muttering behind her back.

"Am I dreaming, or does this boy really want to fight?" one of them says scornfully. "Do you want to kill your father here?" He gives a signal, and the dagger cuts the skin at her throat, making the princess scream with sudden pain. Hasan lifts his head, his eyes flash, and all the rest happens as if in a dream. Moving faster than the human eye can follow, Hasan leaps forward and delivers a precise blow to the bandit holding the princess. He sinks to the ground like an empty sack. Landing on his feet, Hasan turns to face his other two enemies. Two blows that resemble snakebites in their speed and flying grace send them down, senseless, to the stones of the courtyard. Hasan grabs the princess just before she sinks limply into his arms.

"Princess?" he whispers, urging her to pronounce the wish he can easily fulfill.

"Take us back, Hasan," she manages to say, using all her strength to make her barely audible plea. She doesn't remember how she finds herself in her normal shape and in the safety of her chambers. She clings to Hasan, as the djinn gently holds her, and it seems that she will never again find the strength to leave the shelter of his safe embrace. Gradually, she regains her ability to speak.

"You didn't *kill* them, Hasan, did you?" she whispers.

"Of course not, princess," Hasan answers softly. "I just knocked them out for a while."

"It's all my fault," the princess sobs. "You warned me it could happen."

"It was unforgivable for me to let those men scare you, princess."

"I thought you would never come to my rescue after the way I behaved." Tears run down her cheeks and she cannot stop shivering. She clings to Hasan, and suddenly notices a little stream of blood running down her white sleeve. "Blood...they cut me with a dagger," the princess sobs, trembling.

"It will be all right, princess." Hasan gently runs his hand along her neck. "I will touch your wound and it will heal. There, it's all gone."

Hasan caresses her. The movement of his hands is soothing and the princess starts to feel the terror loosen its grasp. Only one thought still has her worried.

"Hasan," she says softly, raising her tearstained face to him, "please don't tell anyone about this! I don't want them to forbid me to see you."

"Of course not, princess," Hasan says, and she sees a very definite smile on his face. Holding her breath, she watches this smile lightly touch the corners of his mouth, gradually changing his complexion and making his eyes, which are gazing down on her, glow with a soft light. This lasts only for a moment, and then he turns away—as the princess, giving in completely to her fatigue and to his caress, lays her head on his shoulder. She feels her body become pleasantly heavy, the tears dry on her cheeks, and she sinks into a quiet peaceful sleep.

Her breath is even, her eyes are shut, and her pale cheeks, salty with tears, gradually regain their natural color. Looking at her, sleeping peacefully after the shock, you slowly let your mind become absorbed in its usual smooth flow of thoughts. You made a serious error, letting her drag you into an adventure that was too dangerous, even considering the precautions you took. It was unforgivable to over-

look anything in this way—unable to help her with your magic—leaving her to suffer such a brutal attack.... You give yourself a solemn oath not to make such mistakes in the future. And, at the same time, you feel surprised at the significance that you put on such a small episode, moreover, an episode with a happy ending.

What makes you care so much for this young girl, this little child? You are, after all, an all-powerful spirit who once chose the path to absolute knowledge and followed the way to its end. What makes you feel so much? The answer, which you have already found before, is put into new words in your mind. Having given in to your destiny, bearing the torture of absolute power, and losing your freedom, you have suddenly met someone who reflects the same feeling that long ago made you, a young fool and a talented mage, recklessly set your foot on the way to absolute knowledge. And now, at the end of your journey, you are ready to apply all your powers and knowledge to protect this someone, your young mistress, from the dangers of the outside world.

Your thoughts wander more deeply into the distant past. You remember your life after you gained immortality. You recall how at first your knowledge served your vanity, giving you immeasurable advantage over the people who surrounded you. How you later confined yourself to your Dimeshqian house, surrounded by books. How, searching anew for the company of people, you started to leave your refuge from time to time and wander around the noisy Dimeshqian bazaar, like the way you did with the princess today around the bazaar in Dhagabad. How those walks sometimes put you into very strange situations and led you to very unusual meetings. And gradually, without noticing it, you sink into memories as old as the burden of centuries that weighs on your shoulders.

The Dimeshqian bazaar on a Sunday morning resembles a thick field of colorful flowers that constantly ripples, changing and mov-

ing around so fast that anyone who happens to look from the side is instantly dazzled. But inside the churning mass, everyone knows his exact place and role, going about his business with surprising efficiency. Approaching the Plaza of Mages you suddenly find yourself engulfed in a stream of people. The powerful current carries you down the street, turns you right, right again, and finally brings you to the plaza, where it turns around to make an eddy and gradually scatters where a crowd is forming.

At the center of the plaza, you hear the sound of an argument coming from a stone platform, built in the shape of a giant pentagram. The crowd, with an enormous effort to lower its usual beehive humming, carefully catches the voices that float in waves above their heads. One—loud and confident, obviously belongs to someone who thinks highly of himself, and the other—is it possible?—is the voice of a woman.

"Repeat what you just said, O miserable one!" thunders the man. "Repeat your words, so that all these worthy people can witness your incredible foolishness!"

"I have been called by many names, mage." The woman's voice rings high above the crowd. "But no one has ever called me a fool!"

Squeezing between two gapers, you find yourself close enough to the platform to see them arguing. The man, whose black velvet cloak falls down his shoulders like a king's mantle, is familiar to you. He is the court mage to the sultan of Dimeshq. Galeot-din al-Gaul is a haughty character who knows the flashy tricks of magic well enough to dazzle a crowd and win a reputation as a great mage. You have never known, never even wondered, about the true limit of his powers; but now, standing in the crowd, you realize for the first time that the force that surrounds him is enormous. His handsome face is grim, and his eyes are shining with anger directed at the woman standing motionless opposite him. And, seeing that woman, you forget for a moment about the crowd, about the Plaza of Mages, about the pentagram, and about the haughty Galeot-din.

The woman is wrapped in a loose silvery-gray robe that enfolds her tall stately figure from head to toe like a cloud of mist. Her pale beautiful face with narrow catlike eyes is frowning. Strands of hair stray from under the shawl wrapping her head and shoulders, hair of a fiery-red color that you have never before seen. Her face and figure are completely enchanting, leaving the impression of flowing grace, further enhanced by the soft shine of a strange misty stone in a ring on her right forefinger. Sending your feelings in her direction, you realize that the woman is familiar with magic, but her powers, arranged mostly around the stone in her ring, are far less than the overwhelming force of Galeot-din. In the now-inevitable magic duel the woman is bound to lose.

The mage's voice thunders above the crowd:

"Are you saying, O miserable one, that you are arrogant enough to challenge me, the great mage Galeot-din al-Gaul?"

"I leave the decision to you, O great mage," the woman says, a quiet threat ringing in her voice.

"In that case, woman, I, Galeot-din al-Gaul of Dimeshq, challenge you to a magic duel! And let all these worthy people be the witnesses to my rightness and your defeat!"

Magic duels in the Plaza of Mages aren't unfamiliar to the people of Dimeshq. But many of them end in the death of the weaker mage, and often considerable damage to the nearby buildings is done. The crowd backs off, crushing the rear rows of spectators, leaving the center of the plaza around the giant pentagram totally empty.

Desperately pushing forward through the thick mass of people, you finally pop out into the open and stand alone in the empty space in front of the pentagram. Galeot-din, pale with anger, slowly turns his face to look straight at you.

"What are you doing here, Hasan?" he asks. "Did you, bookworm, come to challenge my place as a court mage? If that is so, you have to wait your turn."

Keeping your eyes on Galeot-din, you again direct your feelings toward the woman and sense that her fright is gradually replaced by a faint glimmer of hope. The woman is proud and angry—she would rather die than admit that she is wrong. But her magic is strong enough for her to know she cannot equal the power of the Dimeshqian court mage. There is no way for her to get out of this duel alive and well. The sudden intervention of this confident stranger, who in spite of his apparent youth emanates wisdom and power, is her only hope.

"I am not after your title, Galeot-din," you say. "It just seems to me that this woman is new in Dimeshq and may not be familiar with all the rules of a magic duel. And you wouldn't want to win without rules, would you, Galeot-din?"

By the laws of Dimeshq, one who wins the magic duel without rules loses his title as a mage and is thrown out of the city with shame. There is nothing more feared by wizards than to be accused of dishonesty in a magic duel. Even now, at your unexpected words, the crowd stirs in shock.

Galeot-din angrily straightens up.

"No one has ever accused me of fighting without rules!" he storms. "If you, Hasan the bookworm, dare to throw such an accusation into my face before all these respectable citizens, I will fight you immediately!"

"On one condition, Galeot-din," you say. "If I accept your challenge, you will leave this woman alone."

"This woman gravely insulted me!" the court mage announces. "No one has ever insulted the great Galeot-din without paying for it!"

"I am taking her words upon myself," you say. "Let me resolve both arguments with our duel."

Galeot-din pauses, sizing up his two opponents, and you easily read his thoughts. On the one hand, the woman would definitely make an easier target for his flashy magic. He could strike her down with one blow and let the people of Dimeshq fear and respect him even more. But on the other hand, Hasan, the mysterious ageless sage buried in his studies for as long as Galeot-din can remember, the wizard openly mocked as a bookworm and secretly feared for his unknown powers, presents an outstanding challenge. Defeating Hasan in a magic duel would bring him glory among the wise and among the ancient sages of the royal council that have great influence over the young sultan. Besides, this common bookworm dared to question the honesty of the great Galeot-din in front of half the people of Dimeshq. Such a crime cannot go unpunished! No one has ever questioned the great court mage!

"I accept!" Galeot-din proclaims.

You jump onto the platform and reach the woman in just a few strides. Her mask of proud anger can fool no one. The woman's every nerve is strained, and her deadly strain gradually eases at the sight of her protector, who might, she feels, possess a hidden power stronger even than that of the great Galeot-din.

The woman does not say a word. She slightly squeezes your arm, and with her touch you feel something flow through your body. A fleeting smile flashes in her narrow green eyes as she steps to the side of the platform, clearing a space for the magic duel.

Sounds on the plaza have ceased. No one exists in the world except your opponent, with his black velvet cloak streaming down his back, his fiery eyes shining in his face, pale with anger. You haven't demonstrated your art before a crowd in a long while—you got past your vanity a couple of centuries ago. You are now known in Dimeshq as the book-learned sage who has somehow managed to overcome time. You now feel strange, standing on the pentagram above the crowd, facing the famous Dimeshqian mage who is poised to strike you dead.

Spells that you know so well but keep hidden away in some distant corner of your memory slowly come to mind. You feel, rather than see, the black figure at the other end of the pentagram raise his arms. Fiery blasts of lightning stream from his palms, ready to turn you to ashes. You move even before you can think, your hand shoots forward, words form themselves upon your lips, and the lightning, breaking against an invisible wall, falls down in a rain of sparks.

Your sense of vision, touch, smell, and hearing give way to a new kind of perception, much sharper than any of the human senses. You can now guess the intentions of your opponent much sooner than any of your four senses could have warned you. You perceive Galeot-din speaking the incantation of water, and you break his spell before the giant wave that he has called upon can rise above the motionless crowd. The wind created by your opponent only touches you slightly, throwing back a strand of your unruly hair. A stone avalanche falling on you from the sky ends up as a pile of sand at your feet. And then, finally, you see fear in the shining eyes of Galeot-din. His upraised arms pause in midair, slow to choose his next gesture. The haughty mage realizes that your magic power, the limits of which you, buried in your books, could never guess, exceeds anything the great Galeot-din has ever seen. Using this moment of delay, looking with the slightest sarcasm into his fiery, frightened eyes, you utter, unheard by the crowd, a single word. A wave of power, sweeping past you, raises your hair and blows around the folds of your robes. The black velvet cloak of the court mage, torn off in the enormous blast, flies above the crowd like a pair of giant wings. Suddenly seeming very small, the figure of Galeot-din shakes under the blow of a superhuman power, falls backward, his head toward the farthest corner of the pentagram, and lies there in deadly stillness.

You gradually start hearing sounds again. First the humming and rumble of the terrified crowd, then the sound of the breeze that rustles the black clothes on the motionless mage, lying outstretched on the stone platform. You start feeling your body, pleasantly warmed up and heavy as if after a long journey on foot. You move your arms, shaking off the stiffness and making sure that you are still in full command of your limbs. Carefully setting foot after unsteady foot on the stone platform that seems strangely hard, as if it had gained additional firmness during the duel, you approach your defeated opponent.

The face of Galeot-din has lost all trace of color. His eyes are wide open, and for a moment you see in their bottomless blackness the reflection of the blue sky and sparse spring clouds. Looking closer, you notice some signs of life. You sink on the ground by his side, greatly relieved. You never intended to kill anyone, although death is the most common end to the many magic duels that have been waged on this very pentagram. All you wanted was to make sure that another, unfair death would not happen here today before your very eyes.

Automatically remembering the necessary spell, you move your hand over his pale lifeless face, concentrating at your fingertips the pulsing energy of life. Some color returns to Galeot-din's cheeks, his eyes roll toward you, and you see fright and hatred in their black depth. He speaks in a hoarse voice.

"You are stronger than I, Hasan the bookworm."

"It seems that I am, court mage."

"The title is rightfully yours, Hasan. You earned it in an honest battle."

"Don't be foolish, Galeot-din. I don't want your title. We have our own, separate ways that will never cross again."

"How can I remain here, in Dimeshq, where so many people saw my shameful defeat? It would be better if you kill me, Hasan."

"Your title does not mean you must be the best mage in the world, Galeot-din. You know your trade well. And this duel may teach you not to diminish the powers of others."

"This woman—it is all her fault!"

"Remember the condition of our duel, Galeot-din. You promised to leave her alone."

"But—what made you stand up for her, Hasan?"

"We both know you would have killed her, Galeot-din. I cannot abide a senseless death. Our duel is over only if you give me your word never to bother this woman again."

Galeot-din lets out a grim laugh.

"I am not in a position to refuse, Hasan. You were more than generous with me."

Smiling, you help the court mage to his feet. And, gently supporting him, you watch the woman you saved walk toward you along a diagonal line on the giant pentagram.

"I thank you, stranger," she says in a rich melodious voice, holding out her hand to you. And again a thrill goes through your body at her touch, and the feelings that you considered long forgotten, asleep somewhere deep inside you, make you shiver.

"His name is Hasan," Galeot-din says helpfully.

"Will you see me home, Hasan?" the woman asks, and a deep fire sparks inside her narrow eyes. It is not the fear of walking alone that makes her ask you. For a moment you feel your mind clouding, defeated by a magic far older than any wisdom you ever learned. You take her hand and let her lead you to the unknown. The crowd backs off in fear, leaving a wide passage before you, allowing you to move through the bazaar with unbelievable speed, making your meeting with the sweet mysterious future more swift and sure than

the stroke of a dagger. Moving away from the plaza, gradually submitting to her piercing touch, you realize that the magic power that kept quietly growing inside you in the still solitude of the libraries, growing without your noticing it, has finally outgrown anything you have ever seen or heard, and that from someone mocked as a common bookworm you have gradually transformed into the greatest mage.

The princess cries out in her sleep as if pushing someone away, and a tear from under her eyelid runs down her pale cheek. Awakening from your thoughts, you softly place your hand on her brow, and her breath becomes even again, a smile appears on her lips, and the tear dries without a trace. With gladness, you feel a great peace and purity emanating from this sleeping child; and it gradually encloses you, quieting your ancient, restless, all-knowing spirit. You pause, hesitant to remove your hand from her brow, enjoying with all your being a long-forgotten feeling of peace.

II
Awakening

❀

NEW BRIDE

✣

The midday sun shines with unbearable brightness, making the sand covering the riding arena at the back of the palace look blindingly white, with the deep shadow of the palace gallery seeming as dark as night. Narrowing her eyes against the glare, the sultaness is walking along the edge of the shade accompanied by Nimeth, Zulbagad, and the princess's nanny Fatima, a tiny, fragile woman with huge, sad eyes.

"The princess wanted very much for you to wait here, your majesty," Fatima says in her soft voice. "She wanted you to see how well she has learned to ride."

"I am worried about her lessons," the sultaness says anxiously. "The princess is too delicate for horseback riding."

"I heard that her horse is one of the gentlest in the whole stable," Nimeth says with her usual calmness. "Besides, you know how you always exaggerate the princess's weakness. She is no less capable of riding than other fifteen-year-old girls."

"After all, she is old enough to be a bride," Zulbagad agrees. "You shouldn't keep thinking of her as a child."

The word "bride" makes the sultaness feel an unpleasant sting. Unwillingly she glances at the white harem building, whose stones shine in the sun like pearls. For a whole month now the sultan has spent almost all his time in there, enjoying the company of the new Baskarian slave girl, to whom the court flatterers refer in no other words than "the beautiful Albiorita." Faithful Nimeth managed to find out that the new star of the harem has very unusual looks. Her skin is whiter than chalk and her hair is like a cascade of pale gold, as yellow as the endless sands of the Dimeshqian desert; her eyes shine blue-green like turquoise ocean water. The sultan has completely lost his mind over her and keeps calling her "my bride."

The sultaness has long forsaken all jealousy of her husband's numerous concubines, though she sometimes feels the painful sting of memory—how he used to look at her during the first months following their wedding, when she was still a beautiful young girl, before her slender figure was forever lost to childbearing. But the nights and days her husband spends in the harem do not really bother her. She was never in love with him, so, if anything, she perhaps feels some relief at this transfer of his attention. But something about his special devotion to the pale-skinned, golden-haired Baskarian girl hurts her pride. *Where did he find such a wonder of nature?* she thinks bitterly. The Baskarian women, like the women of all other neighboring lands, are usually dark skinned and black haired. But somewhere in the northeastern end of Baskary, in the villages close to the mountains of the Halabean Range, one can sometimes find those fair-haired women who are praised so highly among connoisseurs. Undoubtedly, the "beautiful Albiorita" must be one of them. Is she different enough from the sultan's other women to awaken his hidden manly powers and break the curse of their dynasty? Will she be the one to bear him a healthy son?

She sighs, consciously turning away from the elegant white building. After all, she is perfectly happy and content with what she has. She is the sultaness, the wife of the mighty ruler; and her daughter is, at least for the time being, the heiress to the throne. She may not approve of her daughter being treated more like a boy than seems proper, but that is a minor thing compared with everything else. Truly, what more could she wish for? The princess's husband, chosen from among the princes of neighboring lands, will be the future sultan of Dhagabad, thus placing the fate of the throne in her fragile hand. As for the fact that the princess's father prefers young concubines to his middle-aged wife, that can be seen only as the natural proclivity of a man in his declining years. The sultaness knows her role very well: she must focus on bringing up the princess to be fully prepared for her future role, dwelling as little as possible on her husband's side interests.

And the rest of it is up to the gods who rule their destiny. If it is the will of the gods for the sultan to beget a son and heir with his fair mistress, then the sultaness will step down without much regret. She doesn't care about anything as much as the well-being of her daughter.

"The princess enjoys her riding lessons," Nanny Fatima says. The sultaness realizes that while she was lost in her thoughts, the same conversation has been going on around her. She feels a new wave of anxiety pour over her.

"I hope Hasan is present at all her lessons?" she asks.

"Certainly, your majesty," Fatima answers.

The sultaness sees a smile slide over Nimeth's lips, and she inwardly smiles back. It is hard to believe that not that long ago they didn't even allow the princess to be alone with Hasan. Now the djinn is considered to be the best guarantee of her safety, and the sultaness feels totally happy for the princess and her friendship with her slave. Gone is all fear of his mysterious powers, and gone is the helpless feeling that unknown forces will tear the princess away from her surroundings. Gone, or almost gone, is even concern over the djinn's devilish attractiveness and manly appearance. The princess is much more levelheaded than most girls her age, and she would never find herself in the situation that occurred when her friend Alamid lost all control of her feelings in his presence a couple of years ago. No, the sultaness has great faith in Hasan's wisdom and common sense, which seem to be the best protection for the princess. With Alamid, Hasan never lost control, resolving it in the best possible way. He is so wise that even the sultan, as she has heard, sometimes asks his advice in affairs of state.

The sultaness hears the clattering of hooves and the neighing of a horse, and is once again pulled back from her thoughts.

Looking over the low banister of the gallery, she sees the princess riding a black horse emerge from the side arch. The riding teacher, a short bowlegged man from Halaby, is walking behind, along with Hasan, carefully watching his pupil.

The sultaness looks at her daughter with secret pleasure. During the past year the princess has grown much prettier than before. She is still almost transparently fragile, and still reminds the sultaness of a little peri. But at fifteen, her features have lost some of their soft childish clumsiness, as if an unknown artist, looking over his almost-finished creation, had smoothed some lines in a few sure strokes to turn his creation into a masterpiece. Or, perhaps, it is not the princess's features that have changed but the look of her eyes. It feels as if, over the past three years, her dark-blue eyes have acquired even more depth, coming alive with new life and intelligence, so that they can now look straight into the face of the world and the people who inhabit it.

On her fifteenth birthday, celebrated just last month, the princess reached marriageable age, when many noble families hurry to marry off their daughters. But the princess is heiress to the throne, and her marriage arrangements require much more care than those of any ordinary girl. Her future husband is destined one day to rule Dhagabad in her father's place. Besides, whatever small part the princess must play in all that, she has to be much more educated than other women. For these reasons it was decided by the sultan that the princess's marriage has to be delayed until her seventeenth year, allowing him, the State Council, and her teachers much more time for her preparation. The sultaness feels that the firmness of the sultan's decision may have been enforced by his hidden hope that two more years might allow him to beget a son from his new concubine. But in spite of these suspicions, she is happy to have this extra time with her only daughter, the focus of her life, whom she will undoubtedly lose forever to a brilliant suitor.

Now the sultaness praises with all her heart the princess's grandmother for sending such a wise teacher to her only daughter. The presence of an all-powerful djinn gives the princess a chance to learn things inaccessible to other children, and the princess seems to be using this chance to the fullest.

"Mother!" The princess shouts from the arena. "Look what I can do!"

She sends her horse galloping around the yard, her white shawl flying behind her. Her usually pale face is flushed, and strands of hair scatter over her face. Even when riding she doesn't change from her white outfit to a more practical one, and the sultaness's heart melts at the thought of how the princess must have been longing to wear white when she was still too young and how she must love this particular privilege of growing up. At the tug of the reins the horse turns toward the sultaness, and she notices a white mark on his forehead.

"Which horse is that, princess?" the sultaness shouts, suddenly alarmed.

"Father let me take his Arabian stallion today!" the princess shouts back, pulling the horse to a stop right before the sultaness.

"He must be mad," the sultaness mumbles to herself, as she smiles and waves to her daughter.

"Careful, princess!" Nimeth exclaims.

"Father told me he might come to watch me, too!" the princess says, not listening to her. "Look!"

The princess resumes her galloping around the arena, and the sultaness watches her with terror. She remembers very well how this same horse nearly killed her daughter three years ago, when only Hasan's intervention saved her from the deadly hooves. She heard that since then the best court riders have tamed the stallion, and that the sultan himself rode him several times. But how could he even think to allow this wild beast near his fragile daughter? Is he out of his mind? Is he so obsessed with his desire to have a son that he is willing to treat the princess like a boy and a future warrior in every possible way? Or, the sultaness thinks in terror, maybe he is so overwhelmed by his passion for the new concubine that he forgets even his duty to care for the well-being of his family?

The hollow sound of steps in the gallery brings her back to her senses. Out of the corner of her eye she sees the women around her bow, and she automatically bends her head even before she has time to see the group of people walking toward them. The sultan Chamar Ali walks in front, with his usual firm stride. His black beard is sticking straight out, his long cloak waves behind him with the rhythm of his steps, and his dark eyes are shining with the same fire that has made her shiver with reverence ever since they first met. In his suite the sultaness notices the master of ceremonies, the grand vizier, four bodyguards, and someone else....

A woman wrapped in a shawl from head to toe. The woman's face is completely covered, but the sultaness seems to see a lock of golden hair glowing from within the folds of her garments.

Does it mean that Albiorita, unlike other concubines, is allowed into the inner galleries of the palace to the arena where the princess of Dhagabad herself is undertaking her riding lessons?

"Your majesty," the sultaness says softly.

"How do you like the princess?" Chamar exclaims proudly. "She is really her father's daughter! Not everyone is able to control my Arabian stallion!"

"I am worried about the princess, your majesty," the sultaness says with difficulty, trying very hard not to look at the woman wrapped in shawl. "This horse—"

"Nonsense!" Chamar interrupts impatiently. "The princess is very good at horseback riding, as you see. Don't forget, madam—she is old enough to be a bride!"

That word again—"bride." The sultaness sighs, raising her eyes to meet her husband's gaze.

"Some time ago this horse almost killed the princess," the sultaness manages, gathering all her courage.

"The princess must learn to overcome her childish fears," Chamar says firmly, and, turning away, he walks up to the banister.

"Father!" the princess shouts, trying to turn her galloping

horse and pull him to a stop. The horse, nervous and sensitive like all thoroughbreds, obeys the reins too suddenly, rising on his hind legs amid a cloud of dust. As if in a dream the sultaness watches the hooves waving in the air, the black mane flying in the wind, and a tiny white figure sliding off the horse's back onto the sand.

"Princess!" the sultaness screams, forgetting all fear of her husband, forgetting everything at the sight of her daughter helplessly lying on the ground. Frozen in terror, she watches the bowlegged Halabean teacher run across the yard toward the princess, and Hasan catch the horse by the reins with a firm hand.

But the princess jumps up to her feet, laughing and brushing the dust off her clothes with only slight embarrassment.

"Well done, princess!" Chamar exclaims and, turning, whispers something to his suite, out of which the sultaness can only make out some words about women's hysteria.

"I was doing all right, wasn't I, mother?" the princess asks, her eyes shining. "It's only that your horse, father, is much faster than mine."

The princess runs up the stairs to join them in the gallery and stops, catching her breath and carefully studying shawl-wrapped Albiorita.

"I myself used to fall off when I was learning to ride," Chamar says, patting the princess on the cheek. "I think you exaggerate the dangers of riding, madam," he continues, turning to the sultaness.

"Yes, your majesty," the sultaness replies, bowing.

"Can I ride your horse again sometime, father?" the princess asks with the mixture of shyness and confidence characteristic of polite but spoiled children.

"We'll discuss it with your riding teacher, princess," Chamar says.

Nodding to the bowing women, he turns and walks away in long strides into the depths of the gallery, followed by his suite.

"He is really not that scary, mother," the princess says. The sultaness finds herself confused for a moment about whom she means—the horse or the sultan. "And I just love to ride! Hasan taught me some of his tricks, and now I can control almost any horse!"

The mention of Hasan calms the sultaness somewhat. She looks at her daughter tenderly, smoothing her hair and straightening her shawl, stained with dirt.

"Be careful, princess," she says, sighing at the memory of her fright.

"Is that his concubine, mother?" the princess asks suddenly, looking in the direction of where the sultan and his suite have disappeared.

"One of his concubines, princess," the sultaness answers.

"I thought they never leave the harem."

"Sometimes they do, princess," the sultaness says, hoping that the princess won't hear her voice tremble, but knowing that a thing like that is too hard to hide from her sensitive daughter. After all, she is old enough to be a bride.

THE CULT OF RELEASE

✱

*S*itting *in your usual place near the head of the princess's bed, you look with unseeing eyes at the pages of an open book, listening to her rhythmic breathing beside you. Tonight you read to her from the religious book of the Stikts, and, as usual, the princess fell asleep just as you were finishing the last words of the chosen chapter. The ritual of bedtime reading was established almost from the beginning, and, although over the last three years she has gradually turned from a child into a young woman, the ritual is still followed to the letter.*

You watch her quiet face, not trying and not wanting to penetrate her dreams, thinking of how strangely close you have become to this creature, so different from you, yet somehow similar. You still cannot understand the reason for your closeness; the princess—for all her curiosity and hunger for knowledge—doesn't bear the mark of absolute power which, as you now know, had been hanging over you from a very early age. Perhaps, you think, the reason for your bond is books, which the princess loves so much, and which are, and always were, a big part of your life.

From time immemorial you found more pleasure in reading than in those activities that are usually considered an enjoyable way of spending time. Only later, when you were already an eminent scholar and considered a sage by some people—and by others, a strange, ageless youth with a distant look—did you start to take an interest in oth-

ers and the opportunity to gain more knowledge about human nature. You spent time absently walking around the noisy Dimeshqian bazaar, attending receptions in noble houses, talking to the beggars on the streets, to the court sages, to the owners of the shops adjoining the bazaar, and to the venerable keeper of the Dimeshqian library. Many of them knew your parents when they were still elderly, honorable citizens of Dimeshq. Such people always regarded your unchangeable youth with distrust.

In time, they, too, grew old and died, replaced by other beggars, sages, merchants, and keepers of the books. Your reputation as a mage, which by then had became as natural as your surroundings, made everyone treat you with respect and uneasiness. People didn't shun you, but they kept their distance. Your home on the outskirts of Dimeshq, a large house filled with books, they avoided. Then the sultan of Dimeshq started to send the court sages to seek your advice in difficult matters of state. The sages, looking with wonder and unease at a handsome and somewhat remote young man, wrote down your words on their waxen tablets and left, collecting about them the folds of their long garments on the narrow stairs, leaving you alone with your books.

Through your studies, increasingly, you felt surges of special insight and saw visions of the true nature of objects and occurrences. You moved headlong on the path of knowledge, rapidly discovering the answers to more and more questions. Sometimes, when recalling the Agritian scroll, you searched your mind for indications of the burden and the despair that had marked the way of knowledge for that mighty sage. Marveling at the very age of the ancient scroll, yet not quite believing it, you searched relentlessly for those signs that marked the Agritian sage's approach to absolute power, and you repeated to yourself, sometimes even aloud, forming a harmony of sounds, that mysterious Agritian word, indelibly imprinted on your memory— "djinn." Then, with an outward laugh and some inner relief, you in-

sisted you felt nothing of the kind, that the old sage had made a mistake, and that whosoever were those mysterious spirits called djinns, you, a mage from Dimeshq, would never become one of them.

"That Stiktian book we read last night made me completely confused about religions, Hasan!" the princess says impatiently. She is sitting on the floor, books and scrolls scattered around her in complete disorder. Her face is frowning, her head shawl has slid to the side, falling in folds off her shoulder.

"It wasn't my intention to confuse you, princess." She hears laughter in Hasan's voice, and, raising her head, she manages to catch a reflection of a smile disappearing from his face. But the princess is not in the mood for jokes.

"Tell me, Hasan," she insists, "the head priest of the temple Al-Gulsulim says that there is only one true god who rules all the elemental phenomena in the world. Correct?"

"That is correct, princess," Hasan answers, and the princess cannot hear any appropriate seriousness in his voice. But she is not going to turn back.

"I have been thinking about it," the princess says, frowning again, "and I realized that most of the people in Dhagabad also believe in one god. Only they all call him by a different name."

"Are names so important, princess?"

"Well, the sage Haib al-Mutassim also says that it is not the name but the meaning of god that matters."

"What don't you understand, princess?"

"I heard the sage Haib al-Mutassim also say that there really are many gods, and that every elemental phenomenon should be called a god. And the head priest says that there is no god but the true One, and that the sage Haib al-Mutassim should die a terrible death for such blasphemy."

"What is the difference between an elemental phenomenon and a god, princess?" The smile is shimmering right near the surface, though Hasan is not quite letting it out. "Maybe they are the same?"

"I could have believed that, Hasan, if it weren't for that Stiktian book that yesterday confused me so completely. As far as I could understand, the Stikts say that there are no gods at all and that the divine nature lies in each human being."

"Maybe this is true, princess, and that's why people are inventing so many gods."

"Don't laugh at me, Hasan! You are all-powerful! Tell me!"

"Gods lie beyond my powers, princess."

"In that case, tell me about Stiktian religion. How do they conduct the services if they have no gods? Do they pray to themselves?"

"Something like that, princess."

"Tell me, Hasan! The book says that only the initiated Stikts may know that."

This time she catches a glimpse of the smile, and she suddenly finds it hard to keep from laughing. The merry sparkles in Hasan's eyes are so contagious that the princess gives up and lets out a laugh.

"If you don't tell me, Hasan—I—I will die of curiosity!" She laughs, knowing how ineffective is her threat and how filled with desire she is to learn the answer to her question.

"All right, princess," Hasan says, smiling. "The Stiktian cult is called the Cult of Release. The purpose of their ritual is to release the divine from the influence of mind. Only high priests can do it and only the initiated are allowed to see it. The minds of common people are too resistant to such things."

"If only I could see it..." the princess says, not daring to phrase her wish as a direct order. "Is it true that the Stikts pray in underground temples?"

"Some call them temples, princess. In reality they are natural caves. The Stikts believe that you can pray to the divine only in temples that were not created by man."

"I know what we shall do, Hasan! You will take us to a Stiktian temple and we will see the ritual!" The princess holds her breath, wishing with all her heart to see the mysterious rite, yet giving Hasan a chance to voice his concern.

"Are you sure of the stability of your mind, princess?" Hasan says, sounding unexpectedly serious.

"I *thought* you would say it is too dangerous!" the princess says with relief.

"I don't know, princess." There is a lot of doubt in Hasan's voice. "There is a way to make our journey safe, but you must take care of your mind yourself."

"Is it really so terrible, Hasan?"

"Not exactly terrible, princess. I'd rather say it's *unusual* for the uninitiated."

"I am too curious to turn back now, Hasan. Tell me, what kind of safety do you have in mind? If you are going to turn us into stones in the cave, I'd rather not."

"I will make us invisible, princess."

"Will you really, Hasan?" The princess jumps up impatiently. "I have always wanted to become invisible!"

"But if you start talking or bumping into things, we can get into trouble, princess."

"I promise to be as silent as death and as still as stone," the princess answers with impatience.

"One more thing." Hasan also rises to his feet, and the princess feels her heart jump with expectation. "To avoid any accidents I will make us visible to each other."

Strange forest surrounds Hasan and the princess. Trunks of low, wide trees seem to be composed of massive, intertwined brown snakes with their shining scaly tails flattened on the ground and their heads hidden in the small, hard leaves of the crown. These extraordinary trees cover the steep slopes of a canyon in grayish-green spots. A noisy mountain stream has formed many rapids at the bottom of the canyon, working its way down the rocky foothills of the Halabean Range. Straight ahead, the princess hears the roaring and rumbling of falling water. Looking more closely through uneven rocky spurs, she can just glimpse the crystal-blue water of a mountain lake.

"Is that the noise of a waterfall?" she asks. "Are we going there?"

"Yes and yes, princess," Hasan says. "There is a cave beyond the waterfall and inside it is the most famous Stiktian temple. By the way, you just broke your vow of silence."

"But we are not in the temple yet!"

"We are close enough for unfriendly ears. Keep silent and don't fall behind." Hasan moves ahead along the side of the canyon, stepping lightly on the rough rocks. The princess climbs carefully behind him and soon, around the river bend, a giant waterfall appears before them in all its magnificent power. The wide wall of water, like an enormous curtain, is falling into a smooth stone basin. A wet path carved into the rock girds the vertical wall midway.

"You probably won't be able to walk this path," Hasan says anxiously.

"If the Stiktian women can walk it, I can."

"They are initiated," Hasan reminds her.

"I will hold on to you. If I fall, you will catch me, won't you?"

"You trust me too much, princess," Hasan replies, grinning and again pressing his finger to his lips for silence.

Holding Hasan's hand and trying not to look down, the princess carefully walks along the stone ledge behind the waterfall. Her hair and clothes are soaking wet; but now, so close to the Stiktian temple, she is too excited to notice.

Suddenly she sees a narrow gap in the stone wall behind the waterfall.

"In there," Hasan says.

Trembling with excitement, the princess ducks into the chilly darkness. She immediately sees that it is not dark at all. The walls of the cave are covered with a glowing substance, and as her hand touches the wall, it also starts to glow.

"Luminescent fungi," Hasan whispers. "Don't stop."

Careful not to slip, the princess and Hasan move along the

gradually sloping, winding corridor. The entrance has disappeared behind them and the princess stays closer to the djinn. She can now hear a hollow drumbeat and a monotonous chant straight ahead.

"Don't stop, princess," Hasan whispers again. "Follow me."

The cave suddenly opens before them. It looks like a strange palace with towers, balconies, and passages connected to one another inside a single huge vault. Looking more closely, the princess realizes the most unbelievable thing: these buildings, passages, and walls are natural, as if this mysterious temple was really created at the will of some ancient gods. Myriad torches provide carefully designed illumination that leaves many places in deep shadow to enhance the mood of the enormous space. The princess holds her breath in awe. She could forever admire this magnificence, but Hasan, with a firm hand, pulls her aside to one of the dark balconies.

"The ritual will begin any minute." His whisper is barely audible.

The music becomes louder, echoing resonantly under the arched stone ceiling. The princess can now see the musicians. Dark skinned, in red ritual robes, they are standing in the shadows of five immense columnlike stalagmites that grow out of the middle of the floor and end with their sharp tips midway to the ceiling. The light inside the columns is brighter than anywhere else, making the columns look semitransparent. A carpet of leopard skins covers the floor.

"Where are the others?" the princess whispers.

"Those who are not part of the service are sitting on balconies very nearby. So, if you don't stop talking…"

The princess wants to answer, but the words freeze on her lips. Seven figures clad in white appear as if from nowhere in the space in front of the columns.

"The high priests," Hasan whispers.

The first priest is carrying a stone cup. A blue liquid in the cup is glowing with a faint light similar to the glowing temple walls. The priest steps inside the ring of columns and sets the cup on a stone pedestal. Standing behind the cup, he turns to other priests and raises his hands.

"The release will now begin," Hasan whispers. "Look carefully."

The seven white figures slowly move in a strange dance in front of the glowing columns. Their movements are so smooth that their bodies seem to be boneless, as they easily fold into any shape to the slow rhythm of the chant. The princess can now see that the number of the priest musicians is also seven and, as they chant, they swing back and forth like tall grass in the wind.

The monotonous chant suddenly stops. At the sound of a loud drumbeat, another white figure enters the circle to join the highest priest, the priest with the cup. He dips his palms into the glowing liquid and puts them on the second priest's forehead. They hold still for a moment and then the highest priest removes his hands, at which the second priest, easily bending his slim body, bows down to the cup to take a sip.

The drumbeat grows louder. The second priest straightens up and raises his arms. Carefully stepping on the leopard skins, the priest walks around the blue cup and sits, cross-legged, to the right of the highest priest. And then, accompanied by the drumbeat, the other six priests follow the same ritual, take their place around the cup, and observe in silence how the highest priest lays his hands on his own forehead and drinks the last sip from the cup.

Chanting, the red priest musicians dance smoothly around the motionless white figures. Censer bearers have appeared from the shadows surrounding the center space, and the giant cave gradually fills with sweet incense smoke. The princess feels dizzy, and the figures of the white priests start swimming in front of her eyes.

"Look!" Hasan whispers, grabbing her hand. The princess sits up straight, startled. The priests, sitting in meditation poses, are floating in the air, spinning around the empty cup at the very tops of the stone columns. Their bodies are relaxed, their eyes are closed, and their white tunics slightly sway to their slow circular movement. The chant and drumbeat are rolling in waves, and the light from the torches is pulsing to the rhythm. As the incense gathers in thick clouds around the princess, she gradually sinks into a trance.

A bright flame suddenly bursts from the cup, the torches go out, and in the white light the circle of priests slowly descends to the leopard skins below. The last spark in the cup burns down and everything sinks into darkness.

The princess feels Hasan's strong arms lift her from the stone floor, and he carries her up and along the winding corridor. Suddenly, a fresh wind, splashes of icy water, and the bright beams of mountain sun hit her face, returning her to her senses.

"I must have fallen asleep, Hasan…."

"They have a reason for letting only the initiated into the temple, princess. The incense is designed to cloud your mind and you need to be accustomed to it."

"Does that mean that I dreamt the flying priests, Hasan?"

"Why dreamt, princess? This flight is the most ordinary thing. The liquid in the cup released their souls and they flew."

"Their souls flew? What about their bodies?"

"Did you see nothing, princess?"

"I saw something flying. If they were merely souls, I wouldn't have seen them!"

"They were bodies, princess. There is nothing impossible in flying. The Stiktian priests achieve it with the aid of the drug in the cup. It takes much longer to learn the art of flight without such aid."

"Does that mean you can take a drug to learn to fly?"

"You can, but then you will still have to learn, and, besides, if you stop taking the drug, you will die."

"Well…how long does it takes to learn to fly without the drug?"

"About sixty years."

"You are always so impossible, Hasan! Sixty is four times

more than I am now! That means, if I start learning now, I will become a flying old hag at best. No, thank you!"

"I have to admit, your words do make sense, princess."

"Could it be any other way, Hasan? Listen, can you make me invisible to you?"

"Why would I do that, princess?"

"Well, I would very much like to take a swim in this lake."

You feel a new awakening to life, listening to her merry laughter and the splashing of the cold water behind you—as if her very presence, her joy at simple pleasures, her hunger for knowledge, somehow give you back a part of your physical existence. It's as if being close to her you regain the ability to feel that which you both neglected and cherished, that which you have kept as the greatest of treasures and pushed away as a useless toy long outgrown—the joy of physical existence, the taste of the air you breathe, the cool freshness of the mountain waters, the hard roughness of rocks warmed by the sun, the wondering at what tomorrow will bring, and the pleasant anxiety of expectation.

Joy of life... that which comprises the life of the young princess, the temporary mistress of your destiny, who, against logic, against the power of will, takes over more and more space in your eternal mind. You realize that her wonder and amazement at the sight of the Stiktian temple almost passed over to you, making you, together with her, shiver with anticipation of the Cult of Release—shiver in a long-forgotten way, highly improper for a spirit.

Listening to the splashes and her screams of joy—not having had the nerve to make her invisible in consideration of unexpected danger—but keeping your promise not to turn your head under any circumstances, ready to come to her rescue at any moment, you gradually absorb yourself in thoughts of your existence.

Being a spirit, you are somehow able to feel your presence simultaneously in all the corners of the world. There are no more distant forgotten places in your memory; you know everything and remember everything you know at the same time with the same clarity. This special faculty, which substitutes for all physical perception, allows you to know everything that is happening at this very moment in every corner of every kingdom, city, town, and village. This power, depriving you of perception in the usual sense, allows you at the same time to experience reality in a new way. In taking the princess to the ancient Stiktian temple that you haven't visited for thousands of years, ever since the day of your own initiation, you somehow knew that the temple was not destroyed, that it still stood as it was, and that there would be a ritual performed there today. You knew it with the same certainty as you know that today there is a big birthday celebration in Avallahaim, where the young crown prince, Musa Jafar, has turned fifteen, as you also know that the elderly sultan of Baskary has received as a present today a new slave girl from Megina, as you know that there will be an eclipse in Veridue in a week, and that the Veriduan court sages haven't been able to predict it yet....

You remember how at first this endless knowledge felt like an enormous burden, making you despair at your helplessness before it. How later you slowly started to come to terms with your new life, enclosing yourself in new dimensions of indifference to the earthly existence that rejected you, an all-powerful, powerless slave. But now, serving the young princess of Dhagabad, you start to feel a new awakening to an old interest, to the pleasure of your endless knowledge that can be used, if for nothing else, to teach the mysteries of the world to this small human creature who is ready to absorb like a sponge everything your powers can give her. Unwillingly, you feel your infinite closeness to her, the seamless unity between her eager interest, her irrepressible curiosity, and your own, long lost to the ages....

You see in her the quintessence of that which made you a djinn. And yet, remembering your life before the terrible transformation, you cannot find in her those little things which, as you now know, doomed you to your destiny even before you realized how inevitable it was. Even then, you were already marked by the higher signs that ruled over your destiny. You hardly had time to choose the path of knowledge when, without even realizing it, you had already doomed yourself to walking the path to its end. Only now have you acquired the ability to judge the signs that mark the future. Looking at your young mistress, the princess of the fair city of Dhagabad, you cannot see in her any of those fatal signs. As if she, in the naïveté of her purity, can touch the highest mysteries without danger of being drawn into them. As if her childish curiosity gives her the right to walk unmarked along the way, which was so painful to the many sages and wizards gone before. And, being close to her, you seem to gain this ability to free yourself, at least for a while, from the burden of your powers, an equal partner in her games, like a carefree new-born child.

You hear the splashes behind your back approaching the shore, the crick-crack *of the pebbles on the beach, a short laugh. You feel her mischievous pleasure in the danger that you, in spite of your solemn oath, may turn your head any minute and see her; and, at the same time, her calm certainty that you would never do something like that. Sitting with your back to her, you perceive her every movement better than any mortal standing right in front of her would have—her nubile nakedness, the sharp angles of her slim body that hasn't yet acquired the fullness of a grown woman, how she stands, wet after her swim, drying off in the cool gentle mountain breeze, her downy skin covered with tiny goose bumps. How she takes the comb out of her hair, letting her heavy wet tresses fall in cascades almost to the ground, as she glances cautiously at your turned back. How she squeezes the water out of her hair, pulls it up again into some kind of an arrangement, and how she now dresses herself, collecting her garments that were scattered all over the pebbly beach. And how, finally, she takes a few tentative steps in your direction, hurriedly looking over her outfit for faults she would surely not want you to see, and shyly calls out:*

"Hasan!"

DREAMS

❖

The desert she sees in her dreams seems more real each time. She can almost feel the heat of the sunbaked sand—though her feet still tread lightly—as if she were not walking but flying above the endless dunes held by an invisible hand. Louder is the singing of invisible birds, the rustling of invisible leaves, the tinkling of an invisible brook. Stronger is her desire to see at least for a moment the beauty of the mysterious garden surrounding the ancient majestic temple. Her feet, not sinking into the sand, cover more and more distance in their half flight toward the place where, amid the broiling heat of the desert, she is beckoned by the cool shade of the stone temple. Blindly pushing against an invisible wall, she is searching for a way into this magically sealed space, trying to set her foot on the stone stairs, to walk up them into the semidarkness that she knows hides something vitally important to her. The princess moans in her sleep, longing with all her being to find a way into a place hidden from her for reasons unknown by the will of strange powers that rule her destiny, depriving her of something important, something necessary for her, an unknown but desirable thing....

She wakes in a cold sweat and cannot stop shivering. She moves in her bed to shake off the bonds of sleep. A moonbeam, sliding into the room through the light drape wavering in the night breeze, moves across her bed as a shining line, falling upon her motionless hand and making it look an alien, bothersome object. Frightened, the princess pulls away from the silvery light, and with this movement she shakes off the trance of the nightmare. Actually, the princess thinks, this dream can hardly be called a nightmare, for nothing terrible is happening to her, except for the frightful regularity of its same strangely important setting and the desperate feeling of frustration of over and over failing to grasp the hidden place within. With horror she suddenly realizes that the noise that fills her ears has nothing to do with the rustling of the drape in the draft from the window. She is still listening to the gusts of hot desert wind shifting and moving the sands of the endless dunes.

"Hasan!" she whispers, immediately scared of the sound of her own voice. "Hasan!" she calls out in terror, unable to control herself anymore.

She is startled by the dark figure of the djinn appearing out of thin air beside her bed. Trying to reassure herself she carefully touches his hand, confirming to herself that the nightmare is gone; that this is really Hasan standing by her bed; and that everything around her is familiar, comforting, and has nothing whatever to do with her terrifying dream.

"What happened, princess?" Hasan asks softly.

"Stay with me, Hasan," she begs, unable to control her fear and knowing that if the nannies find him in her bedroom at night a scandal will be unavoidable. But her fright is stronger than her common sense.

"I had a nightmare," she says, deeply inhaling the cool night air, feeling the shivers gradually leave her body.

"Don't be afraid, princess." Hasan puts his hand on her arm lying on top of the bedcover, and the princess feels his touch send pleasant warmth flowing through her body.

"Tell me a story, Hasan," she asks. "Tell me of your life before you became a djinn."

She immediately regrets her words. What if her thoughtless request reminds him of the time when he was free? What if this memory is painful to him? She cannot see his face in the darkness of the room, but his voice sounds as calm and quiet as usual.

"I lived most of my life in Dimeshq, princess," Hasan says. "Most of my time I spent reading books. When I wanted to learn something I couldn't find in books, I traveled to different places."

"You must have had many friends, Hasan," the princess says thoughtfully.

"Why do you think so, princess?"

"I cannot possibly imagine anyone who wouldn't love you...." What is she saying? "I mean..." The princess falls hopelessly silent.

Is he really smiling, or does she only imagine it?

"I was going to say..." The princess feels blood rush to her face, making it burn. At least he cannot see in the dark how red her face is.

"I know so little about love, princess," Hasan says softly, and she hears a smile in his voice.

The princess suddenly feels with her whole body the touch of his hand, still resting on her arm. This touch, so light and calming, so sure and strong, fills her body with a pulsing warmth that suddenly makes her weak and helpless before him. She feels strange excitement rise somewhere in her stomach, pushing up to her burning face, forcing air out of her lungs and making her breath quicken. All her feelings seem to focus on his touch that sends waves of weakness through her arm to the excited knot in her stomach, to the small of her back, and from there, up her spine, crawling with blissfully deliberate slowness right into her head, clouding her mind. Half-consciously, she finds herself wishing for him to move his hand along her arm, along her whole body, to add a new dimension to this wonderful feeling that she has never experienced before. And at the same time, on the edge of her awareness, she seems to hear the collective voice of her mother and nannies, strictly forbidding anything sensual to enter her life. Reluctantly, she forces herself back to her senses. She remembers their reproaching Alamid who, as she now understands, was guided by feelings similar to her own. Blushing, forcing her strange new feeling to leave her, and yet unable to deliberately move her arm away from him, she buries herself deeper into the covers.

"To have friends one must spend a lot of time with them," Hasan says, and the princess realizes with alarm that he completely understands what is happening within her and that he is trying to make the situation more bearable by keeping to the original conversation. "And I spent my time elsewhere."

The princess forces her remaining thoughts back into her head and picks up the thread of the conversation that still, in spite of her unexpected sensations, interests her deeply. It isn't often that Hasan talks about himself like this, and now she is almost angry at herself for not being able to take full advantage of his openness.

"Wasn't it sad to be alone, Hasan?" she asks in a trembling voice, trying to pretend, as he does, that nothing in this situation is out of the ordinary. Her head is light and burning with the mixture of feelings too overwhelming for her inexperienced body.

"I didn't have enough time even to be sad, princess," Hasan answers softly.

It is time for her to sleep, to forget the words that escaped her lips, and to put to rest the disturbance of her awakening sensuality that is filling her with such confusion, and makes you feel a pleasant warmth flowing inside you. You put calmness into your touch, feeling her quieting down, feeling her sink into sleep—this time free of any unpleasant dreams. And at the same time, sitting next to her, you think about her spoken and unspoken questions. Really, weren't you ever sad to be alone? What did you do then, before the end, buried in your books, eagerly searching for new knowledge? What

did you do, secluding yourself for ages in your Dimeshqian house? And what did you do earlier, back then, when people surrounded you with love, antagonism, hatred, glory, and worship, in those times you now call your time of vanity?

In the time of your vanity you had many women ready to praise you and give you anything your exercised mind could think of. Some of them were obedient, others obstinate; some were ready to follow you everywhere, and some wanted you to strive for their affections. You enjoyed them the same way you enjoyed noisy feasts, where your eloquence and unsurpassed judgment made venerable sages listen to your words with respect. The same way you, gaining eternal youth early on your way and giving special attention to your physical training, won in tournaments over the most skilled fighters and performed feats impossible for the best athletes in all Dimeshq.

The vanity left you without notice, without any effort on your part as you were getting deeper and deeper into learning the secrets of the world. It happened all by itself. The women who surrounded you, your friends, your followers, your apprentices, and your defeated enemies were suddenly gone. Noisy feasts, tournaments, and magic duels that brought you such fame among the crowds disappeared without a trace. You separated yourself from the activities the books called earthly pleasures, and finally submerged into the essence.

At first, the defeat of Galeot-din at the Plaza of Mages seemed to return you to a time in your life when the admiration of crowds, your great prowess, and the promises in the eyes of beauties, fascinated with your infinite glamour, gave you in itself an immense pleasure. You enjoyed to the last drop the respect of the crowd in the plaza, hastily making way for you, a promise twinkling in the narrow eyes and reflecting in every smooth flowing movement of that mysterious woman you saved from certain death. From the past, your vanity was stretching out its hand to you, trying to grab you as you moved away, trying to return you to its favorite surroundings. And at the same time something inside you was fleetingly different from the other, old Hasan, long forgotten in Dimeshq. You felt that the past could not possibly be revisited, as you followed the lead of that beautiful woman deeper and deeper into the empty streets and alleys of the upper city, where houses stand more widely apart, surrounded by huge gardens, barely visible over stone walls; where the streets gradually straighten to run upward, right to the palace of the great sultan.

You remember how you felt back then, as she guided you into the streets of the upper city, along the blind walls, as you approached a small, delicately carved door that led you right through into an alley of tangerine trees that guided you, surer than her hands, to the house beyond.

You let the flow of your memories carry you effortlessly on their gentle waves as, once again, you become Hasan of old times, a mere wizard with powers far from absolute, a sage, but not yet a djinn.

The semidarkness of her house takes you in with its warm breeze slightly rustling the soft curtains, a breeze that seems to bring different aromas with every one of its gentle gusts. As you walk in you are greeted by the delicate scent of orchids and sandalwood, so rare in the desert city of Dimeshq. It is the smell of her exotic home, with its subtle luxury and carefully designed comforts, that finally forces you to surrender completely to the power of your sensations, to that long-forgotten feeling that fills your body with a strange combination of weakness and strength, the lightheadedness of a drunken man who, being somewhat unsteady on his feet, believes he is strong enough to challenge anyone to a fight. And, in a way, you really are drunk, drunk with the aromas and rustling sounds of her house, drunk with the touch of her hands that become so much bolder in the enclosure of her rooms, drunk with the honey-like smell of her skin, the smooth brushing of her cheek against yours, the taste of her lips that so far just tease you, kissing you slightly and drawing away as you become more daring.

She pulls off her head shawl, letting it slide down to the floor, and you stop, dazed, beholding the cascade of pure fire that flows in a mass of curls all the way down her back. As she leads you deeper into the room, you carefully reach out to touch her hair, half expecting that this shining magnificence will burn your hand, being surely akin to flame. You see a smile in the depth of her emerald eyes as she finally steps right in front of you and lets go only for the brief moment necessary to slip out of her robe.

You have never felt like this with any one of your women. At the time of your vanity, when you had so many of them, the lovemaking itself, although enjoyable, didn't mean as much as the conquest, having another woman for your pleasure, further supporting your remarkable reputation. That used to be your way with women, but you finally shut the door on that part of your life and devoted yourself completely to meditation and study. And now, admiring this woman's incredible beauty revealed to you so suddenly and completely, you feel that your old way has left you once and for all, leaving room for something totally different and immeasurably more enjoyable. You marvel at this unexpected gift of the purest sensations as you, in turn, give yourself completely to her.

Waves of fiery tresses flow down her fair body, more perfect than a marble goddess's, as her beautiful lines and curves make you wildly hunger for every part of her. As you caress her, every ringlet of her fiery curls seems to burn you, making you mad with desire. You let her undress you, unable to keep your hands, your eyes, your mind—or what little is left of it—off her. You try to hold yourself back, afraid of being too rough in your impatience, and she laughs at your awkward and careful approach as you see the fire in her eyes rise, coming from the very depths of her mysterious, sensual being. You can feel her tremble at your touch, giving in more and more to your caresses, to your kisses, to your own fire, more powerful than anything you have felt before. Her arms become stronger, clinging to you, drawing you down onto the bed, and as her moans of desire become louder, as she opens up, submitting herself to you, your mind leaves you completely, giving in to wild passion beyond control.

She is your match, and more. She is everything a perfect woman should be. She takes you in completely, body and soul. Sinking into the abyss of her arms and lips, to the piercing feeling of her burning body against yours, you feel that you have become one with her to the point of being unable to separate your bodies, your sensations, your very souls that seem to join in their growing desire and soar to reach the point of ultimate pleasure as a single powerful and harmonious beast.

And later, after many hours of unimaginable happiness, emerging into the light and fire of her emerald eyes, you feel as if you have burned and been reborn from your ashes like the legendary phoenix. And then, much later, between kisses, still unable to take your hands, eyes, or mind off her, you finally ask the question, long overdue:

"What is your name, my lady?"

She answers with laughter, her voice ringing like a bell in the cool breeze.

"My name is Zobeide, Hasan."

You feel the princess stir near you and suddenly you remember yourself, realizing that you are still holding her hand and that, before your memories took you away, you were trying to calm her and scare away her nightmares. You cannot help but wonder what kind of dreams you may have sent her just now. And you also wonder how it is that such memories found you and carried you away—you, bodiless spirit in the presence of a pure, innocent child.

A Look into the Past

❁

"**H**asan." The princess shyly raises her head to look her djinn in the face. They are standing on a palace balcony, admiring the garden from one of the side towers. She is still shivering from her feelings of the night before and from her dreams that she doesn't remember clearly but which filled her with sensations even more disturbingly pleasant and somewhat more shameful than her waking thoughts. She knows that Hasan can normally read her feelings and thoughts, and that realization makes her uneasy. She is not quite sure how to behave.

"Princess?" The djinn looks at her with easy friendliness and the princess relaxes a bit. Most of it was probably just a dream, and she cannot really answer for her dreams, can she? Besides, she can hardly hope to deceive Hasan about her true feelings, even if she herself hasn't yet sorted them out. It is best not to spoil their fun with her foolish doubts. Especially today, when she has thought of something of which she is very proud.

"We are always doing what I want," the princess says. "Let's for once do something *you* want."

With triumph she watches the lost expression on his face. It seems that she has finally been able to surprise him!

"I am your slave, princess," the djinn answers automatically. "I always want the same things you want."

"Wouldn't you like to go somewhere?" she insists. "Aren't there any people you want to see? I cannot believe there is nobody in this world you know…"

"Somebody I know and somebody I would want to see are two different things, princess," Hasan says thoughtfully.

The princess is pleased to see something she was hoping for since the very beginning of their conversation. Hasan's face lights up with a very special smile, an absentminded smile addressed this time not to her but to his own memories, his distant thoughts that the princess is unable to penetrate.

"There is one place, princess...if you really want that."

"Very much!" Saying that, the princess immediately regrets the force of her eagerness. What if he guesses that this request, besides her wish to please him, bears a hidden wish to satisfy her own curiosity? But he will guess anyway. She should know by now how useless it is to try to hide her feelings from her djinn.

"Come here, princess," Hasan says, and the princess for the very first time hears a special enthusiasm in his voice. Could it be that her plan is working so easily? Is he really pleased with her unexpected wish?

Before the princess realizes what is happening, the warm sea wind is already blowing her shawl about and hitting her face, leaving a salty taste on her lips. They are sitting in a sailboat, and she can see no sign of land anywhere. Hasan is shifting the single sail with the careless ease of a born sailor, expertly guiding the tiny boat across the endless, rolling waves.

Following his gaze, the princess sees a tiny blue shadow off the bow, barely visible on the horizon.

"Where are we going, Hasan?" she asks.

"You'll see, princess."

"That island?" The princess looks doubtfully at the semitransparent shadow that seems unreal on the edge of ocean and sky. "But it is so far!"

"We are going faster than you think, princess," Hasan says. "We'll be there in a half hour."

Holding her breath, the princess watches the strange island grow larger with unbelievable speed. Cliffs rise in front of them, covered with the curled green of trees. A mountain on one side of the island makes it look like a giant marine animal with its back sticking out of the water. Hasan, maneuvering with ease, guides the boat between numerous underwater reefs, betrayed only by spots of white foam boiling on the dark surface of the water. A narrow passage opens into a cove surrounded by smooth rock walls. Inside the cove the water is mirror still, and a white crescent of coral sand separates the sea from the wild greenery of a tropical forest. The princess doesn't recall ever seeing so much green at once. Peering into the darkness of the forest, she sees marble stairs going up, straight into the canopy of the immense trees.

The bow of the boat creases the white sand, and while Hasan carefully furls the sail, the princess sees a woman standing motionlessly at the bottom of the marble staircase. From a distance the princess cannot see her face, but her long narrow dress, shining yellow in the sun like scaly dragon skin, and her strange flame-red hair almost reaching to the ground are so unusual that the princess freezes in amazement. A wide golden band encloses the woman's brow, and golden bracelets shine on her bare arms.

"Let's go, princess," Hasan says behind her.

"Do you see that, Hasan?" the princess whispers.

Smiling, Hasan jumps out of the boat and carefully carries the princess ashore, then sets her down. The strange woman is already walking to meet them, her hair flying around her like tongues of flame.

"May I be struck by lightning if this is not Hasan!" The woman laughs and extends her arms. Her face bears the perfection of the marble statues of ancient goddesses. Her laughter is carefree like a child's, but in her narrow green eyes there is something as ancient as the world itself and as inevitable as doom. The princess feels shivers going through her body. But Hasan does not seem to share her fright. He laughs in response and takes the woman's hands, and the princess sees a strange ring with a yellowish semitransparent stone on the woman's right forefinger.

"Time has no power over you, Zobeide." Hasan moves away from the woman and looks her over with the delight of a brother looking at his sister after a long separation. Or, perhaps, the princess suddenly thinks, there is something more in his smile, in his eyes, as he looks at the strange woman he calls Zobeide. Fascinated by his new expression, the princess feels at the same time a painful sting of something she has never experienced. She cannot help but wonder what this Zobeide really is to Hasan, and why he wished to see *her* of all the people he must know in the world.

Shaking off these unpleasant thoughts, she returns to reality, as Hasan and Zobeide continue their conversation.

"Appearances are deceiving, Hasan." Zobeide laughs. "I feel older than the rocks that form this island. But when I see you here, just like two thousand years ago...Did my messengers lie to me saying that you had turned into an old bronze piece?"

"Your messengers spoke the truth," Hasan says.

"You lost me....I did not know that a djinn could become free!"

"I am a slave." Hasan pulls back his sleeve to reveal the wide metal bracelet binding his wrist.

"A slave?" It seems that Zobeide has only just noticed the princess standing aside on the white sand. "And this is..."

"My mistress," Hasan introduces, "the princess of Dhagabad. Be kind to her, Zobeide."

"The princess of Dhagabad?" Zobeide leaves Hasan and approaches the princess in a couple of long strides. "Greetings, girl."

"Greetings, Zobeide," the princess says. She is uneasy under the intense gaze of Zobeide's green eyes, but knowing that Hasan won't let her be hurt, she forces herself to look straight at Zobeide.

"Did you order Hasan to come here?" Zobeide asks. "How did you know?"

"I asked Hasan to take me wherever *he* wanted," the princess answers.

"I am happy at your choice, Hasan!" Zobeide turns to Hasan, and suddenly she looks like a little helpless girl. A shiver runs through her body and the princess sees tears brimming in her narrow green eyes. This fleeting impression, though, lasts only for a second and then Zobeide becomes stately and magnificent again.

"Two thousand years is too long, Hasan," she says.

"I would like to be able to disagree, Zobeide," Hasan says with such sadness that the princess freezes on the spot. She has never heard Hasan sound like that. What she hears now in his voice sounds so similar to the pain she saw in his eyes when they first met. She feels a sting again, thinking that this woman, this Zobeide, has brought out Hasan's deepest feelings where she has failed so many times…. She looks searchingly at Hasan's face, but as she manages to catch his eye, he already looks happy and carefree again.

Zobeide straightens up suddenly, as if remembering her duties.

"We shouldn't stay here on the beach," she says. "I haven't had any visitors for ages! Welcome to the Island of the Elements. Let's go!"

They follow Zobeide up the marble stairs into the cool shade of the trees, where Zobeide's shiny dress becomes a natural part of the forest greenery. The princess holds her breath, forgetting all her unpleasant thoughts at the sight of the mysterious forest. It somehow seems like a place where all life began, a place that holds the key to all mysteries in the world. Tall smooth trees rise like arrows to a ceiling of intertwined branches, garlands of strange flowers hanging down. Ivy winds along the huge tree trunks, spreading out its large waxy leaves to the forest moisture. A brook quietly tinkles among rocks thickly covered with moss, forming here and there tiny pools and waterfalls. As she looks more deeply into the endless shade of leaves, she sees vapor rising from the ground between the giant trunks. She feels a breath of the humid air that seems to be born within the trees themselves, bringing the fresh smell of earth and leaves strong and clear, as if this were the place where this smell was created.

Looming ahead, they see the greenish stone walls of an ancient palace, which gradually become more and more visible in the warm dimness of the forest. Walking through an arched gateway along a dark narrow gallery, through a long string of empty rooms and halls, they finally arrive in a giant green hall. The center of the hall is occupied by a marble basin, its clear greenish water moving and rippling as it rises to the surface in boiling domes as if from an underwater spring. Zobeide leads them around the basin to the end of the hall, where giant windows stand widely open in the light breeze, carrying the fresh, heady smells of earth, sea, and pines—not as strong here as in the forest outside but filled with the same primeval, breathtaking richness. Three low armchairs are set around a glass table right next to the window. Zobeide walks up to it, indicating the seats for her guests.

"What did you tell the princess about me, Hasan?" Zobeide asks, settling into an armchair and curling up like a cat. The strange watery stone in her ring now looks like a clot of yellow light with a bright blue beam shining out of its very depths.

"I was hoping *you* would tell the princess about yourself," Hasan says.

"With pleasure." There is a flicker in Zobeide's eyes as she turns to the princess. "Hasan knows how much I like to talk about myself." She smiles. "My name is Zobeide, as you know. I am a sorceress and the Highest Priestess of the Elements. This island is called the Island of the Elements."

"I have never heard of the Island of the Elements," the princess says, "but I know the song about the fay Zobeide who appeared before the caravan traveling from Dimeshq to Megina."

Zobeide pauses to stare at the princess, a look of surprised amusement on her face.

"I was much younger then and liked to show off," she says, glancing at Hasan.

"It is a very old song," Hasan says. "Is it really about you? I must have missed more than I thought."

"It happened just before we met," Zobeide explains, laughing. "You will remember when I came from Baskary to study magic in Dimeshq, and ever since then I couldn't wait to announce myself as a great sorceress."

"Oh, yes, I remember that very well, Zobeide." Hasan smiles at his distant memories.

"Well, somehow I always ended up with a reputation for legendary beauty instead, and I was desperate to prove to the world that I was more than that. At that time the caliph of Megina sent his vizier with rich gifts to ask for my hand in marriage. The vizier was instructed not to take no for an answer, which made his visit more than a bit irritating. You can imagine how angry I was to be treated merely as a beautiful woman. I decided to show these fools once and for all what a real sorceress was. I followed the vizier and his caravan back to his caliph...." Zobeide rolls her eyes upward, sinking into memories.

"Does the song exaggerate or understate what really happened?' Hasan asks.

"I would call it a misinterpretation," Zobeide says. "As you should know, all songs always misinterpret real events." She turns to the princess, slowly coming back to the present. "This happened a long time ago, princess. Right now, I am much more the priestess of the Elements than a sorceress, or a legendary beauty for that matter."

"What are the Elements?" the princess asks.

"The Elements are the great forces that lie at the base of the world, princess. The Cult of the Elements is the oldest of all cults and the first Temple of the Elements, built by its followers, is right here on this island. By now, I am afraid, this temple is also the last...." Zobeide glances around the great hall; and for a moment the princess again sees her as a small and helpless girl, and again this feeling slips away more quickly than a thought.

"The Cult of the Elements requires a lot of sacred knowledge," Zobeide says. "To learn all you need takes centuries, and this makes its followers very rare. Frankly, I don't even know how I had the patience to go through all this. It must have been my drive to match Hasan's great achievements." She glances at Hasan, and the princess fails to read her expression. "Anyway," Zobeide continues, "only by mastering your knowledge and skills can you become a priestess of the Elements. And then you gain the right to wear the Stone of the Elements." Zobeide holds out her hand, and the blue flame from the stone in her ring flashes so brightly and suddenly that the princess jumps in her chair.

The blue flame reaching her from the stone seems to encase her in its light, clouding her mind, making everything in the room step back, molding it into a single background mass. Zobeide's voice now reaches her as if from afar—explaining from the immemorial depths of time—to a part of her that has been ready for this moment, long before her physical birth in this world, explaining to the elements that compose her, the meaning of the stone.

"This stone contains every quality attributed to the Elements." Zobeide speaks with a measured rhythm and the princess completely gives in to it. "It is as transparent as Air and blue as Water; it encloses the Light of Sun, Moon, and Stars; and it is born of Earth. Thus the Stone of the Elements possesses a power that can be used by those initiated in the cult." Zobeide's voice moves away, becomes inaudible; but another voice still sounds in the princess's head, as if completing the thought.

The voice of the stone!

The words shape themselves in her mind, sounding without any audible sound, bringing information in measured waves to the essence of her being. The transparency of Air enfolds her, clothing her in the Light of Sun, Moon, and Stars. From the depths of this transparent shimmering light a blue flame shoots out toward her, piercing her mind. Blue flame, the blue of Water... and all these three qualities—the transparency, the light, and the blue embrace her, pulling her back to the Earth that bore her—and the stone holds her in its power, the Earth that is the beginning and the mother of all Elements....

Suddenly the blue flame disappears into the misty depths of the stone, melting into semitransparent yellow, breaking the ancient magic, returning her to the green hall; to the boiling domes in the marble basin; to the damp air filled with the fresh smells of sea, pine, and life-giving Earth.

The princess stirs, coming to her senses, feeling an unusual silence fill the room. Raising her head, she sees Zobeide and Hasan looking straight at her. She meets Zobeide's narrow green eyes, feeling the terrifyingly beautiful movement of the ancient shadows enchant her, penetrating her very soul.

"The rulers of Dhagabad go back many generations," Zobeide says thoughtfully. "There is a connection between you and this stone, princess... and something else...."

The emerald shadows pull the princess deeper into their enchanting turmoil. She loses her sense of space and time. She is trying to draw away from this all-seeing gaze, to keep at least a small part of herself intact, and yet she is unable to resist the ancient priestess and the power of her green eyes.

"I cannot explain it," Zobeide finally says, "but there is something premeditated in the fact that you, princess, own a djinn, and that this djinn is Hasan."

"I inherited Hasan from my grandmother," the princess says, feeling how inappropriate it sounds after all that has been said here.

Zobeide looks away to stare into the greenery beyond the open window.

"Your grandmother, princess, had decent talents at one time," she says with a slight touch of scorn, "for a mortal, that is. But she never dared to overcome time, partly for the fear of becoming all-powerful. Of course, like any mortal, she was nowhere near absolute power. She grew old and died as ordinary people do."

"Did you know her?" Hasan asks. "Before… "

"She came to the Island of the Elements," Zobeide says. "We never quite made it to great friendship, but if I only knew that she had found you, Hasan…"

"It is just as well that you didn't, Zobeide," Hasan says. "I wasn't able to face my existence at the time."

A silence falls on the room, disturbed only by the tinkling of the water in the basin and the light rustling of leaves outside. The princess slowly recovers, trying to understand Zobeide's strange powers and her mysterious words, feeling completely inadequate to the task.

"The ability to see fates and destinies is a very frightful thing," Zobeide says quietly. "But it is you, Hasan, who should know that better than anyone else. Or, perhaps, an all-powerful one doesn't know the meaning of fear?"

"Alas, we know it all too well, Zobeide."

In his quiet voice the princess hears an echo of the pain that she saw in his eyes on her birthday years ago. With a sinking heart she listens to Zobeide ask him the question she would never dare ask him herself.

"I still don't understand why you decided to become all-powerful, Hasan. You could have been free now, a great sorcerer, your own master. Why didn't you stop? Why did you go all the way to the end?"

Zobeide's voice is filled with despair. The princess has the feeling that this is not the first time this question has passed between them. She holds her breath, trying to become invisible in a conversation in which she doesn't belong, one begun many centuries ago in another time, in another world.

"It is hard to tell where to stop, Zobeide. I never completely overcame the feeling that there was something vitally important just beyond my reach, a whole new field of knowledge of which I was ignorant. It is impossible to tell how much knowledge separates one from oneself and being all-powerful. Impossible until you really are all-powerful. And then it is too late." A shadow runs across Hasan's face.

"Have you never regretted your choice?"

"That is hard to say. The way I chose was long and required so much from me that I simply had no time to call it a mistake and go back. It was much more natural to stick to this way till the end and, enjoying its advantages, put up with the disadvantages as well."

"Are you calling your life putting up with the disadvantages, Hasan?"

"By no means, Zobeide." Hasan's eyes sparkle with amusement. "Most of the time I enjoy the advantages...." He shoots out his hand to catch a brass candelabra that flies at a great speed out of nowhere, aimed straight at his face.

"I never liked it when you started to make jokes in the middle of a most serious conversation," Zobeide says.

"There is no such thing as a serious conversation, Zobeide." Hasan laughs.

"Of course there is," Zobeide insists. "Those are the conversations where I start throwing objects when you joke! At least your reflexes are still good."

"I am glad there are no weapons in this room." Hasan carefully sets the candelabra on the glass table in front of him.

"Do you remember our magic duels?" Zobeide says. "I have to admit, I was terribly vain and proud and I wanted to prove to the whole world, and especially to you, that I was the greatest of all magicians."

"The best way to become a djinn," Hasan points out.

"Never." Zobeide smiles. "I just wasn't talented enough. It is one thing to appear in a purple cloud, levitate objects, and turn water into wine and quite another to comprehend the world to its end."

"What is the difference, Zobeide?"

"You are laughing again, Hasan!"

"I am deadly serious."

"It is so strange to see you again, Hasan. It may sound trivial, but you cannot imagine how glad I am!"

"To be honest, Zobeide, I also have strange feelings. I used to think I had no past...."

"So recently..." Zobeide says absently, "and yet so long ago."

"Do you really feel so old, Zobeide?" Hasan teases. "I could never tell, I mean, just from your looks—"

The candelabra leaps again from the table, but this time it suddenly jerks aside and disappears in the water of the marble basin.

"You forget that you cannot use magic of your own will, Hasan!" Zobeide exclaims, laughing.

"Is this magic?" Hasan asks naively.

"It is more than a Dimeshqian court mage could do. Remember the one that challenged me to a magic duel, and you bravely came to my rescue because I was totally unable to defend myself at the time?"

"It wasn't just that, Zobeide," Hasan says, suddenly serious. "It wasn't chance that brought me to the Plaza of Mages. It wasn't chance that we met. It was a beginning of a completely new phase of my life."

His words hang in the air, almost substantial. It now seems as if there is almost a visible link, a bridge of power, that goes between Zobeide and Hasan, connecting them with a special bond—as if an ancient shadow separates them from the marble hall, the fresh smells from the window, and the princess who sits in deathly stillness, afraid to interfere in this conversation that reveals to her so much of Hasan. Holding her breath, she listens to Zobeide ask another question that she herself would never have dared to ask.

"What is it like to be all-powerful, Hasan?"

Zobeide's voice is ringing with pain that she isn't trying to hide anymore. And, in response to that pain, Hasan's voice sounds very gentle.

"It is very strange to be all-powerful, Zobeide," he says. "You can do anything and yet you are as helpless as a child. Most of all I am glad I did not forget how to be surprised. And even more than that I am surprised that in reality I still know so little...."

"What is the meaning of absolute power, then, if it isn't to know everything?"

"I mostly know that all questions have more than one answer. The more answers, the more questions, and it never seems to end."

The princess listens to their conversation, feeling completely unreal. She can only vaguely understand its meaning—of the looks they exchange, of the power that hangs almost visibly in the green marble hall. The unpleasant stinging feeling she experienced at the beginning is gone. Whatever Zobeide is to Hasan, their relationship is so beyond her comprehension that she cannot feel troubled by it. After all, who is she to attempt to penetrate Hasan's mind? She feels more and more aware of how impossible it seems that her life is so closely connected to this ancient, wise, perfect, all-powerful creature. She is uneasy at the thought that Hasan is her slave, and that in spite of her being so small and unworthy, she must continue to give him orders, because he cannot use even the tiniest fraction of his great powers of his own will. At the same time she feels that the ancient shadow separating Hasan and Zobeide from herself is part of the past, as distant as the centuries and millennia that lay between the present and the time of their youth. Whatever it was that connected these two extraordinary creatures, whatever feelings existed between them, they were resolved two thousand years ago when Hasan became a djinn.

EYES IN THE SAND

✴

Y ou did not yet know you were close to absolute power. You reveled in your knowledge as only a connoisseur can revel in a rare collectible he acquired with great difficulty. With a mere word you could fly up in the clouds or make the waters of the raging ocean part before your feet. You could travel to any distant corner of the world in the blink of an eye. You could do almost anything you liked, and the awareness of your power made you feel invincible. But because your rebellious spirit was never content with any of your achievements, you felt the urge to put yourself to more and more tests, so that you could constantly learn new things and thus prove yourself to be up to your own standards. It was at this time that you first learned about the endless desert.

This knowledge was concealed in a book in the library of Avallahaim, the oldest library known to you, where you, having already learned an unbelievable number of things, kept finding more and more left to learn. The book was written in the magical script of the highest order, the one that can be read only by the wisest of the wise. To common people, the pages appeared blank; and to the mages and scholars who had yet to start on the way to eternal knowledge, the script appeared as strange ornaments of some kind or as chaotic lines, thoughtlessly scribbled by the hand of a child. When you were first able to read this script, you felt as if *suddenly seeing the light. You bristled with excitement when, looking again at the familiar page covered with senselessly intertwined lines, you suddenly saw a text telling of strange, unknown places. Eagerly peering at the lines suddenly filled with meaning, you read with wonder and disbelief something that to a certain extent confirmed the words of the old Agritian scroll. It explained why, to the part of your mind which in spite of everything believed the anonymous ancient philosopher—why you heard so little of djinns, besides the usual tales describing those mysterious creatures as a special kind of lower demon. You learned of the existence of the endless desert lying beyond the known world, where the all-powerful spirits were exiled in order to save the world from the dangers of their presence. You learned of the imprisonment with which the spirits paid for their absolute power, of the helplessness of these spirits in the endless desert, and of the ancient temple that reigned over the sands—the temple that contained the vortex of an unknown power, the temple that could only be seen by those who were privy to the highest mysteries.*

The book described in detail ways of entering the endless desert for those who might have liked to look their destiny in the face before taking any irreversible steps. Entering the desert physically required the creation of a portal, a door between worlds, requiring enormous amounts of energy; and you didn't want to waste energy on something you didn't consider directly connected with your future. The other way, the way of dreaming, allowed you to enter the desert when the mind is asleep to the world of man and to the soul, separating itself from the body, wandering freely in places inaccessible to corporeal men. Back then, you chose this way of entering the endless desert; and now, being an all-powerful spirit, you smile, remembering that the way of travel you chose was, as you now know, the only way possible for a djinn.

In a dream the blazing sunlight and the heat could not touch you. You easily walked upon the unsteady surface of the sand dunes toward the temple, barely visible in the hot crimson haze ahead. You looked the endless desert in the face, trembling with the excitement of learning something unknown, but in no way connecting these ever-shifting sands, these ancient stone walls and domes, with your destiny. You saw in the desert nothing more than another piece of knowledge, similar to that which you had learned from the dusty pages of old books, long forgotten on the shelves of the biggest libraries, from the age-darkened scrolls containing the sacred wisdom you so eagerly sought.

You rapidly approached the temple, barely making out through the trembling haze of hot air the ghostly outline of a beautiful garden surrounding the ancient walls. And, moving faster and faster, you hardly had time to notice a dark glint in the sand at your feet.

Stopping on the crest of a dune, you saw, half out of the sand, a jar made of age-darkened silver. The cork and the mouth of the jar were covered with wax, its dark surface bearing the outline of an unknown seal. Looking more closely, you discovered with surprise that the silver walls of the jar were somehow transparent to your eyes and there, inside the dark jar, you sensed a slight movement. Trying hard to penetrate with your eyes the shadowy depths of the jar, you felt as if someone were watching you from inside. You tried to dig the jar out of the sand, but being present in the desert only in spirit, you weren't able to physically move a single grain. Suddenly, focusing your eyes askance on the space surrounded by the walls of the jar, you saw, looking straight at you, two huge eyes filled with pain unimaginable even in your most horrible dreams.

Reeling from the jar in terror, you fell flat on the thick, unsteady sand and woke up with a scream in your throat, overwhelmed by a

long-forgotten feeling of fear and emptiness. Trying to banish the
horrible vision from your memory you realized that from now on
the stare of those unknown eyes would haunt you forever....

A thin tongue of flame twists and flickers right in front of the
princess's eyes. Listening closely she can even hear the faint
hissing of oil burning on the wick, barely audible above the
sound of the wind rustling the drapes. She always considered
oil lamps to be objects of mystery and enchantment; and now,
tired after a long sewing lesson from the demanding and merciless Zulbagad, the princess is enjoying the quiet of her quarters, stretching out on the floor and setting the only lighted
lamp in the room in front of her eyes.

The princess is rarely alone, and she usually doesn't miss
solitude; but now, after a long and busy day, she is enjoying the
stillness around her, broken only by the rustling of the light
drapes and the faint hissing of the flame. The only person she
wouldn't mind seeing now is Hasan, but she is trying never to
summon him without need. It seems to her that lately Hasan
has started to show a little more interest in the world around
him and a little less of his calm passivity. She is afraid to scare
away this new state of his mind, which is such a big step forward compared with the time they first met, when he was
closed off from her and the rest of the world behind the tiny
iron shutters. She knows that Hasan likes to do many different
things in the palace during the times when she does not require his presence, for instance, during her needlework lessons
with Zulbagad—lessons that her mother insists upon, as if trying to compensate for her otherwise boyish upbringing. She
heard that Hasan spends his free time in the library or visits
various parts of the palace and talks to various people. Alamid
and Nanny Airagad tell her that everyone in the palace, from
the cooks and the stable boys to Selim, the captain of the

guard, eagerly await these visits and show great attachment to Hasan. She thinks with sadness that as she is growing up she seems to be having more and more duties that prevent her from spending time with her djinn, and that the number of these duties will grow even more when she finally becomes an adult. Absorbed in her thoughts, she watches with unseeing eyes the flickering of the light on the elaborate ornaments of the yellow lamp, feeling a growing desire to see Hasan, to sit with him in the semidarkness of her room, to share with him the silence, to feel his comforting closeness and the quiet presence of his thoughts penetrating her confused mind.

Out of the corner of her eye the princess sees a slight movement in the room, a movement without any sound.

"Hasan?" she asks without turning.

"Yes, princess," Hasan replies. She sees from her position on the floor a pair of bare feet appear in her view, feet sinking deeply into the pile of the carpet.

The princess rolls on her side and looks up at him. The lamp doesn't give enough light to see his face, but it seems to her that he is looking her straight in the eyes and that he is smiling.

"Sit with me, Hasan," she asks. "I am so tired...."

Hasan lowers himself to the floor in front of her, leaning back against the wall and crossing his legs to assume the position that the eastern sages call the meditation pose. The princess admires the graceful ease of his movements, forgetting that he can hear her every thought.

She pulls her knees up to her chest, curling on her side and resting her cheek on her hand. Now they form something like a circle—he sitting, she half lying—around the lamp that now throws flickers of light on their faces and hands and on the marble floor around it.

"I wanted to see you very much, Hasan," the princess confesses, "but I didn't want to call you here without need."

"I felt it, princess," Hasan answers softly.

The princess raises her face and looks at him searchingly.

"What were you doing before you came here?" she asks, gathering all her courage. She has wanted for a long time to ask Hasan about his whereabouts when she is not around, but only now does she feel daring enough to venture the question.

"I was playing chess with Selim, the captain of the guard," Hasan says with a laugh.

"How many moves did it take you to win, Hasan?"

"To be honest, I was curious to see how many moves I could make *without* winning, princess, and at the same time learn a lot about the inhabitants of the palace."

"Even about me?" the princess asks, laughing.

"Heaven forbid, princess!" Hasan exclaims in pretended horror. "No one in his right mind would ever dare to gossip about the heiress to the throne of Dhagabad!"

The princess laughs, feeling her tiredness gradually fade away to make room for the happy, carefree feeling she always has when she sits with Hasan in the quietness of her quarters, talking as she does now about nothing in particular. She tries to imagine Hasan playing chess with Selim, a thin, incredibly striking, middle-aged man with a huge gray mustache, whom she has seen many times at palace ceremonies. She cannot imagine Hasan talking to Selim about the inhabitants of the palace over a game of chess, but she knows so little of Hasan and his relationships with other people that she is scared to even think about it. The princess remembers Zobeide with her perfect beauty and the horrifying shadows shifting and changing in the ancient depths of her emerald eyes. Zobeide—the highest priestess of the Elements. Zobeide—the fay that made such a terrible time for the caravan traveling to Megina. Zobeide—the woman whom Hasan calls his friend and who shares a past with him to which the princess has no access. The princess narrows her eyes in the dim light of the oil lamp that suddenly seems painfully bright to her tired gaze. She forces herself to concentrate on the flickering twists of the fiery tongue and slowly, unnoticeably for herself, gives in again to the enchantment of its endless play.

"This flame twists as if dancing, Hasan," she says with a sigh, completely absorbed in a pleasant numbness similar to the effect brought on by music. "If you look at it long enough, you can imagine that the flame encloses a tiny figure circling in an endless dance. It is so beautiful!"

"You would probably have liked the Cult of the Dance," Hasan says thoughtfully.

"The Cult of the Dance?"

"It was one of the cults of the Great Goddess that existed on the shores of the Great River Ghull in the desert land of Aeth. The Temple of the Dance was one of the oldest and most perfect temples created by man. It was built to look very simple, but it was balanced according to the laws of the world equilibrium. Because of that, even when the cult was completely destroyed, the temple retained the spirit of the cult in its walls. There were rumors among the highest mages that, entering the temple, one could see a ghostly likeness of the sacred dance."

The princess listens to him enchanted, absorbed in the endless dance of the tiny tongue of flame.

"Why would anybody need to destroy such a beautiful cult, Hasan?"

"The kings of Aeth, after the establishment of their realm on the shores of Ghull, were suspicious of the cult from the very beginning. The priestesses of the cult wielded too much influence among the people."

"Priestesses?" the princess asks, once again remembering Zobeide.

"Like in the Cult of the Elements, only women could serve this cult. And the Aethian kings didn't like that at all. Finally, King Amenankhor from the Eighth Dynasty ordered the temple destroyed."

"But you just said that the temple stands even now!" The princess looks up, forgetting both her tiredness and her flame.

"The people of the kingdom were unable to move a single stone of the ancient walls, so instead of destroying it the king ordered them to build a pyramid tomb around the temple, the same kind of tomb that was traditionally built for important members of the royal family. It was meant to symbolically bury the ancient cult."

"So, what did become of the temple, Hasan?"

"The temple is still concealed inside one of the pyramid tombs, princess. Unlike other tombs that usually have a secret entrance left behind by the builders, this particular one has solid walls on all four sides. The king believed that the giant stone blocks would prevent evil from getting out."

"I would so much like to see this temple, Hasan!"

"Nothing could be easier, princess."

"But it is almost nightfall now, and tomorrow morning I have a riding lesson. I have so little time, Hasan!"

"Why don't we go there after your lesson, princess?"

"Why do I have to study all the time, Hasan? I mean, I like riding—and history and philosophy are not bad, either—but why do I have to learn needlework, for instance? I can never become as good as Zulbagad, anyway!"

"I think your nannies are generally better at answering this question than I am, princess."

"Yes, I know: the future sultaness must know everything that has to do with housekeeping. But I am so bad at it, Hasan!"

Hasan smiles gently at her.

"Everyone is born for a certain destiny, princess," he says softly. "It is something that's very hard to change."

"True," the princess sadly agrees. "But tomorrow we are going to see the temple, and no one can keep us from doing that!" she adds with finality.

For a while they sit in silence, watching the flame.

"Do you remember when I had that nightmare and I asked you to stay with me?" the princess asks wistfully. She remembers everything that happened that night and blushes, but the dancing flame somehow absorbs her awkwardness, leaving only her wish to share the details of her strange dream with Hasan.

"Of course I remember, princess." The princess feels in Hasan's voice that he also remembers everything that happened, no less than she does, and she feels herself blush again.

"I often have the same dream," she says. "Only sometimes it is much more frightening than usual. I dream of walking in a desert, but at the same time I know I am really surrounded by an invisible garden. And there is an ancient beautiful temple standing in the middle of the garden, a temple I have to enter at any cost...." The princess stops, overwhelmed by her memory.

Suddenly she feels a deadly stillness in the room, as if Hasan has not only stopped moving but breathing as well, as if he has suddenly turned to stone and become one with the wall he is leaning on.

"Hasan?" the princess calls. "What is the matter, Hasan?"

"Please go on, princess," Hasan says, and she hears in his voice something amazingly similar to a plea.

"The temple is beautiful and at the same time gloomy. And I know I would be able to enter it only when something very important happens in my life. I also know very well that the garden is there, but I am completely unable to see it. I can see only the desert."

She looks at Hasan again, overwhelmed by the feeling of a strange significance in her words—as if she suddenly sees a glimpse of a mystery, according to the expression on Hasan's face—so terrible that she would never dare ask him about it. The princess shivers at the sight of his frozen gaze in which she sees newly awakened pain like that she saw the moment when they first met. She feels as if something terrible is going to happen, as if some evil, stirred by her words, will break loose and bring them to some irreversible harm. Fighting through her terror, she calls out to him:

"Are you listening to me, Hasan?"

You are listening to her, holding on to her every word. And yet, at the same time, your thoughts are transported a great distance, to the long-forgotten past, outside the world you know so well. How could this child, who has seen nothing of life, know of the endless desert? How could the ancient mysterious temple possibly enter her dreams? How could this sacred knowledge, open only to the wisest of the wise, touch her mind? Where does she get this inner perception that allows her to see the endless desert and the temple that reigns over its sands? Perhaps there is another way of obtaining absolute knowledge, a way undiscovered by any sages and scholars, a way that allows one to become all-powerful without walking the path of wisdom. Perhaps this young girl, with one step, can reach the stage that took you millennia to attain. Perhaps very soon she will undergo the terrible transformation.

But feeling with the depths of your being the pureness of her childlike mind, the sharpness of her curiosity, and her desire to learn as much as she can, you feel that her mysterious involvement in the high secrets of eternity makes her inaccessible to the suffering that you had to undergo. You feel with your all-knowing mind that, in spite of her unusual vision, in spite of her interest in everything new, in spite of all you share in common that brings you so close together, she will never be a djinn.

Suppressing the ancient pain now awake inside you with a new force, seeing her confusion, and trying to reassure her and calm her, you break out of the bonds of your terror and, meeting her eyes, gently smile at her.

THE SACRED DANCE

✿

A sudden whirl grabs the princess, and the palace walls disappear without a trace. Looking down, the princess shuts her eyes for a moment and gets a firmer hold of Hasan's arm. They are flying in the air without any visible support. Right below their feet, endless sands are shining an unbearable yellow under the blazing desert sun. Straight ahead, the princess sees a rapidly approaching line of green, with glimpses of water barely showing through the leaves.

"Where are we, Hasan?" the princess yells through the wind.

"There, ahead of us, is the Great River Ghull, princess."

Adjusting to the breathtakingly fast flight, the princess finally finds enough courage to look around. The riding lesson that ended only a few minutes ago seems to her now as distant and unreal as a chapter in a book read in a hurry. She is completely absorbed in the whistle of the wind in her ears that brings the smells of the sun and the sands, in the endless open space of the desert crossed by the wide, blue-green line of the river and the thicket surrounding it. To the right, between them and the line of green, she can see something that looks at first like a rough spot on the smooth desert sand. Then the roughness shapes itself into something resembling the castles that children build out of sand. From where she is, the princess can see five big castles and several small ones, scattered at their feet. Each castle points at the sky with a sharp tip, flat surfaces running down its four sides. Each castle casts a triangular shadow on the sand, black as darkness itself.

"The pyramid tombs!" the princess exclaims. "Hasan, I see the pyramid tombs!"

The stone giants appear to be slowly growing as they approach. The princess can now see the rough spots etched by time on the walls of the giant pyramids. Descending closer to the ground, she also realizes that even the small pyramids at the feet of the large ones could easily accommodate the al-Gulsulim mosque in Dhagabad with all its domes and towers. As for the bigger pyramids, from that distance she cannot even comprehend them as something made by man.

The princess slowly flies down to the sand, and for a second she feels as if in front of her, on the edge of the desert, stretch a ridge of mountains and peaks of unusually even, triangular shapes. She can now see about ten pyramid tombs that, crowded together, shielding each other, seem to extend endlessly into the desert.

"They are so big, Hasan," the princess whispers, holding the djinn tightly by the arm. "The smallest of them is probably bigger that our palace."

"Actually, they are not quite so big, princess," Hasan says, narrowing his eyes to observe the unusual view with hidden satisfaction. "They were built to appear bigger than they really are."

"Which of them hides the temple, Hasan? Or, rather, let me guess. I think it must be the biggest one!"

"It would be too obvious to hide the temple in the biggest one, princess. The king wanted to conceal it for the ages to come."

"In that case, is it the smallest one?"

"The smallest one would be also too obvious, princess. It would be too easy to find."

"They are so much alike, Hasan. And yet, they are very different. I cannot even tell how they differ, but it seems to me I would always be able to tell them apart."

"First of all, they are slightly different in size, princess. But King Amenankhor thought of that, too. He ordered two identical pyramids built, one of which should have served as a tomb for his younger brother, Ptahankhtep, and the other—to bury the accursed temple."

"Those two pyramids seem identical to me, Hasan."

"Only from the point where we stand, princess. Actually, the identical pyramids are those two. They are built some distance apart from each other in the group, so they would be very hard to compare. At the same time, if you look for two identical pyramids, sooner or later you are bound to find them. Yet, even then, you wouldn't be able to tell which pyramid you should enter to find the temple—to say nothing of the difficulties of entering a pyramid without any kind of door."

"Do all these precautions mean that there were people who actually wanted to find the temple?"

"The Cult of the Dance had its followers, princess. By no means everyone wanted to get rid of the old temple."

"How would we be able to reach the temple through this desert, Hasan? It is so far from here...."

"Hold on to me, princess."

Together with Hasan the princess takes a step forward and cries out, covering her face with her hands. The wall of the furthest pyramid suddenly moves toward her at such speed that it seems as if, completing the step, she will smash herself against the rock. But, carefully putting down her foot, she feels under the sole of her sandal the rough grains of the dense sand that surrounds the pyramids. Cool shade cast by their walls in the setting sun surrounds her with soft dusk, so different from the blazing yellow of the open desert they just left. Turning back, she thinks she can see the place where she stood with Hasan only moments ago. From here it looks as if this place is right on the edge of the thicket that runs along the shoreline. The princess carefully exhales the air that, as she just realized, froze in her lungs during that terrifying step.

"What was that, Hasan?" she asks with a slightly trembling voice.

"I thought it would be faster this way."

The princess seems to hear a chuckle in his voice, but she has no energy to pursue that. Somewhere deep inside, along with fright, she also feels like laughing. And something else—a breathtaking desire to repeat once again that headlong step, safely holding Hasan's firm, reliable hand.

"Where is the entrance to the temple, Hasan?" she asks.

"All the ancient temples have their entrances facing east, princess. That's why we approached the eastern wall of the pyramid."

"Are we going to pass through that wall, Hasan?"

"By all means, princess."

The next moment the princess feels her body sink into a cold gray substance that surrounds her. She can feel Hasan's hand firmly holding hers, but she cannot see anything except the dense, impenetrable mist. Hasan's hand pulls her forward and, pushing with difficulty through the strange substance, she finally finds herself in complete darkness. By the faint movement of air that gently touches her face, and by the hollow echo of the slightest sound she makes, she realizes that the space inside the pyramid is huge.

"I can't see a thing, Hasan," she whispers, scared by the sudden loudness of her voice. "Is there no light at all in here?"

"Don't worry, princess. We'll make some light in a second." Hasan releases her hand; and the princess sees a red flash above her head, blinding to her eyes, already accustomed to the darkness. The giant space suddenly lights up with something resembling the uneven flame of oil lamps. A huge lantern is now floating above the princess's head, scaring away the ancient shadows that inhabit the mysterious pyramid.

Holding her breath, the princess looks around. The wall they came through angles upward, disappearing into the darkness above their heads. Rows of strange painted signs and figures run along this wall as far as the eye can see. Looking ahead, the princess can barely make out in the depths of the pyramid the dim outline of a strange stone structure. A building, almost square at the base, running upward in large tapering steps, is surrounded by a row of columns. Unlike all the temples the princess has ever seen—usually covered with inscriptions, ornaments, and decorations—the dark stone walls of the Temple of the Great Goddess are hewn smooth, with their polished surface reflecting the light of the lantern, so unusual in this place.

The princess more guesses at than sees the entrance in the shadows surrounding the temple by the interruption in the uneven reflection of the lantern. She slowly follows Hasan inside, walking under the mysterious vault, feeling the spirit of the strange ancient magic close around her with smooth solemnity.

The lantern above the princess's head illuminates a giant square room. Smooth stone floor reflects every movement, making the princess feel as if, instead of walking in the temple, she is flying in a strange space with no sides and directions, without top or bottom, where the intertwined lines on the ceiling fold into a spiral, reflected in the endless mirror of the floor, twisting all shapes and distances, so that the square hall gradually turns into a sphere, giant as the universe.

The princess can now see that all the walls of the room are covered by a continuous row of murals depicting the figures of dancing women. Dark slim bodies of the priestesses are frozen in different movements of the same, extraordinary dance. Following the dancing figures with her eyes, circling in the middle of the giant hall, the princess picks up, row by row, gesture by gesture, step by step, the smooth movement of the Dance of the Great Goddess. And gradually it starts to seem to the princess that the priestesses leave the walls, moving toward her; and in the center of the endless sphere—without top or bottom, without time or space—they combine into one phantom figure, the essence of the dance of the old sacred cult. A ghostly priestess—with unclear features of no known race, carrying inside her something from every dancer in the world, from all the dancing priestesses depicted on the temple walls—shifts her body in smooth, endlessly flowing movements.

Looking at the Dance of the Great Goddess, the princess

forgets everything. She wants to admire forever the perfection of the slim figure; she wants to rush forward, to unite into a single being with this ghostly deity, to turn into one of the dancing figures on the walls, so that she can forever be a part of the sacred dance. She forgets her name, forgets all about the world that splinters in blasts of fresh wind and sunbeams somewhere outside these walls. She stretches out her arms toward the dancing figure that is at the same time so perfect, so close, and so distant from her; and tears of joy, happiness, and unbearable sadness run down her cheeks.

A low rumble shakes the stones of the pyramid. The floor trembles underfoot from a blow of unknown strength. The ghostly priestess of the dance falls apart into separate movements, separate figures that step back into the walls and freeze in separate poses, continuing in a single smooth flow. The princess starts to realize who she is and where she stands. She feels Hasan's hand in hers and looks around, slowly coming to her senses.

The second blow, even stronger than the first, makes her stagger. Uselessly pressing hands to her ears, trying to shut out the sounds of the deep rumble that fills the temple, the princess loses her balance; and only the firm hand of Hasan keeps her from falling. A blaze of white light shines ahead of them, right under the vault of the spiral ceiling, blinding the princess. Reaching unbearable brightness, the light starts to slowly fade and finally disappears, leaving behind a dark outline of a human figure.

In the reddish light of her lantern the princess studies the man standing before them. At first he seems very young—lean, muscular body; dark, lively face; black, dryly sparkling eyes. But looking closer the princess starts to feel an ancient power in the strange man, somewhat resembling the power that flows from Hasan. And something else, more human—nervous restlessness, forcefulness, aggressiveness—and a complete lack of kindness. His clothes, like Hasan's, are simple and elegant. The princess looks with curiosity at the stranger's wrists, seeing no metal bracelets, nor anything else that could signify a slave. Perhaps their new companion is a great mage, but he is not all-powerful. The man standing in front of them is not a djinn.

"How dare you, O miserable ones, disturb the peace of the ancient temple?" The stranger's voice rings with force. The princess helplessly looks at Hasan and, to her surprise, sees a smile of amazement on his face.

"Abdulla?" Hasan says slowly.

The stranger freezes on the spot and peers at Hasan's face.

"Hasan?" he exclaims. "I'll be struck by darkness!"

He impatiently snaps his fingers to summon a whole swarm of floating lanterns. The square hall is illuminated as brightly as in daylight, revealing every last detail of the ancient temple. It seems to the princess that the figures of the priestesses depicted in dance press harder into the walls, pretending to be simple murals drawn by the awkward hand of an ancient artist, and thus hiding themselves until the moment when the dusk will again rule this place.

The strange man and Hasan move toward each other.

"I never expected to see you here, Abdulla," Hasan says.

"If you talk of expectations, Hasan, I was told some completely unbelievable things about you. I was told that you became a djinn!"

"It is true, Abdulla."

"In that case, how did you end up here, in my secret place? Aren't djinns supposed to stay in their containers?" Something in Abdulla's voice makes the princess tremble. At this particular moment he is smiling, and the smile on his pale face seems extraneous, nearly frightening.

"Apparently you don't know very much about the djinns, Abdulla." Hasan laughs. "By the way, I didn't know this temple became your secret place."

"Many things changed in this world in the last two millennia, Hasan," Abdulla says sharply.

"I know that, Abdulla," Hasan says with a chuckle. "As for

the secret places, I think I was the one to bring you here for the first time. Remember?"

"I never forgot you were my teacher, Hasan," Abdulla says with hidden displeasure. "True, you were the one to show me this temple, but during the last two thousand years it became mine. No one except me ever came here to enjoy the vision of the sacred dance."

"I came here to show the sacred dance to my mistress," Hasan says calmly.

"Your mistress?" Abdulla's dark eyes fix on the princess's face and she unwittingly steps backward. A wicked sparkle shines in his gaze.

"She is mortal, Hasan!" he exclaims. "The mortals cannot see the sacred dance without help from the priestesses."

"I thought so too, Abdulla. But it seems that we know even less about mortals than you know about the djinns."

"I never liked your sarcasm, Hasan!" Abdulla's face turns even paler; his dark eyes shine even brighter; and the princess, shivering with fright, moves back several more steps.

"I stopped being your teacher because you couldn't control yourself, and this lack of control interfered with your learning, Abdulla. On the other hand, such unruliness ended up serving you well. Thanks to that, you are still not a djinn."

"Don't pretend that being a djinn is such an honor, Hasan! Where is your valor, if you cannot move a finger without somebody's orders?"

"I never said it was an honor, Abdulla," Hasan says calmly.

"By the way, I was never unhappy with what you call my unruliness, Hasan! True, because of that I lost the wisest of teachers that ever walked this earth—" Abdulla sarcastically bows to Hasan "—but you shouldn't think that I ever regretted that! At the time when you buried yourself in piles of books that filled your dusty hole of a house, I was the fame and glory of Dimeshq! The wisest sages bowed to my knowledge! The fairest beauties that ever existed placed themselves completely at my disposal! Each of them was honored to gratify my wildest fantasies, the same ones that you call my unruliness with such distaste!"

"I also passed through that stage at one time," Hasan says with a smile.

"And foolishly rejected that! You couldn't hold on to your happiness and are now paying for that with your slavery!"

"You can put it this way if you like, Abdulla. I passed through the stage of vanity, and you seem to have stayed there for a much longer time."

"And I don't regret that, Hasan! I have everything one can ever dream of!"

"I am glad for you, Abdulla. Your way does not hold wisdom, but probably it holds happiness—"

"Enough philosophy! I am stronger than you are, O wise teacher!" Abdulla is now laughing and his laughter sounds as disturbing as the screech of metal. "You always won in our magic duels, but now you cannot even move a finger in your defense! Finally, Hasan the mighty, Hasan the wise himself is in my hands! I can smash you like a bug any second!"

"I am not sure this will make you happy, Abdulla." Merry sparkles are dancing in Hasan's eyes, and he smiles with his careless smile looking straight at Abdulla.

"You want me to destroy you, Hasan?" Abdulla asks sharply. "You, an all-powerful djinn, wish for your dumb apprentice to put an end to your suffering in slavery?"

Hasan silently meets his gaze.

Sudden tears fill the princess's eyes. What if Hasan really wants to die, hating his immortality as her slave? What if this angry, restless, unruly boy with wisdom of centuries behind his back can really destroy Hasan with a single movement? What will her life be like without Hasan? How could she live without her best friend who is so dear to her? No! She would rather die with him than allow this to happen!

Shaking from withheld tears, the princess wants to throw herself forward between them, between Hasan and his former apprentice, throw herself in the way of his terrible destructive powers she knows nothing about. Suddenly she remembers something and wild hope awakens in her heart.

"You cannot do anything to Hasan, Abdulla!" she yells. "I will order Hasan to defend himself and he will destroy you! Hasan is stronger than you are."

Abdulla's narrow eyes slip in her direction with cold carelessness.

"I completely forgot about the girl," he says thoughtfully. "She can really be in the way. How about me freeing you from slavery, Hasan? Or, even better, I could get you all for myself, to use as I please. Yes, that would be nice, wouldn't it?" Abdulla raises his hands.

"Don't touch her, Abdulla," Hasan warns. "I can use my magic to protect her."

"In that case"—Abdulla lowers his hands—"let's stick to the original plan. I won't hurt your mistress, Hasan. But you cannot possibly disagree that she can be in the way of my plans. I will distract her by giving her a toy no child has ever refused."

A wisp of white smoke, coiling and twisting like a serpent, rises from Abdulla's outstretched palm. Holding her breath, the princess follows the movements of the white line that grows, slightly diffusing on the edges, and slowly walks off Abdulla's hand onto the floor, turning into a dancing shape. A strange sexless creature of grotesquely thin and long proportions circles and twists in the movements of a beautiful unknown dance that doesn't resemble at all the Dance of the Great Goddess, but nevertheless in a different way attracts and absorbs all the princess's attention. Again she forgets where she is; she doesn't feel her body anymore, sinking with all her being into the movements of the white creature. She forgets Hasan, the temple, and the wicked Abdulla. She does not remember the magic duel in which Hasan is going to die because he cannot defend himself without her orders.

A flash of energy shakes the walls. Through the twists and turns of the white dancer's movements the princess feels something invisible, possessing enormous destructive power, fly off

Abdulla's fingertips, fly with horrifying slowness—or is it the flow of time that is so slow in this temple from the other world?—toward Hasan, standing motionless in the middle of the giant hall. Soon this wave of energy will reach Hasan and then... The princess shakes off the enchantment; and the white figure falls apart to turn back into the smoke that formed it, falls apart leaving behind nothing but a slight quiver of air.

"Defend yourself, Hasan!" the princess yells at the top of her lungs. The wave of energy sweeps past her, throwing her against the wall, pressing her hard into the space between two dancing figures. *I am turning into one of the ancient murals, so that I can forever be a part of the sacred dance*, the princess thinks, even while the blanket of complete darkness softly falls upon her head.

ON THE BANK OF THE GREAT RIVER

❈

*T*he setting sun shines on her face through the holes in the giant palm leaves. She can hear the singing of birds and the splashing of water somewhere nearby. For a while she tries to collect all these sounds and patches of sunlight, pushing with difficulty through a circle of dancing figures filling all the space around her. Then she starts feeling the smells—damp freshness of the slightly wet ground she is lying on; sharp smell of grass, and delicate, barely perceptible aroma of lotus. Finally she recovers the sense of touch—she feels the bumps of hard, uneven ground digging into her back; a slight touch of cool breeze; and something else on her brow. A hand?

Enjoying her newly acquired senses, the princess tries to move. It seems that her arms and legs still respond to her commands, although she seems to feel her limbs as something foreign to her body, something not completely belonging to her....What is that hand doing on her brow? Or is she only imagining a hand is there? The princess is trying to remember where she is and how she got here. Gradually, some pictures float in her mind. The pyramids, the darkness, the temple. The sacred dance, the terrible underground rumble. And the restless, wicked Abdulla...

"Hasan!" the princess exclaims. She tries to sit up, but her body is not responding very well; and this strange object on her forehead, so much resembling a hand, does not allow her to move her head.

"Don't move, princess." The voice that speaks these words

makes a lump come to her throat. So familiar, so dear, so beloved a voice…

"Hasan!"

"You sound surprised, princess." In spite of the irony, the princess seems to hear in Hasan's voice something that sounds very much like relief.

"Where are we, Hasan?"

"We are on the shore of the Ghull, princess. Everything is fine."

"And where is—Abdulla?"

"He disappeared in an unknown direction." She can now hear Hasan chuckle to himself.

"Did you—fight?"

"Of course not, princess. There is no point in my fighting him. First, I am stronger than he is. And second, he used to be my apprentice, and I would never fight someone I taught. Although I cannot honestly say I was a good teacher for him."

"But he—he wanted to destroy you, Hasan!"

"Abdulla cannot control his anger, princess. He regretted it as soon as he returned to his senses."

"What did happen, Hasan? I cannot remember a thing. Something was wrong with me—"

"He shot a wave of energy at me, princess. Unfortunately, Abdulla does everything beyond measure. The wave was so big that the edge of it hit you, too."

"It could have killed you, Hasan!"

"You ordered me to defend myself at the right time, princess."

The princess suddenly feels a stinging under her eyelids. Her eyes fill up with tears, depriving her for a while of the eyesight she regained with such effort.

"Hasan…" she whispers. "If he had killed you, I would have died, too. I don't want to live without you. Did you really want to die at his hands?"

"Of course not, princess."

Do you ever regret your immortality? Do you ever dream of release from your slavery by such simple and unattainable means as death by the hand of a mighty wizard? Perhaps you, knowing of the uncontrolled temper and constant jealousy of the proud Abdulla, provoked him on purpose to challenge you to the duel. Perhaps you were secretly cursing the resourcefulness and recklessness of your mistress who saved you in the last second from the deadly blow. Or perhaps you just weren't sure of what would happen to an all-powerful immortal spirit hit by a skillfully thrown offensive spell. Perhaps you were just trying to bridge the gap in your knowledge of the only field where the unknown powers know more than you do, in the field of knowledge about the djinns and absolute power.

Do you know what made you call Abdulla's anger upon yourself and stand still, in silent expectation of the destructive blow? Can you forgive yourself for letting part of that blow land on her, completely innocent, ready to sacrifice her own life to save you or to share your horrible destiny? Can you ever forget her reckless bravery, her piercing scream, her lifeless body that you are now trying so hard to fill with new life force, and her tears, sacrificed for the sake of your release?

They are sitting side by side among the reeds on the wet bank of the Ghull, looking at the sun slowly sinking behind the sharp line of the horizon. The princess, still weak and slightly shivering with chills, is wrapping herself tightly in the blanket that Hasan, as usual, pulled for her straight out of thin air. From where they sit they cannot see the main part of the river. A backwater pool, looking very much like a lake, lies in front of them, surrounded by a tall reed thicket. The turbid greenish water of the pool is so still that it seems like a window into the upturned sky, reddened by the sunset. Several lotuses in the middle of the pool appear to be hanging in midair, gently rocking with the breeze or an underwater current.

"They probably won't be happy back at the palace with our staying out so late," the princess says unwillingly, torn between the desire to forever sit with Hasan on the bank of the river like that and the late-coming sense of duty.

"Don't worry, princess," Hasan says. "I arranged it so that no one will even notice you are away."

The princess relaxes at the thought that she doesn't need to think of her duties for a while, and gives in completely to her feelings, imagining herself to be a part of the clear evening air, of the smell of the river water and strange plants, of the rustling of leaves and the distant cries of birds. She feels in a new way how great Hasan's power is, allowing him with such ease to resolve any of her problems, and how little she knows of the limits of his abilities.

"I feel scared every time I think of how many things you can do, Hasan…" she says quietly. "Although 'scared' is probably not the word."

"It may seem scary sometimes, princess."

"Not with you, Hasan. But I think it is only now that I finally understand that the magic can really be scary." The princess shivers, remembering Abdulla's cold, restless gaze. "Of course, I read about the evil sorcerers, but it is one thing to read about them and quite another to see them with your own eyes."

"Abdulla isn't necessarily evil," Hasan says thoughtfully. "Although I wouldn't call him good, either. I would say that in terms of good and evil the sorcerers are just like ordinary people. Only they can use stronger means to show their feelings."

"Could he really have killed you, Hasan?" the princess asks, trying without much success to suppress the trembling in her voice.

"I don't know, princess. I know so little about djinns, especially because they, or we, are created in a world that I know nothing about."

"And you really couldn't defend yourself without my orders?"

"Apparently not, princess."

The princess slowly exhales the air she found she had been holding back during his reply, trying to stop the terrible pictures popping up in her head. She cannot bear to think that all her happiness, everything important in her life, everything that seemed so permanent and reliable, could have disappeared so easily!

"When I ordered you to defend yourself, I was thinking only about myself, Hasan." Her voice is still trembling and she is not even trying to hide it anymore. "I couldn't imagine life without you."

She stops with a thought so terrible that everything she just survived seems pale in comparison. She needs several moments to gather all her strength and half whisper the horrible but inevitable question.

"Tell me, did you really even for a moment want him to kill you?" She immediately regrets her words, just as a man who throws himself into the abyss to end his life immediately regrets the irreversible step. "No, don't answer that!" she almost pleads.

But Hasan is already speaking, looking straight in front of him.

"I think I never seriously believed Abdulla would raise his hand against me, princess. I was his teacher for so many years. But probably there is no one left in the world who could really restrain him in any way."

The princess madly regrets her question now, and she is willing to accept this answer as neutral enough to convince herself that everything happened as it should have. She starts to speak, hurriedly trying to smooth the awkwardness, trying to leave the horrible question behind.

"To think that he really entranced me with his strange smoke! I was almost too late!"

"You showed incredible strength, princess," Hasan answers softly. "Had Abdulla even suspected that you could overcome his spell, he would have thought of something much more powerful."

The princess feels chills of pleasure running down her back at these words, and she wraps the blanket tighter around herself to hide her emotions. She completely misses the smile sliding over Hasan's lips as he, turning away from her, looks into the distance.

"Tell me what happened in the temple, Hasan. Where did Abdulla go?"

"I averted his blow, princess, and he realized he had lost the duel. I am much stronger than he is when I am allowed to use my powers, and he knows it as well as I do. He also saw you fall near the wall and he assumed that he killed you. He was terribly afraid I would try to avenge you. To escape without losing face, he disappeared in a brilliant flash, as usual. I think we won't be seeing him for a while."

The princess finally feels calm enough to ask him another question that bothers her.

"What if he had killed me, Hasan?" she asks carefully. "Whose djinn would you be now?"

"Probably your father's, princess," Hasan answers with calm thoughtfulness. "Or perhaps I would have just returned to my bottle."

"I am so glad we are both unharmed, Hasan. To think of the danger we escaped!"

The princess feels slightly weak again, and she leans against Hasan beside her, feeling the pleasant firmness of his shoulder and his usual, barely perceptible juniper smell.

"How long was I unconscious, Hasan?"

"Longer than I liked, princess. I had to spend quite a while trying to bring you back."

"Does it mean you saved my life, Hasan?"

"That is difficult to say, princess. You might have recovered without my help."

The princess inhales deeply, feeling strange freedom from all fears, feeling that some unpleasant part of her past has been left behind forever.

"It is so nice to sit here by the water, Hasan," she says softly. "Let's stay just a little bit longer."

"As long as you like, princess."

Her head, leaning against your shoulder, turns heavier; her breath becomes quiet and even. Turning to her and seeing that her eyes are closed, you carefully lay her down onto a bed of reeds that you crush and flatten for that purpose. It is probably time to take her home where she can rest much better and completely recover from the shock. But you feel reluctant to leave this wet bank of the river, the transparent dusk, the stars appearing in the sky one by one, the cries of the frogs and night birds, and the light breeze that you, as a spirit, are unable to feel, the breeze that slightly moves a strand of hair over her face, so peaceful in sleep, and brings from the shoreline thickets the sweet aroma of the flowers.

Whatever your intentions at the beginning of the duel with Abdulla, you are glad everything turned out the way it did; and now you and she, alive and well, are able to spend this beautiful evening on the shore of the Ghull. You are thinking that you, an all-powerful spirit, can learn something from this little girl who, without giving much thought to wisdom and eternity, can simply name her wish in a way that it will immediately come true. You suddenly realize that when she dies, running out of her sparingly measured human lifetime, you will miss her terribly, that you enjoy your long talks, your trips to mysterious

places, the expression of joyful amazement on her face. You inhale
the night air as if you, a spirit, are able to feel its taste, inhale to
the last bit all its aromas, all its fresh coolness, overwhelmed by
an unknown feeling of happiness.

The invisible garden surrounds her with the magnificence of
smells and sounds; but she can still see only the dunes. She
knows where the temple is and she walks straight there; her
feet infallibly find the path ahead, where her destiny lies.
Domes rise before her—domes and arches and columns—she
takes a step and, instead of the sand, feels the chill of the rough
stone surface. All is going well today, and, without looking
back, she climbs the stairs into the dark gallery under the
arched ceiling. Through the open doors she sees a giant hall
ahead and, holding her breath, steps inside.

III

Ancient Bonds

✳

THE HEIR TO THE THRONE

✦

"The great sultan wishes to see you, your majesty."

The sultaness nods, forcing herself to rise from her seat unhurriedly, with the appropriate royal dignity, suppressing the urge to jump up like a little girl at the sight of the master of ceremonies. Fighting her impatience, she straightens out her shawl with deliberate slowness, wrapping it around herself, making herself look fit to appear before the sultan. She beckons Nimeth, silently standing at her side, and walks toward the door, ready to follow the master of ceremonies to the hall of the State Council.

The sultaness's heart is racing with anxiety, and she is barely able to retain her majestic calm. She knows that today is the day when the princess's future is to be decided. Now, in only a couple of hundred steps, in only several turns of the corridor, she will finally learn who was appointed by the State Council of Dhagabad to be the chosen suitor of her daughter. Though the sultaness knows that the choice of the sultan and the royal sages will definitely fall on a prince of one of the neighboring countries, most likely even an heir to the throne, the very predetermination of this choice makes her heart sink in fear for the princess.

In a week the princess will turn seventeen. By the law of Dhagabad this day is considered to be the day of her coming-of-age; and on this very day the princess must choose a suitor from a number of the sons and younger brothers of the kings, sultans, caliphs, and pashas—the rulers of the neighboring lands. The gods have never lifted their curse from the sultan's dynasty. The sultan has no living sons, and it is now up to the princess to assume the unwomanly role of heir to the throne, the role for which she was prepared ever since she was three. It is now up to her to fulfill her destiny, if only by serving as wife of the future sultan, securing by her marriage the presence of a male ruler for her country.

No one has any doubts that on the day the princess turns seventeen the number of suitors arriving in Dhagabad to seek her hand will be greater than anything ever heard of in other kingdoms. Besides the incredible beauty of the princess, praised even in the realms lying very far from Dhagabad, the sultan's lands are rich and fruitful, and the country is so prosperous that any one of the rulers would be happy to join forces with it.

The sultaness knows that for the past few months the State Council has faced a difficult task. The sultan and the court sages were in session day and night, studying books, scrolls, and maps, learning all they could about the kingdoms that could be expected to send their heirs to Dhagabad. It was necessary not only to prepare for the visit of the noble guests but to make a decision about who would be the one capable of making the sultan's only heiress happy, and at the same time of properly multiplying the riches and glory of the great Dhagabad. The sultaness has no doubt that the best minds of Dhagabad have made the right choice, but the very thought of their discussing her daughter's future the same way merchants discuss selling their precious merchandise to make more profit fills her with protest.

"Her majesty, the sultaness!" the master of ceremonies announces, swinging the doors open in front of her.

Gathering all her strength, the sultaness steps forward, over the threshold of the horrifying room. She moves her gaze, which she hopes is full of dignity, over the rows of gray-bearded sages who rose at her entrance, and, nodding to them, fixes her eyes on the sultan, sitting on the pillows at the head of the gathering. His dark face, still handsome in spite of some new lines around his eyes and mouth, is serious; his bushy beard, now slightly shimmering with gray, is sticking out in a particularly unruly way. His gold-embroidered turban is pushed to the side of his head, and his robe has swung open, baring his dark hairless chest. The sultaness can see that whatever the decision reached by the State Council, it was not an easy one.

Walking with effort on her stiff legs, the sultaness covers the last ten steps and stops right in front of her husband.

"Madam." The sultan pauses and she suddenly feels against all logic that he is almost as nervous as she is. "Thanks to the wise counsel of these learned sages—" the sultan nods at the room and the gray heads respectfully bend in response "—we were able to reach a decision regarding who will be the future husband of the princess."

Feeling completely unable to speak, the sultaness bows her head in waiting.

"We were able to find out," the sultan continues unhurriedly, "that one of the richest kingdoms sharing a border with Dhagabad is Veridue. We know the sultan of Veridue very well and we were informed that the heir to the Veriduan throne is the noble Prince Amir."

The sultaness raises her head. Veridue doesn't sound as terrible as, for instance, Megina or Avallahaim. Veridue is separated from Dhagabad only by the river Hayyat el Bakr, the same river that flows in its upper reaches right across the lower city of Dhagabad, crossing her usual path to the bazaar. Veridue, as she heard, can be reached on horseback in only one day. Filled with joy, the sultaness feels enough strength to join the conversation.

"What do you know of Prince Amir, your majesty?" she asks shyly.

"Only the very best," the sultan replies patronizingly. "He is young, only a little older than the princess, and rumors grant him all the fine qualities of a future sultan. We are quite certain that Prince Amir will be capable of making the princess happy."

The last words sound almost gentle, and the sultaness throws a searching glance at his face. Is it possible that her husband is worried not only about the interests of his country but also about the well-being of his daughter? The sultaness notices a new, more human expression on the sultan's face and feels the invisible hand that squeezed her heart somewhat relax its grasp, letting her breathe easier, letting her shed part of the unbearable burden of her worry for the princess. It seems that everything is going to be settled in the best possible way. The princess will be living close to Dhagabad, her husband will be young, handsome, and noble. Maybe the princess won't even be afraid of him as much as she herself is afraid of *her* royal husband.

The sultaness is startled out of her thoughts by ringing laughter sounding clearly in the giant hall—the laughter of a child, so unusual for the meeting place of the State Council.

A little child no more than two years old runs into the hall, awkwardly moving on its short legs. The sultaness freezes at the sight of its blue eyes and soft golden curls. There is only one woman in the entire palace who could be the mother of this fair-haired child.

Albiorita!

The beautiful Albiorita, the sultan's "bride," as he affectionately called her a couple of years ago when this extraordinary concubine appeared in the palace. A fair-haired beauty from the mountains of Baskary who made the sultan Chamar Ali forget his beloved harem. The woman who gave the sultan the new hope of begeting a son, who made him, as the sultaness believes, postpone the princess's wedding and the official appointent for the Dhagabad heir.

And now she sees the fruit of all these efforts. A fair-haired child.

But why does this child run alone in the hall of the State Council? All the children of the sultan's concubines live with their mothers in the harem until they turn twelve. Perhaps Albiorita is not living in the harem anymore? Can it be that the sultan allows one of his concubines to live in the palace itself? Can it be that the sultan finally has a son?

The sultaness strains her eyes to make out the gender of the little child. Its clothes look more like a boy's, but at this age it is so hard to tell. Especially with the sultan's desire to have a son that drives him to treat not only the princess but also the daughters of his concubines more and more like boys.

The child runs straight to the sultan and, laughing like a spoiled favorite, buries its face in the flap of the sultan's robe. Putting on a look of displeasure, the sultan pushes the child aside, throwing an irate and slightly embarrassed glance at the sultaness. But the sultaness is not looking at him. With wide-open eyes she is looking at the side door of the room where she can now see a woman with long flowing hair, as if clad in pale gold. The woman's face is covered by a veil, but the sultaness can clearly see her eyes—the color of turquoise—of the endless waters of the sea.

"Eleida!" the woman calls softly and her voice sounds like music.

Eleida.

The sultaness lets out a sigh.

A girl. Chamarat Eleida. Another daughter.

The sultaness transfixedly watches the golden-haired child happily running to her mother, grasping at the folds of Albiorita's garments with her tiny hands. She watches the concubine throw a frightened glance, hold her daughter tightly against herself, and disappear behind the door. Her heart stands still at the sight of the tenderness in the eyes of the sultan, following them with his gaze.

"I would like the princess to be happy," the sultan says gently, and the sultaness suddenly feels unexpected closeness to her husband. The scene she just witnessed, which by every right should have filled her with rage and jealousy, makes her look at the sultan in a new way. For the first time during the many years of their marriage she can see beyond his outward glamour and terrifying gaze; beyond his gloom and anger at the whole world that has denied him a son and a heir; beyond his singular beard sticking straight out from his face. She suddenly sees a man like everyone else who loves, makes mistakes, and feels guilty. She suddenly realizes that she was wrong to worry about letting the sultan decide the princess's future, for he is concerned about the happiness of their only daughter no less than she. And she feels enormous compassion for this man's lost hopes, for his failure to change the will of the gods, who cursed him by denying him that which he longs for most —a son and heir.

With boldness that she found impossible before, she steps forward and affectionately pats her husband's arm.

"I will inform the princess of your decision," she says, and, turning away quickly to hide the grateful tears filling her eyes, she collects her garments about her and hurries out of the hall.

The sultaness chooses a long way back. She feels the need to walk without rushing along the side gallery of the palace, along the edge of the garden adjoining the palace, reveling in the suddenly acquired peace. A little later she will discuss these events with Nimeth, now silently walking beside her, feeling with infallible instinct that her mistress and friend needs to be alone with her thoughts. For the first time in many days the sultaness feels capable of simply enjoying the nice day, the waving greenery of the garden, the light breeze on her face.

The sultaness and Nimeth stop, hearing voices ahead of them.

"If a place is described in a book, it should exist somewhere in real life, Hasan!" they hear the princess exclaim. "At least, that's what my philosophy teacher says."

"It doesn't have to be the case, princess," Hasan says.

The sultaness hears her daughter's clear laughter, and crossing the length of floor that separates her from the turn of the gallery, stops to admire the peaceful sight.

The princess and Hasan are sitting side by side on the stairs leading from the gallery to the garden. A giant wood-bound book is hanging in the air in front of them, a book which, most likely, no one in the palace has ever read, if only because of its being so heavy that even lifting and opening it is not an easy task. Hasan is saying something in a quiet voice and the princess is laughing, flushed, her eyes shining. Looking at them, at how carefree they are, sitting there together, how easy they seem to feel with each other, the sultaness feels a slight sting of longing. *If only...* she thinks, letting the flow of wild dreams pull her into their turmoil. If only Hasan was a man and the princess could marry him... There is no one else in the world with whom the princess likes so much to spend time. There is no one else in the world to whom the sultaness could entrust her daughter with such an easy heart. Is it possible to even imagine another couple so carelessly happy with each other, seeing how they sit on the steps of the palace, laughing, engaged in their conversation?

A wave of reality sweeps over her without warning, falling on her like the blow of a hammer. To marry the princess, Hasan has to be free. But unlike other palace slaves there seems to be no mortal, and no immortal for all she knows, who could free him from his slavery. Besides, how would it look for the people of Dhagabad if their princess, the heiress to the throne, married a freed slave? And, the sultaness admits with a sigh, nobody says that Hasan, were he to become free— Hasan, an ancient, wise, all-powerful mage—would wish to tie himself forever to her young daughter. From his point of view, however much the princess might enjoy his company, she most likely remains for him just one of the many women he has known, a temporary mistress who is destined to die within an unnoticeably short time compared to the millennia of his life.

The sultaness sighs again, looking through the tears filling her eyes at her happily laughing daughter, who will have to leave this palace so soon to move to a new home and to fulfill her duty. She admires the princess, who by age seventeen, has turned into the incredible beauty she always promised to be, enjoying the easy precision of her movements that she has never seen in anyone else, the shifting expressions of her sharply intelligent face, the shine of her dark-blue eyes, resembling now more than ever the shine of sapphires in the sunlight. The sultaness signals Nimeth and both of them turn back unnoticed, disappearing behind the turn of the gallery.

LABYRINTH

�֍

"So you really mean that a place described in a book doesn't have to exist in real life?" the princess asks, her curiosity piqued.

"Of course, princess."

"But where does the description come from, then? After all, to think of a place one has to see it somewhere, at least in a dream."

"Or in the imagination."

"The place described in this book would be impossible to imagine, Hasan!"

"The connection between books and real life is not as simple as you think, princess," Hasan says calmly.

"All right," she says, giving up. "Let's say for a moment that it is possible to describe a place that doesn't exist in any reality. What I want to know is whether it can happen the other way around."

"What do you mean, princess?" Hasan asks with a smile.

"Are there any existing places that are not described in any book?"

"Of course there are, princess."

"How could you know they really exist, then?"

"As I told you, princess, the connection between books and real life is not simple. I know of at least one place that is not described in any book, but knowledge of which can be obtained from reading books."

"I don't think I understand...."

"There are books one can read *only* after acquiring a certain amount of knowledge, princess," Hasan explains. "One basic step in the progressive chain of knowledge is the secret of immortality. In this way, therefore, some books cannot be read by mortals."

"But the place you are talking about is still mentioned in those books!" the princess insists.

"No, it is not. But after reading the books the knowledge of the place comes to you by itself."

"What kind of a place could it possibly be, Hasan?"

"The Dimeshqian Labyrinth, princess. The search for this labyrinth has always been a kind of test for the highest mages."

"Is it hard to find?"

"If you haven't reached the prerequisite stage of knowledge, princess, it is impossible to see the entrance into the labyrinth. Many mages, who considered themselves to be the greatest wizards, spend years in Dimeshq in search of the labyrinth. And many of them leave without finding anything."

"Were you able to find the labyrinth at once, Hasan?"

"I started looking for it at the right time, princess. For that reason it wasn't hard for me to find it."

The princess puts her arms around her knees, pulling them up to her chest, forgetting the argument and thoughtfully gazing at the intertwining branches of the garden. She feels a sudden sharp realization of the wide abyss that separates her from Hasan and his endless knowledge and wisdom. The thought of a place where he can go, but that she in her ignorance would never find, suddenly becomes a symbol of the eternity that separates her from this person—closest to her in the whole world—to whom she can never be equal.

"I am so sorry I could never see the labyrinth, Hasan," she says softly.

"Actually..." Hasan says unexpectedly.

The princess looks up at him, filled with sudden hope. Hasan laughs at the passion in her eyes.

"Were you going to say that there is a way for me to see the labyrinth, Hasan?" The princess jumps up, unable to wait any longer. "I would so much like to see it, Hasan!"

"Your wish is my command, princess." The djinn bows, still laughing.

Raising her head, the princess sees that they are no longer sitting in the palace gallery. They are standing on stairs that lead up to a large building, just above a plaza crowded with people. The unbelievable human chaos, bursting with a rainbow of colors and a wide variety of sights and sounds, resembles the main plaza of the lower city of Dhagabad on a market day.

From where they stand, the princess can clearly see that at the center of the plaza, free of people, there is a giant stone platform in the shape of a strange-looking pentagram. The diagonals of the pentagram are painted blue, forming a star that shines brightly on top of the dark stone background.

"Where are we, Hasan?" The princess raises her voice, trying to shout over the buzzing crowd.

"We are in the Plaza of Mages in Dimeshq," Hasan says.

"What is that platform in the middle?"

"That is an arena for magic duels, princess."

"Why would you need a special place for the magic duels?"

"It is the official way for Dimeshqian mages to determine who is the stronger."

"Did you ever see such a duel, Hasan?"

"I have to confess I even took part in some of them, princess."

"You?"

"I told you I was a Dimeshqian mage once, remember?"

The princess sees with new meaning the outline of the blue star shining in the middle of the plaza. This time she notices that the seething crowd is not only avoiding the pentagram itself but also leaving clear the space within a few steps of the edge of the platform. The princess cannot help wondering how bad were these duels, and whether they still happen now, thousands of years after the Dimeshqian era that Hasan must have known so well.

"Has anything changed here, Hasan?"

"Of course some things have changed, princess. But that is true for any place. Actually, the changes are not that significant. Most of the buildings are different, but somehow, the feel of this plaza is still the same."

"Where is the labyrinth, Hasan? And how will I be able to see it—not being a mage?"

"The labyrinth is inside the Dimeshquian library, princess," Hasan answers. "As for not being a mage, I can help you see it," he adds, chuckling.

"Where *is* the library, Hasan?" the princess asks, dancing with impatience. She is fascinated by the plaza in Hasan's home city, but the thought of seeing a labyrinth open to only the highest mages completely overwhelms her.

"Right behind us, princess. We are standing on the steps."

Turning, the princess sees in front of her large double doors covered with gold-painted stars. One of the doors is half open, letting out dim library light and beckoning with a very familiar smell of ancient dust and parchment.

Stepping inside, the princess looks around carefully. She sees endless rows of bookshelves stretching out into the distance straight up to the arches of the wide dome—its skylights being the only source of weak, scattered light in the giant space. She is dazzled by the sight of the innumerable spines of books: large and small, greasy and worn from constant use, shining with gold imprints, and scribbled with strange ornaments—probably the letters of some unknown languages. Being reasonably well-read, the princess still could never have imagined a library of this size; and now, frozen with amazement at the sight of such magnificence, her heart pounds with the thought of how much knowledge must be contained in this wonderful place.

"Have you read all these books, Hasan?" she whispers.

"I am amazed by the thought myself, princess," Hasan confesses.

In the quiet of the library every sound seems too loud. Trying to walk as lightly as she can, the princess follows Hasan, who is confidently making his way between giant bookcases into the dusty, darkened depths of the room.

"Is anyone here besides us?" the princess asks.

"That door over there leads to the library keeper's room. The keeper is always here; it is his job to open the doors in the morning and to lock them at night. Also, there is usually a boy who climbs up the bookcases to get books from the top shelves for patrons. I am also sure that there are at least several people sitting here right now reading books. One of the beauties of this particular library, princess, is that however many people may come here at one time, they may not even be aware of one another's presence."

He suddenly stops in a dark corner free of bookcases, and the princess nearly stumbles over him.

"What happened, Hasan?" she asks.

"This is the place, princess."

"But...there is nothing here, Hasan!"

"That's what the mages and wizards thought when they came here in search of the labyrinth. They examined every crack in this wall and found absolutely nothing."

"Are you telling me that right now, in this very corner, there is a door leading into the labyrinth?"

"Let me show you, princess."

Hasan slowly moves his hand over her eyes, and the princess feels as if she has suddenly acquired sight after being blind. In the dark corner of the library she can now see a faint glow emanating from the stones of the wall that softly outline a rectangular, delicately carved door. The surface of the door is covered with ornaments. As the princess tries to look at them more closely, the fine lines start to diffuse and spread out, forming a single, extremely complicated ball of intertwined shining threads.

"Is something written here, Hasan?" the princess asks.

"'He who seeks wisdom should open this door and enter the unknown,'" Hasan reads out loud.

"Does it mean there is wisdom beyond this door, Hasan?"

"Of course not, princess. It is just that those who created this door wanted the mages who found it to feel rewarded for their labors as when people leave some significant-sounding inscription on carefully hidden treasure."

"It is hard to believe that we can just open this door and walk in," the princess says, shivering with her closeness to the sacred mystery.

"It is the same feeling any mage has when he finally finds this door, princess," Hasan says, and she hears in his voice a reflection of her own excitement.

At his touch the door noiselessly moves inward, leaving behind the shining rectangle of its glowing frame. Following Hasan, she carefully steps inside, sinking her body into the soft glow. She feels the door behind her slam shut, leaving no trace on the blind stone wall.

They are standing in a round marble hall, with identical doorways leading out of it on all sides.

"What do we do now, Hasan? Which doorway shall we choose? And where is the door we walked through?"

"I forgot to tell you, princess. This is the second trial for mages who succeed in entering the labyrinth. They have to find their way out."

"But how, Hasan?"

"You have to be even more powerful than when you found the entrance. Many wizards, seeing the door, never gather enough courage to walk through it. Others enter the labyrinth but can't find their way out and wander here forever, gradually turning into ghosts. Some, taking time to consider all the knowledge they have, manage to find new meaning in some things they already know, and finally walk out of the labyrinth—only to refuse to follow the path of knowledge further. The labyrinth is the true test of magic powers."

"But you—you know how to find the way, right, Hasan?"

"Of course I do, princess. See for yourself."

For a second time Hasan moves his hand over her eyes, and

the round marble hall changes slightly. The princess can once again see a faint glow on the walls, but now the glow fuses and focuses to form a fiery arrow hanging in the air pointing straight at one of the doorways.

"How did you do that, Hasan?" the princess demands.

"The arrow was always here, princess, just like the door before that. I merely helped you to see something that is usually visible only to the initiated."

"Do we need to go where the arrow points?"

"Exactly, princess."

They slowly move through the marble corridors and rooms of the labyrinth. Now that the fiery arrows floating in the air infallibly show the way, the princess feels safe enough to look around. The walls of the labyrinth are decorated with beautiful ornaments, carved from stone with a level of skill that would seem impossible for any mortal. Most of the rooms and corridors look exactly alike, making it impossible to find your way without the guidance of the arrows. Some rooms they see on their way are breathtakingly beautiful—filling the princess with admiration. One of them has a fountain in the middle made completely of green marble set with inlays of gems. The princess, familiar with jewels, realizes they are incredibly large and pure emeralds. Another room resembles an illuminated cave, with numerous crystals hanging from the walls and ceiling, sparkling and shining with unbearable brightness in the light emitted by the walls. The last room, painted in various tones of blue, has almost the entire surface of the floor covered with a pool of what looks exactly like sea water, with fountains flowing out of the walls with great force creating currents and whirlpools that make the crystal-clear water boil like a mountain stream. This room is much bigger than the others, so that the princess can barely make out its far end quite a distance away. A wide staircase in front of them leads straight into the pool, leaving no other visible way to cross the flooded room.

"Where next, Hasan? Do we have to swim through this room?"

"This is the third trial, princess. It is impossible to swim in this water. This pool has no bottom, and the fountains create such a strong current that anyone who gets into the water is pulled straight down."

"It's such a pity, Hasan! I would so much like to swim here!"

"I would not advise that, princess, but you may touch the water and then you will understand what I am saying."

Walking down the marble steps to the edge of the water where small splashes greedily lick the smooth marble surface, the princess carefully dips her hand into the pool. For a few moments the powerful current that entwines her hand feels soft and soothing. But then she starts feeling some unknown power pulling at her hand, slowly dragging it downward, deeper and deeper, where the crystal-clear water reveals no sign of a marble floor beneath—and where as far as the eye can see, there is only the transparent blue, ever swirling in constant circular movement.

Frightened, the princess hastily pulls her hand out of the water.

"Is there no bottom at all down there, Hasan?" she asks.

"None, princess."

"It cannot be that there is absolutely nothing down there. This water is bound to end somewhere!"

"This is one of the miracles of the labyrinth, princess—one of the few places in the world where you can really come close to eternity."

"I don't understand what eternity is, Hasan. Everything has some kind of an end somewhere!"

"Look into the water, princess. This water does not end anywhere."

For a while the princess thoughtfully looks into the depths of the clear water, trying to understand what Hasan told her. Not managing to understand a thing, she finally steps back from the pool, turning to the problem at hand.

"How do we cross to the other side, Hasan?" she asks.

"Like everywhere else in the labyrinth, you just have to see the right path," he says, for the third time moving his hand over the princess's eyes.

The princess looks at the water again and shuts her eyes for a moment, unable to believe the things suddenly apparent to her improved vision. A winding path runs across the water, a glowing path made of the same fire that made the guiding arrows in the passageways.

"What happens to those who can't see the path, Hasan?" she asks, her voice trembling.

"The same thing that nearly happened to your hand, princess. Those who come this far are often aware of the existence of such a path and sometimes attempt to walk across the pool, knowing that the way is there and hoping to feel it with their feet."

"What a terrible trial, Hasan," the princess says quietly.

"Don't forget it is completely voluntary, princess," Hasan reminds her. "There is no way to learn of the labyrinth by accident. Everyone who comes this far knows exactly what the risks are."

Throwing cautious glances at the turbulent water by her feet, the princess easily walks upon the shining path and steps with some relief onto the dry marble surface of the next corridor. They wend their way through several more marble passageways and finally step through a doorway to find themselves outside.

The princess looks around, amazed. They are standing in the most beautiful garden she has ever seen, the most beautiful garden, she is certain, that could ever exist in the world. Intertwined branches over their heads create a kind of roof, where only glimpses of the blue sky can be seen through the dense bower. On the sides, through the leaves of exotic plants, she can see rows of giant strangely shaped flowers, retreating into the green depths of the garden, filling the air with sweet aromas.

"Where are we, Hasan?" she asks.

"We are still in the labyrinth, princess. But we are now approaching its center."

"What's in the center of the labyrinth?"

"You will see, princess."

The fiery arrows point the way through a network of paths between strange trees and bushes unlike any the princess has ever seen. There are no look-alike places here, so the princess, walking close beside Hasan, can devote all her attention to admiring fully the beauty of the garden and the anticipation of the next beautiful sight around each corner they pass. Everything in the garden is planned to perfection—the shapes and colors, the leaves and crowns of trees growing together, the openings between branches making beautiful natural frames for the exotic flowers. It seems as if the gardener who created this beauty, even as he was putting each seed into the soil, knew exactly how these plants and flowers would go together when they grew. Or did this garden, like the labyrinth, appear out of nowhere, created by the will of some all-powerful immortal god?

Walking beneath a wide arched trellis covered with bright-red butterfly-shaped flowers, the princess and Hasan suddenly find themselves in a circular glade. The bushes around the glade create a smooth wall. It looks as if the bushes are strictly forbidden to extend even a single sprig into the open space of the glade, with its thick carpet of low, evenly growing grass. The princess stops to enjoy the feeling of unusual spaciousness after the long walk in closed corridors and thickets.

A marble wellhead filled to the brim with water stands on a platform in the middle of the glade with steps leading up to it. The surface of the well is covered with the same faintly glowing inscriptions that they saw on the door leading into this enchanted place.

"This is the center of the labyrinth, princess," says Hasan.

"What sort of a well is this?"

"It is said that if you look into the water you will see the most important event of your future, although like any prophecy, whatever you see in the well may need interpretation."

"Do these signs on the well explain the prophecy in any way?"

"No, princess. This inscription, just like the one on the entrance to the labyrinth, is designed to make he who reads it feel satisfied with his achievements."

"And what does it say, Hasan?"

"'There is no pain in the world worse than the pain brought by knowledge.'"

"What sort of a reward is that?" the princess exclaims. "Who would ever want to look into such a well?"

"Many mages *only* feel rewarded by something like this, princess. Passing the deadly trials in the labyrinth, they want to read something frightfully serious. Otherwise they won't feel it to be a serious challenge to look into the well."

"Did you look in there, Hasan?"

"No, princess, I didn't. When I walked through the labyrinth for the first time I thought that knowing the future could bring only harm."

"What about now, Hasan?"

"Now I have stopped taking such things seriously."

"I would like to look in there. May I?"

"Certainly, princess."

She takes several cautious steps toward the well but stops in a moment of indecision.

"Are you afraid?" Hasan laughs.

"It's not that…it's just…I thought…let's look into it together, Hasan. I don't want to go through with it alone. And each of us will see something of his own anyway, right?"

"As far as I know, yes."

"You really *don't* take it seriously, do you, Hasan?"

"I don't, princess."

"Come along, then."

They approach the well, walk up the marble steps, and bend over the sparkling surface of the water. At first the princess can see only a kind of gray mist, surprised that she doesn't see their own reflection as she expected. And then…

The mist slowly evaporates into the hot beams of a setting crimson sun. She sees endless sands surrounding a temple reigning over the desert. The domes of the temple run down in cascades toward rows of columns, surrounded by the ghostly outline of a beautiful garden like the one that surrounds them now, here at the center of the Dimesqian Labyrinth. The princess strains to see the faint outline of the garden…but she still cannot see it clearly because there, in the desert, she is slowly walking away from the ancient temple, and someone is walking beside her. Someone, whose hand she holds in the same way as she is holding the hand of Hasan….

You look into the well with her, knowing that you won't see your reflection in the water and never believing for a moment you will see in there something important for you. With one part of your all-knowing being you see all that the princess sees in the sparkling surface of the water. But another part of you is looking into the well by yourself, and the two visions—against all you have ever heard about prophecies, against all judgment, against all knowledge—blend into one. With a special double sight that makes the vision much deeper and more dimensional, you see as if looking from two places with two pairs of eyes, the sinking crimson sun, endless sands, ghostly garden, and ancient temple…. You are present in the desert as if in a dream beyond suffering, seeing every detail, every grain of sand as clear as ever. And, holding her hand, overwhelmed by a long-forgotten feeling of surprise, you realize that by some strange will of the ancient magic, you, an all-powerful djinn and she, your mortal mistress are seeing one and the same thing in the prophetic depths of the marble well….

You lied, saying that you didn't look into the well during your first encounter with the labyrinth. You lied because the vision sent to you foretold your end, but you realized it only when it was already too late. Back then you saw in the well the surface of a dune with its grains of sand right before your eyes as large as rocks. You saw the crimson haze on the horizon with its deadly beams coming straight at you. You saw beyond the crest of the dune closest to you endless waves of sand beyond your field of vision and the approaching blast of the merciless wind that shifts the rippled crests from place to place according to its ever-changing whim. You saw your future, and knowing nothing of eternal suffering, were unable to interpret that vision.

How can you interpret the vision sent to you now? Is it your destiny to return to the desert, to continue your terrible suffering because your spirit is unable to submit completely to its new form? Will the princess become a djinn as well, since she sees the same vision as you do? Were you mistaken when you couldn't see any signs pointing out her passage to absolute power? Can you do something to help her avoid the same end, even if it requires you to stop revealing the most sacred mysteries of the world and sharing your knowledge—even if it takes giving up the new something that you feel every moment you spend with her?

By the law of Dhagabad she will soon become the property of her husband and her life will be filled with duties that will occupy all her time and all her mind—duties that will make her forget her hunger for knowledge. Although you still don't believe that she will become a djinn, you know she will never lose her passion to learn. And, despite your strangely intense regret that she will soon be unable to spend time with you, you know that you must make a solemn oath to help her however much you can in her chosen path.

Can an all-powerful spirit be interested in the deeds of mortals? Can you, who know the truth about the world, who have seen the depths of eternity with your own eyes, pay attention to such minor things as a mortal girl, even if you are her slave, even if you spend almost all your time with her, even if she is the daughter of a sultan and the most beautiful woman in the world?

Did those millennia in the desert really cloud your mind? Aren't you exasperated by your slavery? Aren't you despairing at the thought that with all your power you cannot lift a finger without the wish of your little mistress? Aren't your dreams troubled by thoughts of the grandeur that you gained and lost and aren't the nightmares about the piercing beams and shifting sands torturing your soul? Perhaps you are finally doubting whether the way meant for you was really the way of knowledge and not the way of the mortals. And what finally broke your will was not the suffering in the endless desert but gentleness, kindness, and beauty.

Can any immortal really know what is the strongest power in the world, the power that defeats suffering, pain, and loneliness? Maybe this power is infinite knowledge. That is what you have always thought. But another possibility now crawls into your mind and grows, easily gaining more and more space among the infinite number of things inside it.

What if you were deceived? What if the strongest, most overwhelming, most victorious power is really the ability to feel friendship, closeness, and unity with another living creature? Such is this friendship, this closeness, this unity, that you don't care that this creature is mortal, weak, fragile, and helpless; you don't even care about the future. All you care about is being together with this creature, so weak, so imperfect, and yet so close to you.

And for this feeling that grows inside you, this feeling that is possibly stronger than suffering, wisdom, or immortality—this power that everyone feels in his own way and calls his own name—poets and storytellers that think it important to invent a name for everything, find a single, improper, and awkward word—love.

THE CHOSEN WAY

✿

*T*he princess rises unwillingly to her feet, watching the curtain move to the side, watching a procession of women solemnly enter her quarters. She knows that this is not a usual visit from her mother and nannies and that the serious expression on her mother's face, reflected in the faces of the slave women and nannies comprising her suite, bears upon something very important. The princess throws a quick glance back to make sure that Hasan is still with her, supporting her. He has also risen to his feet, having put aside the book they were reading.

"Princess," the sultaness begins solemnly. By the slight trembling of her lips the princess can see how hard it is for her to maintain this slow, measured manner of speech. "You know that tomorrow, on your birthday, you must choose a suitor from among a number of princes who will come to Dhagabad to seek your hand."

"Yes, mother," the princess says, suddenly feeling small and defenseless.

"You also know that although it must appear to be your choice, you have to choose the suitor selected for you by the State Council of Dhagabad, with the approval of your father and myself."

"Yes, mother," the princess says even more quietly than before. She knows very well the whole procedure of selecting a suitor, but for everyone in the room, including the sultaness and even the princess herself, there is a special significance in a mother instructing her daughter on the eve of her coming-of-age.

"Your suitors will bring rich and exotic gifts," the sultaness continues in her measured voice. "But remember: you mustn't accept gifts from anyone except the suitor you choose."

The sultaness pauses; and the princess stands absolutely still with her eyes wide open, unable to even nod at this moment of high tension, waiting for her next words.

"Your chosen suitor will be Prince Amir of Veridue."

Having gathered all her strength, these words are like a burden she has been forced to carry a long distance, until it was finally time to bring it into her daughter's quarters and drop it at her feet. The tension in the room visibly subsides as the women start to stir and sigh. Old Nanny Zeinab shakes her head, and the princess sees tears sparkling in the deep lines under her eyes.

"Yes, mother," the princess says again, feeling it her turn to say something.

The sultaness looks away uneasily. She wants to get past the formalities, to step forward and to hold her daughter in her arms—the daughter she was forced to raise almost like a son, the daughter she will soon have to let go. But there are still some details they have to discuss, so she hurries to finish with them as soon as she can.

"Tomorrow morning Zulbagad and other slave women will bring your outfit. You must appear on the balcony exactly at noon."

"Will you be there, mother?"

"Of course I will, princess. Your father and I will sit beside you on the same balcony, but you will have your own canopy closer to the railing. You may talk to me, but you must try to pay more attention to the ceremony."

"What if the suitors don't come, mother?" the princess asks.

The sultaness cannot help smiling. It seems her naive daughter doesn't realize how precious she is—the only heir to the throne of Dhagabad and a rare beauty on top of that. It seems she doesn't understand what an upheaval there will be tomorrow on the palace plaza on her behalf.

"Of course they'll come, princess," she says, smiling. "Most of them are already here, setting their camps at the city walls. Tomorrow there will be more princes in Dhagabad than you could ever imagine!"

The princess sighs. Her role, the choosing of a suitor, stepping on the path she was born for, doesn't raise any questions in her mind. She has known for many years that it would be like this, and now she is flattered at the thought that tomorrow there will be princes in Dhagabad who have come for her sake. She turns to Hasan and meets his encouraging gaze.

"Where will Hasan sit, mother?" she asks.

"Hasan..." The sultaness stumbles—she foresaw this question but failed to prepare for it.

The princess feels her hesitation and addresses her mother with an air of finality.

"I want Hasan to be with me, mother."

Looking at her, the sultaness remembers the moment, five years ago, when the princess disobeyed her for the first time, refusing to order Hasan to go back into his bottle in spite of her knowing exactly what the consequences would be.

"You know how the Veriduans feel about djinns, princess," she says helplessly. "Prince Amir's great-grandsire died at the hand of a djinn..."

"I want Hasan to be with me, mother," the princess repeats even more firmly.

"Very well." The sultaness gives up. In the depths of her heart she completely understands her daughter's wish. After all, Hasan is her best friend, and tomorrow's events are probably the most important of her life. She doesn't feel it right to try to deprive the princess of her djinn at such a time. But as a responsible person she must think of some precautions.

"Let Hasan wear a long cloak with hood, princess," she says. "Even if you want him to be near you, it is not necessary for him to attract any extra attention."

"But, mother..." the princess begins, as she hears Hasan's quiet voice behind her.

"Let me wear the cloak, princess. I am certain it will be better that way."

Probably the most frightening thing on your approach to absolute power was the sudden realization that there would be no one in the world who could be any kind of authority over you. It was that realization, and not the burden of knowledge described by the Agritian sage, that became the first foreshadowing that your chosen way had a terrible end. You felt that everything that was happening in the world didn't and shouldn't have any reason or purpose unknown to you, and that it was within your power to change anything in the world you didn't like. But then you faced your first trial.

You knew it was in your power to defeat anything unfair, illogical, or unreasonable, and that none of the sages and wizards you knew had the power to stop you. And yet, at the same time, you knew that the world is as it should be and that no one, however much power he has, should try to change the world to his liking without knowing the risk of shifting the world's equilibrium and causing even greater mishap. Knowing that, you suffered in frustration with a powerful helplessness, and it was then that you started to curse the knowledge you had so eagerly sought before. It seemed that everything you learned only increased your despair and brought you no satisfaction. Only then did you finally start to read the Agritian scroll over and over again, finding familiar feelings in the descriptions of your ancient predecessor. Only then did you wish there were a power in the world stronger than you, restraining you, capable of destroying you. But even then, suffering in the face of your might, you kept searching for more and more knowledge. And, gradually, the suffering passed, leaving room for indifference.

In your indifference, as in the suffering you felt before, you recognized with a shiver all the conditions from the Agritian scroll. That was the time you really believed you had made your final step toward absolute knowledge. You knew that the end was near and could come at any moment. But you never wanted to change your chosen way.

This evening most of the palace sinks into quiet as usual after nightfall. But in the south wing, the sultaness is overwhelmed by feelings of both excitement and sadness. On the one hand, tomorrow when the princess comes of age, she will merely choose a suitor and become engaged; the wedding itself will not take place for at least another month. But, on the other hand, something important in the princess's life is going to change tomorrow when her little girl, a child she raised, cared for, and watched grow into a beautiful young woman, will have to point out from the palace balcony a suitor chosen by her, or rather *for* her, to be her future husband. This symbolic moment when a girl becomes a woman, a "bride," fills her with a touch of sadness.

The nannies, preparing the princess for sleep as usual, hesitate to leave her quarters. After dressing the princess for sleep and serving her usual bedtime glass of warm cinnamon milk, they sit in the armchairs and on the pillows around her bed, outwardly busy with their needlework, yet forming an inward circle connected by their shared ritual. Nannies Zulfia and Fatima, helplessly lowering their hands, sigh and look into the distance with their needlework resting on their laps. The young and headstrong Airagad is embroidering with an expression of independence on her face; but looking more closely, it is easy to see that her hands are not moving as fast as usual. Old Zeinab, in her favorite armchair at the head of the princess's bed, looks at the princess with tenderness, not even trying to pretend to do anything useful. The princess, who at this hour usually says good night to her nannies and calls for Hasan to read a book to her, also feels caught up in the mood, reluctant to break the atmosphere of silent farewell.

"Tell me a story, Nanny Zeinab," she asks.

"Not about your grandmother again, princess!" Airagad exclaims and the princess smiles, remembering how, when she was a little girl, she would never go to sleep without the nanny's story about her grandmother and the bottle.

"How quickly have you grown up, princess," Zeinab says. "How quickly have you become a bride."

"Have you ever been married, nanny?" the princess asks.

"Never, my beauty," Zeinab answers. "I had a suitor once who asked for my hand, but your grandmother told me not to marry him. I was looking after the little sultan at the time...."

"Did you want to marry him?"

"Of course not!" The nanny waves her hand in dismissal. "I hadn't even seen him before!"

"Why did he ask for your hand?"

"I was said to be very beautiful back then." Zeinab laughs. "But it was much better to live as a nanny in the palace than a wife in somebody's home. Ask Airagad why she doesn't get married."

"What good is it for me to marry?" Airagad says crossly. "I could just as well decide to bury myself alive!"

"Stop frightening the princess!" Zulfia exclaims as her round, middle-aged face becomes even redder. She shifts her large, strongly built body in the chair, looking at the princess with kindness and compassion. "Don't listen to them, princess," she says. "There is nothing wrong with getting married!"

"Of course, not," Zeinab agrees, good-naturedly. "Just wait, princess, we will be bringing up your children yet...."

The princess tries to imagine herself as a mother and a sultaness, a full-figured majestic woman, the way she sees her mother. She looks helplessly at her thin arms lying on top of the blanket, feeling completely incapable of performing this new role for which she was destined from birth.

She feels that her life, which she always enjoyed so much, has suddenly gone out of control and is flowing away into the distance slowly and smoothly, but inevitably like a river to merge somewhere with the waiting ocean. She tries to imagine what her groom, Prince Amir of Veridue, will be like, but the image in her mind mostly resembles her father, the sultan, with his beard sticking out and his dark eyes shining from beneath heavy eyebrows, making her fear him all the time. She is trying to remember what her father looked like when she was younger, and suddenly she sees in her mind the face of Abdulla, the restless, unkind apprentice of Hasan from distant Dimeshq.

The princess shivers, suppressing her desire to call Hasan right away—trying to remove the unpleasant image from her memory, trying to convince herself that Prince Amir will turn out to be handsome and kind, perhaps even resembling Hasan himself. Trying to call forth to her mind a pleasant image of her future husband, she suddenly realizes that she is unable to remember what Hasan looks like.

CEREMONY

✢

The turban on her head is crowned with a white ostrich feather that waves whenever she moves. This dazzling white feather tells the crowd at the palace plaza what is happening on the royal balcony. Right now the princess is following with her eyes another procession—rejected. Their banner, a serpent entwining a lion, is already disappearing under the arch of the palace gate. No matter who the princess chooses to be her husband, all the foreign guests will feast at the palace tonight to honor her seventeenth birthday.

The princess, never before having seen so many different and unusual people gathered on her behalf, cannot hold still. All the worries of last night and about the morning's preparations have disappeared at this joyous occasion and at the sight of the plaza filled with people, the bright flags and banners. The princess feels like the hero of a magic tale, absorbing every little detail around her. Different processions float by the balcony one by one as the princess forgets how curious she was to see the party from Veridue—to find out what her future husband looks like. She is not feeling a part of the mysterious ritual anymore. She is twisting and turning back and forth on her pillows under the canopy while the sultaness vainly tries to call her to order.

"Prince Musa Jafar Avallahaim spent a month traveling to bring to the feet of the beautiful princess of Dhagabad this statue of a dragon carved from northern malachite!" the master of the ceremonies announces.

Two slaves pull a light cover off a huge shape on a wheeled platform and the crowd freezes in amazement. Sunlight bursting into rainbows on the green scales, a black and green forked tongue hanging between the open jaws of green stone, and the fiery beryl of the eyes, breaking the uniformity of the statue by their brightness, bring shivers. Startled, the princess recalls the Avallahaim myth of the dragon that Hasan read to her from an old book found in the palace library. The dragon—a mystical protector and symbol of prosperity in Avallahaim—was described in the book as a creature with the body of a snake, the claws of an eagle, the wings of a bat, and the head of a lizard. Transfixed by the gaze of its beryl eyes, she has to force herself to look away from this fairy-tale dragon, so real in its green stone flesh.

Enjoying the effect to the fullest, Prince Musa Jafar, a pale, feeble youth with dark cold eyes, signals to his suite.

"Aware of the great knowledge and wisdom of the princess of Dhagabad, Prince Musa Jafar brings to her feet the oldest manuscript in the great Avallahaim library!" the master of ceremonies continues.

A venerable old man with a long, white beard steps forward, carrying a pillow with a golden case on it and, bowing, holds it out to the balcony.

"Look, mother," the princess whispers excitedly. "Do you know that no one is allowed to read this scroll? Rumors say it bears the secret of eternal life...."

"Nonsense, princess," the sultaness says. "Go on, announce your decision. You are making the prince wait."

With a deep sigh the princess slowly shakes her head, the white feather wavers and bows to the side, and the crowd breathes out in disappointment. Alas, this suitor was not to the princess's liking, either. Stretching their necks, the citizens of Dhagabad are trying to see how many banners are still visible at the far end of the plaza. How many more noble princes are still waiting to seek the hand of their young princess?

"Prince Said Abdulla Ahmed of Halaby!" the master of ceremonies announces.

Prince Said carries with him a feeling of unusual physical strength and might. His skin is almost black from sun and wind; his slanting dark eyes pierce the princess.

"Prince Said devoted his life to the search for something as beautiful as the fair princess of Dhagabad!"

"How did he know?" the princess whispers, pulling an end of her long scarf to her face to hide a smile. "He has never seen me before!"

"It is just a figure of speech, princess," the sultaness whispers back. "Pay attention!"

"Spending years in travel, Prince Said finally came to the conclusion that the gods haven't yet created anything to equal the rare beauty of the princess!"

The princess throws a mischievous glance back toward Hasan, who is wrapped in a dark cloak from head to toe.

"You see, Hasan, someone is finally appreciating my true value."

"I admit, princess, I am blind, foolish, and appalling, even to myself." Hasan laughs. "How could I ever miss something like that?"

"Prince Said brings before her highness two sapphires, borne by the earth in its very depths to praise the eternal shine of the divinely blue eyes of the princess of Dhagabad. Prince Said begs the lady to accept these stones, his most valuable possession, as a humble gift to her immortal beauty."

The prince is holding a box and, keeping his eyes on the princess, he slowly raises the lid. A deep blue shine flows out of the box. Even the sultaness cannot hold back a gasp of admiration. Two large sapphires, sparkling with many facets, for a moment overshadow the sunlight itself.

"Mother!" the princess bursts out, forgetting her duties with the gift of the Halabean prince, "can I marry Prince Said? I have never seen anything so beautiful!"

"You cannot choose a husband by his gifts, princess," the sultaness says with strictness, "it has to be someone you can spend your life with."

"Look how handsome Prince Said is," the princess insists, forgetting how long it took the State Council of Dhagabad to reach a decision about her future husband. "He looks like a real warrior and the ruler of his people!"

"But, princess—" the sultaness hesitates for a moment and finally names what she believes to be the real reason for the impossibility of this marriage "—Halaby has a very small army. It is a mountain land and it has no border with Dhagabad. On the other hand, the union of Dhagabad and Veridue would be practically invincible. Besides," she says, concluding her strategic speech, "the best minds in all of Dhagabad came to the decision about your suitor, and it is not our place to discuss it!"

"What if Prince Amir is ugly, mother?" the princess asks, giving up.

"We are not giving you away as a concubine." The sultaness shrugs her shoulders at the ridiculous thought, having by now completely convinced herself that Prince Amir is the perfect match for her daughter. "If you don't like him, you won't have to see him at all."

Another sigh runs through the crowd when the white feather bends to the side, and the Halabean banner slowly and sadly moves to the palace gate.

"The caliph of Megina, Abu Alim Agabei!" is the next to be announced.

A fat, cheery little man with an enormous mustache bursts forth in a complicated series of bows before the balcony, and the princess again brings the scarf to her face to hide her smile.

"Caliph Agabei puts beauty before all virtues and dance before all arts. The caliph brings before the princess a perfect creation of the gods that combines these two virtues. This dancing girl is beautiful as houri and as skillful as the ancient goddesses of dance."

Again the slaves pull off the cover, this time to reveal a woman's slim dark body, clad with well-designed negligence in narrow strips of soft fabric.

In her movements, the dancer resembles a snake. Her body shifts so smoothly that the spectators sink into a kind of trance. Sharp sounds of the zither frame the softness of the dance, just as a hard metal setting can frame the deep softness of a gemstone. Only with the final sharp chord does the dancing girl stand still before the balcony, so the princess can take a close look at her. At first she appears very young—a tender childlike face with huge eyes and full mouth, an unusually thin yet strong boyish figure, black hair scattered in many braids along her back, and dark skin like that of a Ghullian slave girl. But as she looks more closely, the princess seems to see in the girl's eyes and in her flowing grace, a strange something that resembles the ancient murals of the Dance of the Great Goddess entombed inside the pyramid in the desert land of Aeth. Shivering at the mixture of scorn and impassiveness this goddess of dance bears on her face, the princess comes to her senses and hurriedly shakes her head to reject the marriage proposal of the cheery lover of arts from Megina. Even then, as the procession from Megina moves away, throwing back glances full of polite disappointment, something in the eyes of the caliph and his dancer slave makes her uneasy and she is relieved at the sound of the next announcement:

"Prince Amir of Veridue!"

The princess sits up straight. Whatever her future husband is like, he should see her as a majestic and beautiful daughter of a sultan, not as a little girl frightened by a strange, fat, cheery little man. She slowly raises her eyes to look at her chosen suitor, and, fixing her gaze upon him, she forgets for a moment the palace plaza, the crowd, the fancy speech of the master of ceremonies....

Prince Amir looks exactly as she imagined a perfect prince should look. She sees a handsome, stately young man, just a little bit older than herself, surrounded by a magnificent glow, the very essence of majesty and ease of manner characteristic of a born ruler. His rich garments embroidered with gold and a saber in a gem-encrusted scabbard at his side enhance his aura of nobility. The direct gaze of his dark eyes is set right on the princess, bearing the winning expression of admiration with which a conqueror looks at a beautiful city he has just taken. It seems to the princess that Prince Amir has no doubt that the princess likes him more than any other suitor, and that if she rejects him it would be done not because of his personal qualities, but only because of matters of state. The princess feels so affected by his confidence that she is ready to give in completely, overwhelmed by her admiration for his looks and manners. She blushes deeply under his gaze.

The prince turns to his suite as she regains her senses, able to hear once again the words directed at the balcony.

"Prince Amir brings before the princess..."

After all the treasures that have been offered to her, the gifts of Prince Amir don't seem so special—three boxes of old craftsmanship filled with black, pink, and white sea pearls. As far as she remembers from her geography lessons, Veridue has access to the sea, making it especially advantageous for Dhagabad and Veridue to join forces. It would have been strange for her if she had known then that she herself would become the means to achieving this union. She slides her eyes with indifference over the rest of the Veriduan gifts: a precious necklace, in which the sparkle of large diamonds is carefully matched by the smooth shine of pearls, amazingly round and even, somewhat resembling peas in the pod; and, of course, books—ancient volumes bound in gold-carved wood, with age-yellowed pages. The first book is called *How to Overcome a Djinn* and the princess feels uneasy. How would Hasan live with her in a country where people dislike djinns so much?

But the decision is already made for her, and she solemnly bows her head in acceptance. The white ostrich feather leans forward, opening wide before the crowd, motionless with expectation. The fanfares sound, and the herald announces:

"Hail, Prince Amir of Veridue, the chosen suitor of the princess of Dhagabad!"

The yelling of the crowd sweeps across the balcony. Prince Amir walks up the stairs as the sultan and the sultaness rise to meet him. Two slave girls help the princess up from her pillows and, as a token of their engagement, the prince puts the Veriduan necklace around her neck.

The rest of the ceremony reaches the princess through a growing numbness—some speeches and gestures, the shouting of the crowd, voices, hands embracing her, polite congratulations from the splendid young men of Prince Amir's suite. Automatically answering everyone, the princess cannot wait to leave the balcony, to retreat to the safety of her chambers, to recover, and to prepare herself for the ceremonial feast. Although she has known since early morning that she would be engaged to Prince Amir, she cannot get rid of the feeling that just now something in her life has come to an end.

You will never be able to forget your end—the page of an open book on the desk in front of you shining with a faint, mysterious glow that indicates the presence of the greatest secrets of magic. The flame of a single candle quivers and fades before the sacred glow of the book. You are carefully reading the complicated array of symbols—a magic language of the highest level. You can clearly see the end of the page in front of you and you know that it is the end of the book; but still you raise your hand to turn the glowing page, hoping for more knowledge. With every word you read you reconsider every aspect of your existence. You know that you have already passed through every possible stage of dependence, attachment, affection, disdain, and indifference, and there is nothing more to separate you from eternity. And yet you want more. You search with your hungry mind for new knowledge yet undiscovered as you finish the last words of the book in front of you....

Shafts of lightning strike you from all sides, piercing your body with terrible pain and meeting somewhere at your center, then flying apart in waves of energy—turning your body to ashes, leaving only a pile of dust in the place where you have just been. You feel every moment of your burning, torturing every bit of your body that no longer exists, but you don't die. Burning with an unearthly flame, you keep seeing, as if looking from afar, the open book, the lifeless candle on the desk, the pile of ashes that was your body just now—ashes that rise with the blasts of wind coming out of nowhere, slowly curling into a bigger, more substantial shape, resembling...

A molded bronze bottle.

You see the mouth of the bottle moving straight at you; you see darkness itself gaping at you from the depths of this newly created container. You see yourself, surrounded by bronze walls that crowd and press you much too tightly for your mighty spirit. You see your room filled with books fall apart around you into endless dunes. You feel yourself burning, feel the shafts of lightning inside your mortal body. You look with terror as the wind hurls hot sand at you; and you feel the sand go through your body as through thin air, making you writhe in pain with every grain of its fiery-hot surface... trying in vain to find a place to hide from the deadly crimson light coming straight at you from the merciless sun.

You realize with terrifying finality that you have learned all there is to know of the world, that your physical existence has ended, that the prophecies of the Dimeshqian Labyrinth and the Agritian scroll have turned out to be true, and that you are not a wizard or mage anymore but an all-powerful spirit that since time immemorial has been known by a strange, unclear, gently ringing name—djinn....

CRIMSON FLASH

❁

*T*he desert surrounds her, and yet she can hear the tinkling of water, the singing of birds, the rustling of giant leaves; she can smell the sweet aroma of exotic flowers. She is walking toward the temple; her feet are not sinking into the sand.

The cool shade of the temple covers her. Walking up the wide rough steps, she feels drawn inevitably into the soft semi-darkness of the columned gallery hiding the entrance. If she were to look behind her, she would see a magnificent garden surrounding the temple; but she cannot draw her eyes away from the transparent blackness where she can almost see an arched gateway and heavy doors standing wide apart. She smiles, remembering how, in the past, she could not make it into the temple. She easily steps inside.

The light that streams into the temple from high, arched windows falls upon half of the great hall—its walls invisible behind rows of columns on three sides. She is standing between two columns under the low roof of the gallery, gazing into the half-lighted expanse under the huge dome, trying to see him. But he is nowhere. Looking ahead, she sees a dusty sunbeam and a bronze bottle, standing on a carpet beside a prayer niche. And then music starts, barely audible, floating upward into the heights of the great dome.

She feels she must go deeper into the hall to the bottle, and she helplessly rushes back and forth between the columns, trying to find an entrance. She sees the bottle starting to open like a giant flower, gradually turning into a massive bronze cup.

Soft light pours out of the cup toward her that she must at any cost catch in her palms; but the light scatters before reaching her. Gathering all her strength, she throws herself against the invisible wall.

"Princess. Princess! Wake up! It is time."

Nanny Airagad's voice comes to her as if from afar, forcing her out of the bonds of her dream; and coming back to her senses she slowly opens her eyes.

"She is tired, poor darling," Nanny Fatima says beside her. "Can you imagine, receiving all those suitors with the crowd watching and everything?"

The suitors, the princess thinks as she tries to concentrate on the fuzzy ornaments of the bed curtain. Yes. Something in her life has changed today. She is not what she was before. She is— *betrothed.*

As her mind slowly comes back from the dream to reality she feels a strange anguish fill her heart. She desperately wants to see Hasan—she wants to so much that tears come to her eyes. She sits up sharply in her bed.

"Nanny, is that you? Where is Hasan?"

"I don't know, princess," Zeinab grumbles, standing closest to her bed at the moment. "Why would you need Hasan? Your chosen one, your groom, Prince Amir, is waiting."

"Hasan!" the princess exclaims, feeling that her entire life depends on his appearance in her quarters right this minute.

"Please calm down, princess," Fatima coos in her soft gentle voice. "You are tired. Let me comb your hair....Hasan is not here."

"*Hasan!*" the princess commands at the top of her lungs, feeling the tears that stood at the back of her throat break loose and rush in streams from her eyes. Then she hears a quiet voice beside her.

"I am here, princess."

"Hasan..." she whispers, suddenly drained of all strength,

sobbing, not even trying to hide the tears running down her cheeks.

Hasan sits next to her on the bed and gently touches her hand.

"Why are you crying, princess?" he asks softly.

"I had that strange dream again, Hasan...," the princess whispers, the nightmare leaving her—feeling his presence, his soft touch, make everything right as it usually does. "Where have you been, Hasan?"

"The sultaness asked me to help prepare the ceremonial hall, princess," Hasan says. "The feast is to begin any minute."

"The feast," the princess whispers helplessly. "I completely forgot that I had to go somewhere...to dress up...to comb my hair."

"If you just sit still I will comb your hair in no time, princess," Airagad says firmly, seeing this turn of the conversation as a chance to speed up the preparations. Feeling lost and empty the princess bows her head, submitting to the nanny. But in her brittle state she is unable to bear even the slightest pain, and the first sharp pull of the comb makes tears run down her cheeks again.

"Leave me alone, nanny—it hurts," she begs so plaintively that even the merciless Airagad steps back with indecision.

"You must appear at the feast, princess."

"She's had a very difficult day," Fatima says gently, sitting on the bed next to the princess and hugging her shoulders. "You just need to hold on a little bit longer, princess. Be patient. Let me—very gently—comb your hair."

But the princess is already beyond reason. Over her head Fatima throws a helpless glance at Hasan, sitting on the bed next to the princess.

"Princess?" Hasan calls out softly.

He reaches out with his hand, putting it gently on the princess's shoulder. Her sobs gradually quiet as she raises her tearstained face to him.

"Hasan," she sobs. "I don't want to go to that feast. I don't want *him* to see me like this. I simply cannot go there now!"

"Everything will be fine, princess," Hasan says softly. He keeps his hand on her shoulder, and Fatima, holding the princess in her arms, somehow feels that it is his touch that makes her sobs become quieter; the strain in her body gradually relaxes. Fatima carefully draws away from the princess, gets up, and moves away to join Airagad, Zulfia, and Zeinab. The nannies watch the scene with mixed expressions, showing both relief that someone strong and wise is taking it upon himself to resolve the problem and terror at the idea that the princess is sitting on her bed with a handsome man who is touching her on the shoulder.

The princess slowly sinks into a state of relaxed quietness and leans against Hasan's shoulder, making the nannies freeze in terror. Under any other circumstance they would have definitely interfered. But now some inner voice tells them everything is for the best, and nothing short of this will allow them to deliver the princess to the engagement party in a suitable condition for her role of the new bride. Transfixed, they watch Hasan gently put his arms around the princess and caress her hair; they watch as the princess stops crying and calms down to the point when her now-dry and surprisingly fresh cheeks start to glow with their usual faint color. And every one of the nannies feels a half-conscious, strongly suppressed desire to see Hasan in place of Prince Amir, to be the man with whom the princess is about to bind her future. They think of it simultaneously, like a single creature that wishes its young ward well, and at the same time is ashamed that such well-being could only be achieved by unconventional means.

"It is time to go, princess," Hasan says softly.

"Yes...," the princess says, pulling away from him with reluctance. She sees Airagad approach her with a comb and pulls back in fear.

"Hasan," she exclaims, "can you do something so that I

won't have to dress up and comb my hair? Can you use your magic to make me dressed up with my hair all done?"

"Nothing could be easier, princess." Hasan smiles.

"Gods forbid, princess!" the large, rosy-cheeked Zulfia exclaims, blushing even more, satisfying everyone's urge to call the princess to order. "How can you even think of having a man help dress you?"

"But it is magic, nanny," the princess pleads, turning to Hasan. "Can you dress me in this outfit that Zulbagad left for me?"

"Certainly, princess."

The nannies jump up in surprise, seeing the princess's long dress change into white, silver-embroidered pants and blouse, similar to the ones she wore when she turned twelve.

"What have you done, princess!" Zeinab helplessly drops her arms. "Dressing like that is completely unheard of!"

"I've done nothing wrong, nanny!" the princess answers back.

Zeinab mumbles to herself, knowing that there is really nothing indecent in all this, but feeling that as the oldest nanny she shouldn't have allowed it to happen. Ever since his arrival, Hasan's presence in the princess's bedroom has been a frustrating contradiction in itself; and Zeinab, like the other nannies, could not find a best way to react. She feels it to be her duty to grumble; and, saying something indistinct, she turns her back to the princess.

"Well, Hasan," the princess says, seeing that at least for a while she is free to do as she wishes, "I think I was told to put my hair in braids around my head...and something else...."

"The Veriduan necklace, princess," Fatima reminds her.

"Oh, yes...but it is so big and uncomfortable...such large pearls. All those diamonds...it must be very valuable."

"It certainly is," Zeinab grumbles, rejoining the conversation.

"Anything else, princess?" Hasan asks.

"The shawl, princess!" Zulfia exclaims. "And the sapphire diadem."

"Yes," the princess agrees, "that seems to be all."

She looks in the mirror, making sure that her outfit is perfect and her face bears no trace of tears. She inhales deeply, enjoying the feeling of calm that Hasan has brought with his touch.

"This is wonderful, Hasan—so easy. From now on I want you always to dress me!"

"What are you saying, princess?" Zulfia exclaims dutifully without much conviction in her voice. "Someone may hear you, gods forbid!"

"Oh, nanny, what did I say?" she says, accepting the game. "Are you ready yourself?"

"We are always ready," Zeinab grumbles.

"I want Hasan to walk beside me," the princess says in a voice that dismisses all possible objections.

"But your mother said…"

"Otherwise, I am not going anywhere!"

"All right, all right," Fatima says.

The great ceremonial hall is shining with a magnificence it hadn't yet seen during the entire rule of the sultan Chamar Ali. But the splendor of the best decorations fails to outshine the glamour of foreign rulers, princes, and guests in their rich, exotic raiments—representing the glory of their lands. The display of power, riches, and majesty leaves everyone crowded into the hall completely breathless.

Even this giant hall, during the centuries of its faithful service to the rulers of Dhagabad, has seldom seen so many guests gathered for a holiday feast. This time, not one but two rows of tables and cushions extend in a circle along the periphery of the hall, leaving in the center not the usual open space, but something more akin to a stage for entertaining the noble guests. The front row of tables, with larger cushions and more lavish decorations, is reserved for the foreign princes and noblemen of their courts. The back row is left for the members of their suites and for the lesser courtiers of Dhagabad.

The royal canopy at the end of the hall has been extended to accommodate two new members of the royal family—the princess—the heiress to the throne, now old enough to take a seat beside her parents—and her bridegroom, the noble prince Amir, who will become the future sultan of Dhagabad.

The reduced open space in the hall is not able to accommodate all of the guests waiting for the feast. The doors stand wide open and guests are also crowded outside the hall in the adjoining space that leads to the kitchens. The delicious aromas coming from the kitchens make heads swim and mouths water in anticipation of a feast that promises to equal the splendor of the gathering.

In addition to the traditional *sankajat* and sweets, the servants carry on their trays foods of foreign lands meant to please the noble guests—to make them feel more at home. Cinnamon apricot cakes of Avallahaim are found in the unlikely neighborhood of sour sesame bisquits of Baskary, dark bean candy of Dimeshq, and spicy cabbage rolls of Megina. Princes and their guests eagerly devour these delights, as they inhale their heady aromas and strain their ears for the signal that will start the ceremonial feast.

The sultan, the sultaness, and Prince Amir have already made their appearance and are now standing in the hall surrounded by a group of Veriduans. From time to time the sultaness throws impatient glances at the passage that leads to the south wing of the palace. She regrets that she left to the nannies the important job of escorting the princess, and now, for some unknown reason, all the noble guests are made to wait.

She throws an uninterested glance at a tall girl with a wide face and straight thick hair, who walks toward their group with determination in her dark slanting eyes.

"Your majesty," the girl says, bowing and glancing sidelong at Prince Amir.

The sultaness catches a sparkle of interest in the young prince's eyes as recognition dawns on her.

"Alamid!" she exclaims and adds, collecting herself—ignoring the irritation on her husband's face—"Prince, this is Alamid, the daughter of the master of ceremonies. She is the princess's playmate."

"Charmed," the prince says politely, making the girl blush and lower her eyes. Used to his effect on women, the prince turns back to his conversation with the sultan with a winning smile.

"Alamid, dear," the sultaness says, "why don't you run along and see what is taking the princess so long? The guests are waiting."

"Yes, your majesty—" Alamid says, only to be interrupted by fanfare and her father's announcement:

"The princess of Dhagabad!"

A sigh of admiration is heard in the great hall at the sight of the princess. As it was on her twelfth birthday, she is dressed in white. A light semitransparent shawl covers her from her black hair, arranged in a crown around her head, to the silver sandals on her small feet. A band of silver around her brow holds a large sapphire in the middle of her forehead. On her right, one step behind, walks Hasan. Metal bracelets shine on his bare wrists, his face is impassive, but his very presence at the head of the princess's suite is like a gauntlet thrown down by the princess to all the gathering—especially to the Veriduans. The sultaness bites her lip and glances at Prince Amir. The young prince, though, is a perfect gentleman. The friendly expression on his face never changes. He smiles across the hall at his bride.

Before the feast can begin the princess has to walk around to all the noble guests and the rejected suitors, speaking in turn to each of them. By custom no one can feel neglected today. The guests are arranged in groups; and the princess with her small suite, hurriedly joined by the master of ceremonies, moves toward them, feeling strangely uneasy. Something in this hall—in the crowd of strange faces—scares her. But Hasan is beside her. She steps toward the first group that awaits her.

"Prince Said Abdulla Ahmed of Halaby," the master of ceremonies whispers from behind.

Here in the hall Prince Said looks even bigger and taller than he did on the palace plaza, and the princess regards him with interest.

"Greetings, Prince Said," she says. "It is a great honor."

"The honor is mine, princess." His rich low voice is trembling slightly as the princess gives him an encouraging smile. For the mighty warrior that he looks, he seems to be very shy with women.

"I dare to ask your permission," Prince Said says suddenly, "to give you, in honor of your coming-of-age and your engagement, one of the two sapphires that you have rejected today. The other sapphire I would treasure forever as a poor reminder of your beauty."

Prince Said opens his huge hand, revealing a tiny ebony box of the finest carving. Taken by surprise, the princess seeks out her mother, standing, alas, too far away to solve such an unexpected problem. She was never taught how to behave in a situation like this. Can she accept the gift, being a promised bride? Can she reject it without offending the noble prince? Fortunately, the sultaness, who is carefully watching her daughter from across the hall, nods her head; and the princess, smiling, holds out her hand to receive the box.

"Thank you, Prince Said," she says. "This is indeed a kingly gift and the most beautiful gem I have ever seen. I will cherish it as a memory of our meeting."

"You are beautiful, princess," Prince Said says. But her suite is already leading her away to the next group, and she has time only to smile charmingly at the sad giant.

"Caliph Abu Alim Agabei of Megina," the master of ceremonies whispers.

"I am happy to see you, caliph," the princess says. "It is a great pleasure to have this opportunity to thank you for the dance of your beautiful slave."

The caliph, a short man with an enormous mustache, elaborately bows to the princess.

"I can confess to such a one as you, princess," he says, "I sometimes feel that this dancing girl, Shogat, is not an ordinary slave but a goddess that chose to serve me for reasons unknown. To honor you today, O matchless one, Shogat will dance again."

"This is a divine pleasure, caliph," the princess says automatically. The caliph's small eyes seem to hypnotize her, and she doesn't understand how she could have rejected such a charming, sweet, kind man, whatever her parents ordered her to do. Nice caliph, he would be a perfect husband for her....

"Allow me to kiss you hand, princess."

She hears his words as if from afar. She holds out her hand—she couldn't possibly refuse anything such a wonderful, beautiful man asks....

Someone pushes her aside, and a body appears between them, breaking the enchantment. She wants to look at the caliph, but someone is looming before her eyes, and gradually she starts hearing sounds again. She hears Hasan's voice in front of her:

"You dropped your bracelet, princess."

"What bracelet?" The princess suddenly realizes that she is standing in the great hall, there are lots of people everywhere, she is surrounded by her suite, the Megina delegation is grouped in front of her, and Hasan is kneeling before her, holding out a bracelet she does not remember wearing. Behind Hasan she can now see the fat and cheery caliph of Megina trying with some irritation to get to her past Hasan. But Hasan, awkwardly swaying at her feet—how is it possible...he is always so quick and efficient?—is not letting the caliph reach her.

Her suite is already leading her on to the next group, and giving the caliph a farewell smile, she sees such cold malice in his eyes that her heart nearly stops.

"Prince Musa Jafar of Avallahaim," the master of ceremonies whispers. The princess absently fastens the bracelet Hasan has given her, as she meets the dark, impenetrable eyes of the prince.

"Greetings, Prince Musa Jafar," the master of ceremonies whispers.

"Greetings—" The princess stops for a second and pulls herself together.

"Greetings, Prince Musa Jafar," she says, smiling. "It is a great honor to see you in Dhagabad. Your way here was long indeed."

"All the hardships of our journey are nothing compared to the pleasure of seeing you, princess." The prince is haltingly speaking these polite phrases, as the princess realizes that he is actually really offended by his rejection and that nothing she could say could possibly make him smile.

Exchanging a few meaningless words with the prince, she moves on.

Princes and caliphs are sweeping before her. Even the old sultan of Baskary has honored her with his visit. The princess talks to everyone, smiles at everyone, but something inside her is broken. Feeling as if the marble floor under her feet is as unsteady as quicksand, finally she approaches Prince Amir of Veridue.

The prince smiles at her with his usual winning look, and she suddenly feels as if a burden has been taken off her shoulders and placed on more appropriate ones, those of her future husband. She feels as she has never felt before—being brought up like a boy. She feels like a *wife*, an inferior being that belongs to someone more glamorous to and revered by the outside world than she will ever be. She feels some strange relief at this new feeling, and something else deep inside—something disturbing that she doesn't want to listen to.

Forcing away all other feelings except relief, she takes her place beside her groom.

The master of ceremonies signals the beginning of the dinner, as the princess automatically takes the hand offered by Prince Amir and follows her parents to the royal canopy at the head of the feast. She has time to glance back and make sure that Hasan is still following her, and that he is taking his seat, as intended, at the second-row table directly behind her.

"Have you met Hasan, prince?" she asks, settling down and feeling secure enough to rebound from her strange fears.

She sees a frown of displeasure on the prince's handsome

face, and the disturbing feeling she felt inside her just moments before helps her to hold his gaze firmly. She wants to convince herself that her disturbing feelings are not a protest against her new, secondary role. She tries to maintain that her outwardly innocent question, directed to her magnificent groom whose whole nation hates djinns, is not an attempt to show him his place. His place is and always will be ahead of her, proper and right for any woman, princess or not.

She sees her harmless question merely as a test of how Hasan will fit into her new life. Everyone seems to think now that she is getting married, she will forget all about Hasan. But she is not going to give him up so easily!

"I saw him beside you on the balcony." The prince throws a mildly disgusted glance at Hasan and smiles to the princess. "I heard this slave is dear to you, princess. But in Veridue you will have as many slaves as you wish."

"Hasan is not just a slave," the princess points out. "He is my friend."

"For the lack of a better one," the prince says with polite firmness. "I dare to point out that you are talking to the happiest of all men who humbly hopes to be your faithful servant and an even more faithful friend."

The princess smiles, feeling cornered. Here, for the first time in her life, she is forced to be something she has never been before—merely a *woman*. She feels like a toy in the hands of merciless etiquette who has to keep up the appearance of splendid calmness.

She absently picks up a piece of warm rosemary bread and dips it into the sesame oil. The table is covered with delicious foods, but somehow she doesn't quite feel like eating. A servant offers her a dish of quail, but she waves it away before she has time to question her decision. She puts the crumbly, aromatic bread in her mouth as she watches Prince Amir attack a bowl of thick lamb soup fragrant with a mixture of spices. To keep up the appearance of eating she picks up a handful of dark, glistening olives from the dish in front of her and smiles at her mother, who from two seats away looks at her with concern.

Her conflicting thoughts are interrupted by the unfaltering voice of the master of ceremonies:

"The caliph of Megina, Abu Alim Agabei, wishes to please the noble guests with the dance of his skillful slave girl, the matchless Shogat!"

The princess feels a strange wave of anxiety as she watches the center of the hall being cleared of lamps and decorations.

The hall quickly sinks into a hushed silence. The sharp sound of a zither startles everyone, as Shogat appear as if from nowhere before their astonished eyes. She is dressed only in leather sandals and silver snakelike bracelets around her arms and wrists. Her nakedness is pure and perfect as if she were a goddess bringing to mortals the gift of a divine dance. A crimson rose is shining in Shogat's hair, which is pulled back into a smooth knot. The princess is somehow observing the dance through the crimson glow of the flower.

All sounds gradually leave the great hall. Shogat's slim body is moving smoothly within the crimson beam, crimson light cuts through the darkness, as the perfect movements of her body are bordered by a crimson glow.

And then silhouettes of waves start pulsing through the darkness, rolling over each other in perfect symmetry. Waves— not of water—but of sand. A secret garden spreads over the sands, as the domes of a temple rise through it—domes— steps—columns…

Shogat suddenly thrusts her palm upward with the crimson flower already in her hand. This sharp change somehow shifts a balance as the columns start slowly collapsing inward like a house of cards, raising noiseless clouds of sand. The giant dome turns over in an unreal way, folds inward, and disappears.

With a long swing, Shogat throws the crimson flower toward the princess. The flower flies and flies, turning over and over in the air, as the temple silently collapses. The princess holds out her hand to the crimson flash, knowing that touching it will mean escape from suffering, release from a terrible sight of destruction and then—afterward—peace....

A strong hand pushes her aside, as fingers close around the flower and sounds suddenly return to the hall. Caliph Agabei is now standing in the center of the hall beside Shogat. Both are speaking to the princess, but she cannot hear them because everyone is cheering and applauding and loudly praising Shogat's divine art. Hasan is now standing in front of the princess, shielding her with his body; Prince Amir is looking angrily at him. And the sultaness, the only one who feels something has gone wrong, looks from Hasan and the princess to the caliph and Shogat with visible alarm.

"Princess!" Hasan swiftly turns to her as she looks up, slowly coming to her senses. "At any excuse leave this hall now! I'll go with you."

"You are forgetting yourself, slave!" Prince Amir exclaims, but the princess is already rising and holding her hand out to Hasan.

"Excuse me, prince, I am not feeling well. Mother—"

"Go, princess. What is the matter, Hasan?"

"I'll tell you later, your majesty. Don't let the caliph or his slave girl leave the hall."

The princess senses something near her foot and, lowering her eyes, she sees on the floor beside her seat the crumpled and broken crimson flower. In a sudden flash of crimson light she sees again the masses of sand running in endless waves and the collapsing dome in a billowing crimson cloud.

The princess releases her grasp on Hasan's arm and, sinking into a noisy, whispering darkness, collapses on the floor.

GLASS DUNES

✻

Dark, broken clouds fly low through the sky. A wild wind is tearing off her shawl and ripping his shirt. They are together in the desert, but this time there is no sand. The dunes that run in smooth waves seem to be made of dark glass, and the moonlight through the breaks in the clouds shimmers on the wavy surface.

Someone is waiting for them straight ahead—Caliph Agabei—only here he is not a caliph. The tips of his black cloak are flying in the wind like giant wings. And Shogat, the goddess of dance—only here she is not a goddess, although still a great dancer—a black cloth clings closely to her, imparting frightful grace to her slim body.

Two black and two white figures meet on a smooth shiny crest.

"Why don't you want to give me the girl, all-powerful slave?" Agabei's voice is rolling like thunder above the desert.

"Her destiny lies elsewhere," Hasan says. "She is not for you."

"She is hungry for knowledge," Shogat says softly. "We shall help her gain absolute knowledge."

"She would make a good slave," Agabei says. "I have never seen the stars point so definitely to one person. She has a part to play in absolute power and djinn making."

"Only charlatans read the stars," Hasan says, grinning. "Didn't Shogat tell you that?"

"Step aside, slave!" Agabei's voice threatens. "Give me the girl!"

"Her destiny lies elsewhere," Hasan says again. "She will never be a djinn."

"Let her speak for herself." Shogat's deep voice hypnotizes. "Tell us, girl, do you want to know everything? Do you want to be able to dance like me, so that kingdoms fall at your feet from seeing you dance? Do you want absolute power and absolute might?"

The princess floats away upon her beautiful voice over the smooth glass dunes. She can see herself dancing in a great hall, as all around her kingdoms fall, scores die, temples collapse....Temples! She suddenly remembers the soundless hall, the crimson beam, the clouds of sand.

"You destroyed my temple!" she exclaims.

"It is not your temple," Shogat says. "That temple has been standing in the desert since the beginning of time and will remain there for ages to come. Neither I nor you can foresee its end. You saw the vision of the temple falling because you don't need the temple anymore. You will never go to your temple again. It is unimportant compared to eternity."

"Think, girl! You will have absolute knowledge and absolute power," Agabei says. "We will save you from suffering in the endless desert. With our guidance you will become all-powerful without paying the terrible price. True, you will be a slave, but is that really so bad? Is it so bad for Hasan to be a slave?"

The princess is floating again and all the world, everything she sees beneath her, belongs to her.

Except one thing.

"Hasan! What will become of Hasan?" she exclaims.

"Hasan will serve me too," Agabei replies. "You will be together. Think of it."

"Three all-powerful slaves to one ordinary sorcerer?" Hasan laughs bitterly. "You have big plans, caliph!"

"I am not so foolish as to become all-powerful when my slaves have absolute power," Agabei hisses. "I am not such an idiot as to comprehend all the knowledge and then let myself be tortured for thousands of years in a bronze bottle in an endless desert."

"Wait a minute." Hasan laughs. "If your soul is worthy enough, the bottle could be made of gold!"

"Silence, slave!"

"I am not your slave," Hasan points out. "Although, it seems, you are greatly tempting my mistress to become your slave girl. I am sure she cannot possibly resist."

"Are you a djinn, too, Shogat?" the princess asks.

"Yes, girl," Shogat says sadly.

"How did you become all-powerful?"

"I was the priestess of the Great Goddess and became all-powerful through dance. It is hard to explain."

The princess feels small and weak among these perfect, mighty, immortal creatures; and again she shudders at the sharp feeling of injustice. Agabei and she are masters here, and Shogat and Hasan, far more worthy and wise, are slaves.

"Are you happy, Shogat?" she asks.

"Luckily, Agabei saved me from the tortures of the desert. Everyone admires me and I can dance however much I want. How can I possibly be unhappy?"

The sadness in Shogat's voice is unbearable. "I am happy, happy, happy—happy because I cannot be unhappy. Happy at the will of my master."

What about you, Hasan, are you happy…? You are a slave but you are always at the side of someone you love. She is attached to you, but, although you belong to her with your heart and soul, she will never be yours. Never, because you are a slave, a spirit, a djinn.

"I don't want to be a djinn," the princess says. "But more than that I don't want to be your slave, Caliph Agabei."

The glass that covers the dunes cracks, sand breaks loose, and, swept by the wind, flies all around, settling over the writhing crests, covering all in sight. Broken clouds fall apart into tiny grains of sand and fall on the ground like dry rain. A crimson sun rises over the horizon, and the princess sees the temple in the distance, ghostly but unharmed. A beautiful garden surrounds the temple, but the princess hasn't the power to see it.

The sifting sound of dry sand falling on the ground in an endless curtain is broken at times by a disorderly choir of voices coming from a great distance. The princess is trying without much success to catch bits of words as she slowly comes back from her trance, beginning to make out phrases, recognizing distinct voices in the noise around her.

"Praise the gods, she is coming to!" *That sounds like the voice of Nanny Zulfia.*

"Sand! There is sand on her!"

"It must be the wind. Close the window, nanny," another, commanding voice says; and she recognizes, this time without doubt, the voice of her mother. She slowly opens her eyes to see her mother bent over her, and makes out a word spoken clearly as if addressed directly to her: "Princess!"

Does it mean that I have completely come to my senses, if I am being addressed? Does it mean that if I try hard, I may be able to answer?

"Mother..." she whispers, barely audibly, having a hard time forcing her lips to obey her.

"You scared us to death, princess!" She hears in her mother's voice great relief and a less obvious doubt that it is yet time to feel relieved. "You were unconscious for several hours!" the sultaness exclaims. "Prince Amir has sent servants to inquire about your condition three times."

Who is Prince Amir? the princess thinks and reality suddenly comes back to her with a snap.

"Where is Hasan, mother?" she asks, trying to sit up on the bed and feeling very weak from the effort.

"Hasan again, gods forgive!" Zeinab grumbles, and the princess hears the relief in her voice—she grumbles more from habit than from displeasure. "I told you, your majesty. She is always like that. The first thing she asks when she wakes up: 'Where is Hasan?'"

"Let it be, nanny," the sultaness says firmly. "The princess is ill." And, turning to the princess, she adds gently: "Hasan is sitting over there, princess. While you were unconscious he was meditating all the time. Maybe he helped you."

The princess turns her head with difficulty and sees Hasan sitting on a pillow in the corner of the room, his legs crossed, his arms relaxed along his body. His face looks drawn, his hair is covered with sand, but he is smiling at the princess.

"Hasan..." she whispers.

"It is all over, princess. Everything's all right." Hasan smiles at her; and she feels in his voice the secret that connects the two of them as with an invisible bond, a secret to all but themselves.

The princess turns back to her mother.

"Did Caliph Agabei leave, mother?" she asks anxiously.

"Not yet." She can hear the displeasure in her mother's voice. It seems, the princess thinks, that the sultaness must have asked him to leave but was turned down. "We cannot force him to leave," the sultaness continues reluctantly, as if repeating someone else's words. "He is our guest—but we won't let him near you," she adds hurriedly. "Hasan told me everything."

The princess turns to look at Hasan again and meets his gaze that tells her that the secret stays just between the two of them and that the sultaness will never understand it.

"Told you what, mother?" the princess asks.

"Let's talk about it later, when you feel better."

"Tell me now, mother!" the princess insists, not from fear but from curiosity. She knows very well that Hasan told no one of what really happened, and she is curious to know what his version was.

"Very well, princess, I'll tell you," the sultaness agrees with hidden anxiety. "But don't be afraid. Hasan is here, he can protect you from anything."

"I am not afraid, mother." The princess urges, "Tell me."

"Listen, then. Caliph Agabei is a sorcerer. He fell in love with you and was trying to use his magic to make you marry him. And when his magic failed he asked his mighty slave Shogat to help enchant you. All her evil power was in the flower she threw at you. If Hasan had not caught the flower, had you but touched it, you would have fallen in love with the caliph and nothing could have possibly made you feel otherwise."

Well, that version seems to be accurate enough, the princess thinks. Suddenly she remembers something that bothered her all this time, something she doesn't understand herself.

"What about the bracelet?" she asks.

"What bracelet?" The sultaness looks disturbed, and helplessly turns to the nannies.

"This one, mother. The one Hasan gave me." The princess raises her arm with the bracelet still on her wrist, and only now takes a closer look at it. Green, semitransparent stones set in silver form a chain running around her wrist. The princess admires the soft glow of the stones, the color of which, she now sees, is formed by tiny green dots, dispersed throughout the stone.

"She is feeling worse, your majesty. She is talking nonsense again," Zulfia suggests.

"This is not nonsense, your majesty," Hasan interrupts. "I really did give this bracelet to the princess. I just did not have time to tell you."

"Tell me now, Hasan," the sultaness urges him impatiently, studying the unusual piece of jewelry on her daughter's wrist.

"When the princess was walking around the guests and approached the caliph," Hasan explains, "he started to work his magic on her. He wanted to kiss the princess's hand, and if he had touched her she would have been enchanted. To stop him, I pretended I was picking up a bracelet the princess dropped."

"Hasan threw himself between me and the caliph, mother. He did not let the caliph touch me. I did not understand what was happening. Hasan was crawling on the floor so awkwardly—and you should have seen how dismayed the wicked caliph was!"

"Nasty old man!" the sultaness exclaims heartily, looking toward the door with newfound determination. "Listen, princess, I will make the caliph leave sooner. But neither your father, nor Prince Amir, will ever believe such a story. All they know is that you were not feeling well at the feast, do you understand? You are a big girl now, about to get married. It's time for you to learn to deceive men. A little lie and everyone is happy. It's the truth that can sometimes get you into trouble."

The princess looks at her, not daring to believe that she is hearing such words from her mother, and understanding at the same time that the sultaness is trying hard to make her life easier for her. Her entire being resists such a way of dealing with the problem, but she has no energy to discuss it now.

She turns her head again and meets Hasan's eyes, immediately forgetting her everyday problems, enjoying a new feeling of closeness to the djinn—the special feeling of a secret that binds them together.

"I am happy you are feeling better, princess."

"Thank you, Prince Amir."

They are sitting in a gazebo on a low, wide sofa covered with a bright Baskarian rug. A light wind through the ornate window gratings is gently blowing the fine shawl that is wrapped around the princess's shoulders. She is studying Prince Amir through lowered eyelashes: dark handsome face, slim muscular figure, rich elegant clothes—all this seems too good to be real. The princess catches herself at the thought that in studying Prince Amir so closely, she is really just trying to find some fault in his splendid perfection. She calls herself to order. Why should he have any faults? It is only fair that her future husband should seem absolutely perfect to her. *I am going to spend my life with him*, she thinks. *He is so nice and kind to me. I cannot lie to him, whatever mother says.*

"I wasn't ill, prince," she says. "Someone was trying to bewitch me."

"Bewitch?" The prince looks at her in disbelief.

"Caliph Agabei wanted to make me a djinn and take me as a slave. This way he was hoping to get Hasan too, although he already has Shogat...."

"Why would the caliph need you and Hasan when he already has Shogat?" There is sarcasm in the prince's voice that the princess does not want to notice.

"He thought that having three djinn slaves would enable him to conquer the world. Two would have probably been enough, but without me he wouldn't have been able to get Hasan."

"And he wanted to bewitch you to get Hasan?" The prince is barely holding in his laughter.

"Why are you laughing, prince?"

"You are not well, princess. Let me walk you to the palace."

The princess makes a great effort to suppress her rising anger.

"Why don't you believe me, prince?" she asks hotly.

"Caliph Agabei is the closest friend of my father," the prince says. "I have known the caliph since early childhood. He wouldn't hurt a flea, let alone bewitch anybody."

"You did not see how wicked his eyes were when Hasan did not let him approach me!"

"Hasan must have told you a fairy tale and you took it seriously, princess," the prince says patronizingly. "Don't be afraid. No one will try to bewitch you in Veridue and you will never need a djinn to protect you."

"Why do you hate djinns so much, prince?" the princess asks.

"I don't hate djinns at all, princess. I think they are very useful but only when they know their place. There is nothing worse than a slave trying to be too familiar with his master."

"Do you know that djinns are all-powerful?"

"If they were all-powerful, they wouldn't be slaves, princess."

"They are slaves exactly because they are all-powerful," the princess explains hurriedly, hoping to straighten out the misunderstanding. "At one point every djinn was human. And then they come to absolute power and are imprisoned in containers because—"

"Forgive the interruption, princess, but your information is not accurate. It is generally known that djinns or ifrits, as they are sometimes referred to, are a special kind of demon born in a land called Djinnistan. Their powers, by the way, are very limited. As for what Hasan tells you about the djinns, it only serves one purpose: to make the mistress treat her slave better."

"How do you know all this about djinns, prince?" the princess asks with sarcasm.

"From books, princess. From the palace chronicles. I dare to point out that my honorable parents and myself chose the books for my wedding present with a meaning. My noble wife cannot allow herself to be ignorant about djinns."

"I know about djinns from the best possible source, prince!"

"Your source is not impartial, princess. We in Veridue have our own sources of knowledge about djinns. My noble ancestor had a djinn, and it came to no good…. Besides, you now have no need for such a dangerous slave. I will be able to grant your wishes better than anyone else."

Where do I get this feeling of helplessness…? The princess wonders how exactly Prince Amir imagines their life together. *Does he believe that I will always submit to his opinion?*

"Do you want me to give up Hasan?" she asks.

"I am not the tyrant to force you, princess, but I am convinced you will soon understand that a respectable marriage can never go together with childish fantasies."

"How exactly do you see that, prince?" the princess bursts out, unable to hide her feelings anymore. "Do you think I will give Hasan to someone else? Or do you want me to seal him in a bottle and hide him?"

"By no means, princess. A djinn can be very valuable if you use him correctly. With my knowledge of djinns, we could agree to sometimes let him out of the bottle and put his abilities to work for the glory of the kingdom. You look faint, princess. You have barely had a chance to recover from your illness. I do not want to tire you out. Don't a bride and a groom have better things to talk about?"

A lump in the princess's throat makes it hard to continue the argument. Prince Amir is so perfect, so nice, so kind to her. How is it possible that he cannot hear what she is telling him—that which is so important to share with a husband? How can it be that by marrying such a splendid suitor she has to refuse something so dear, so important to her? Should she really have to lie from now on, lie to make everyone happy, as mother tells her to? Or should she make a choice between a lie and a misunderstanding, between unending quarrel and intolerable peace?

The Princess and the Djinn

❁

With a trembling hand the princess opens a book, the title of which runs in golden script across the carved wooden cover: *How to Overcome a Djinn.* She is certain that her disagreement with the prince is a result of some discrepancy in the information he has, and she is ready to take the first step in resolving their misunderstanding.

Sitting in the garden, where slaves have carried the Veriduan books, she is turning the age-yellowed pages of the ancient volume. The princess begins to read:

> The demon was horrible in looks. His legs were like giant masts, his arms like pitchforks, his head swept the clouds like a dome. His mouth was like a cave, his teeth like sharp rocks on the shore, his eyes like lamps, and all his appearance was dark and disgusting. His hollow laugh made the earth shake, and he spoke in a voice that sounded above like the trumpets of doom.
>
> "Beware, O wretched one! Your time has come, for I am going to kill you this very minute in the worst possible way!"
>
> Horrible was the djinn indeed, but the fearless Almansor did not lose his presence of mind.
>
> "Why do you want to kill me, O mighty ifrit? I was the one to release you from the jar, to free you from your imprisonment!"

And the merciless djinn exclaimed:

"Know, O mortal, that you see before you a djinn apostate who was imprisoned in this jar at will of the great prophet Suleiman ibn Daud. Four hundred years have I spent in the jar, and nobody came to set me free. And I swore to give eternal riches to the one who opened the cursed jar. But nobody came. Another four hundred years went by, and I swore to grant any three wishes to my savior. And again nobody came to break the seal of the great Suleiman, and I languished in captivity four hundred years more. And finally, O mortal, I felt great anger in my heart, and I swore the third horrible oath. In the name of the great prophet I swore to kill the one who saved me from this jar in the worst possible way. You freed me, O wretched one, after I was bound by this oath. Prepare to die."

And the fearless Almansor realized that it was useless to enter into an argument with the ungrateful monster. And, being gifted with valor and wisdom, Almansor decided to trick the vile demon. Bowing his head in pretended submissiveness, he said:

"So be it, O mighty ifrit. Like any true believer I respect the oaths sworn in the name of the great prophets of Allah. I accept my destiny."

And the evil djinn exclaimed:

"Indeed, my heart rejoices at the sight of such commendable acceptance!"

Meanwhile, the fearless Almansor went on.

"Allow me, O mighty one, to satisfy my curiosity by asking you just one simple question before I die."

"Speak, and be brief!" the revolting demon roared.

"My mind is confused by one odd thing," Almansor said. "How could you, so huge and mighty, fit into such a tiny jar? For, as Allah is my witness, this jar cannot hold even a little finger on your hand!"

"You don't believe I can fit into this jar?" the ifrit asked threateningly.

"I don't, O mighty one, and I am willing to accept death for this lack of faith!" Almansor answered firmly.

"Look, then, O mortal one!" And the djinn, spinning into a wild whirlwind, turned into a dusty cloud and momentarily drew himself into the narrow mouth of the jar. And at the same second the fearless Almansor closed the jar with the lead stopper bearing the seal of the prophet Suleiman, ignoring the angry wails coming from the ancient container. Thus Almansor overcame the ugly evil djinn, because the perfect human mind is always greater than the vileness and the treachery of the lower demons.

"Do I interrupt, princess? Your nannies told me you were probably reading in the garden."

"Prince Amir?" The princess absently raises her eyes from the book, watching him walk toward her with his light, assured steps. He sits on the bench next to her, elegantly throwing aside his white cloak.

"I was just reading one of the books you gave me."

"My heart rejoices at the sight, princess. You who own a djinn should really know the things that we in Veridue know, alas, from our own bitter experience."

His confident, patronizing tone makes the princess angry against her better judgment.

"Regretfully, prince, the description of djinns in this book is prejudiced and inaccurate, to put it mildly," she says, much more harshly than she intended.

"Please, princess," the prince says peacefully, "let's not begin our fruitless argument again. To my greatest happiness you have had no misfortune to feel upon yourself the bad sides of owning a djinn, and I will try to do everything I can so that you won't have to regret your ignorance. On the other hand, if you care to spend some time learning..."

"What are the bad sides, prince?" she asks.

"I'd rather not talk about it, princess."

The princess frowns, and a thought suddenly crosses her mind that he is unhappy not about the memories of what the djinn did to his family but about her insistent questions. But, once started, she is not going to turn back.

"But to understand you completely, I have to know, prince! So far I cannot find any real facts in these books you gave me."

"These books were created with the wisdom of centuries, princess. Undoubtedly, you can understand it completely only by reading them more carefully."

"Did you read them yourself, prince?" she says with sarcasm that she regrets. But the prince seems not to notice.

"Choosing books for the wedding gift, I looked through all of them," he says matter-of-factly. "Thanks to the great knowledge gathered in our family, I could appreciate them at first sight."

"Tell me about your family's experience, prince. Maybe this story will put an end to our misunderstanding!"

"Very well, princess." The prince gives in, making himself more comfortable on the bench, preparing for a long story. "As I told you before, my noble great-grandfather owned a djinn."

"I also heard that this story has a sad ending, prince. But I don't understand...."

"If you insist on hearing it, princess, I'll tell you. I heard that you got your djinn as an inheritance from your noble grandmother. I also heard that your grandmother had studied magic and understood completely how dangerous her slave was. Therefore, reaching her declining years, she confined the djinn to his bottle."

"Unfortunately, I know little of my grandmother's motives, prince."

"Only the sad experience of our family allows me to be so sure of my words, princess. Alas, my noble ancestor did not possess cryptic knowledge of magic and he never fully realized how dangerous was his mighty slave. For that reason, even when very elderly he continued to use the djinn's powers for his noble needs."

"I still don't understand...."

"Listen, princess. I am certain this story will dispel all your doubts. My noble ancestor did not tolerate traveling very well. Once he had to make a trip to Megina to ask the caliph for the hand of his daughter in marriage to my great-grandfather's only son, the future sultan of Veridue and, as you probably guessed, my noble grandsire. At that time traditions called for very formal marriage arrangements. Mindful of the difficulties of the long trip, my noble ancestor decided to use the djinn to get to Megina by magic. Unfortunately, the evil demon had long planned to arrange the death of his master. Taking my great-grandsire in his arms, the djinn carried him so fast that the heart of the elderly man could not endure the strain. The djinn brought to Megina a lifeless body. The caliph's daughter escorted the body back to Veridue to conduct a royal funeral worthy of the great ruler. The beautiful maiden became the wife of my grandsire, but their union was forever affected by the sad event preceding their marriage."

"This is a sad story indeed, prince," she says thoughtfully, trying to feel more compassion toward Prince Amir's great-grandsire. "But I fail to see the djinn's fault. He was just following his orders. As for the weakness of heart—natural in an elderly man—"

"Your judgment is clouded by the unnatural affection for an unworthy slave, princess!" Angry, the prince rises from the bench and starts pacing back and forth. "As for the djinn that belonged to my noble ancestor, were he even half as wise as you claim a djinn should be, he should have known what a man in his declining years is capable of and what goes beyond his strength!"

"And what happened to the djinn after the death of your great-grandsire?"

"His son, my grandsire, personally sealed the bottle with a holy seal and threw it into the ocean so that the foul monster would never again bother mortals with his evil deeds!"

The princess winces at her utter failure to reach understanding. If, after all they talked about, after all he knows about her, Prince Amir still finds it possible to call the djinns foul monsters, they can never come to an agreement! Feeling anger rise in her, the princess allows herself another bit of sarcasm.

"Could that be the very same djinn the fearless Almansor found in this book here?"

The prince stops his pacing and looks at the princess with cool dignity.

"I am sorry, princess, that you can mock the sacred story this way. This book contains ancient wisdom that I am sure you will someday understand."

The princess suddenly feels ashamed of herself. After all, he has just told her a sad story about his family, and she never showed any compassion, if only out of politeness. She feels the need to smooth down their argument, to salve the stings and forgive their misunderstandings.

"Forgive me, prince," she says with genuine regret. "I never wanted to mock anything. I am really sorry about your noble ancestor."

She looks up at him and to her amazement sees again an expression of patronizing confidence on his face. She feels another rush of anger, and finishes her sentence with unnecessary sharpness: "But I still think that the role of the djinn in his death is somewhat exaggerated."

"Let's leave it be, princess." The prince waves the conversation aside with his usual winning smile. "I hope that you will gradually get rid of your prejudice, and then you will undoubtedly understand how right I am."

The princess feels strangely awkward. Was she really less than fair in her quick-tempered judgment? Really, a wise and all-powerful djinn could not possibly be ignorant about the limited abilities of an old man. Maybe Prince Amir's ancestor was so cruel to his djinn that the djinn did not care about his master's well-being and in the swift flight never bothered to account for his master's old age? Alas, this mystery is hidden in the depths of the ocean for ages to come. The princess's heart sinks at the thought of the terrible destiny of all-powerful slaves, whose wickedness she simply can't accept. At the same time, she feels unexpected compassion for Prince Amir, who seems to be so sure of knowing right from wrong, and who tries so hard to win the trust of his bride, patiently tolerating her willfulness. But can she possibly put up with the role of obedient wife when so many things with which she is being forced to agree are so obviously absurd, like the story of the fearless Almansor?

Someone calls out to her in a dark passage.

"Is that you, princess?"

"Who is it?" the princess asks, slowing her angry stride and straining her eyes to see the figure that approaches her in the darkness.

"It is I, Selim, the captain of the guard."

"Hello, Selim." She stops and relaxes a bit. She remembers Hasan's stories about playing chess with Selim while gossiping about the inhabitants of the palace, and a smile lights her face, scaring away her anger at Prince Amir.

"Have you seen Hasan, princess?" Selim asks anxiously, his mustache standing on end with excitement.

"No, I haven't." *Why would he be looking for Hasan in this dark passage?* "Is anything the matter?" she asks.

"Well, princess..." Selim falters. "We made a bet."

"A bet?"

"We were playing chess this morning and I, well, I said something about our guards being the best in the world, and Hasan started to laugh at me and, well, we made this bet."

"What bet, Selim?" the princess asks impatiently, feeling irritated again. *I don't have all day to stand in this dark passage and talk to the captain of the guard. I am not as good-natured as Hasan!*

"Hasan said that he can enter the palace without any magic and go as far as your quarters, and none of my guards will catch him. By gods, this is really too much, even for Hasan!"

"I can tell you one thing, Selim." The princess smiles, starting to walk away. "If Hasan says he can enter the palace without being caught, he can."

"We'll see about that, princess!" Selim hurriedly walks past her, disappearing around a bend in the corridor.

One of the doors in the passage leads into the library. This refuge fits her mood perfectly. Here she can stay in quietude by herself, without the constant noisy fussing of her nannies. Here she can choose any book or any scroll she wants and read it until dark, curled in a cozy armchair.

She barely has time to close the heavy door behind her when the brass knob turns again and somebody slips inside the library after her.

"Hasan!" the princess exclaims softly.

Winking, Hasan puts a finger against his lips and presses his back flat against the wall beside the door. They can hear voices and the tramping of feet coming down the passage.

"I think he went over there!"

"Are you sure it was Hasan?"

"Who else would sneak along the dark passage in broad daylight?"

"Look, the library door is slightly open! He must be in there!"

"Get back!" Selim yells from behind. "I just saw the princess herself walk into the library. Don't disturb her highness reading, you idiots."

"Yes, captain, sir!"

"Let's go to the stairs. He must be here somewhere!"

Holding still, the princess and Hasan listen as the voices and footsteps fade into the distance.

"We made a bet," Hasan explains.

"I know—Selim told me." The princess smiles.

After the strain of the past few days she feels surprisingly easy and peaceful. Suddenly she realizes that standing beside her now is the only true friend she has ever had, a friend to whom she can talk about anything and who understands her probably better than she understands herself. All her anger at Prince Amir, all her frustration with their fruitless argument, all the noisy feasts and strange guests bearing presentiments of a new life that scares her—all seem unreal next to Hasan, so familiar and comfortable, so close to her that she feels his light breath on her cheek and enjoys his usual, barely perceptible juniper scent.

The princess feels a strange inner freedom. She shakes off the bonds of etiquette, duty, and habit...that which she does not dare to dream of, now seems real and close...the most natural thing in the world. She gently touches Hasan's face with her fingertips. She runs her hand down his face, his muscular neck, feeling for the first time the smoothness of his skin that burns her fingers with pulsing energy emanating from him and flowing through her slender fingers into her veins. She trembles, giving in to a feeling she has never let loose before. She draws him closer, running her hands through his thick, unruly hair, pulling him toward her, clinging to him with every part of her shivering body. She lets out a slight moan as she feels his hands, sure and strong, move up her back, catch her in their grasp, and hold her in an embrace that captures every part of her being in an infinitely sweet bond.

She feels his lips touch her hair, her brow, her eyelids with a mixture of passion and tenderness, as if holding back, afraid to hurt her with the strength of his desire. In turn, she is kissing everything she can reach, his sweet-smelling skin, his neck, his chin—until their lips finally meet and become one.

After what seems like an eternity—an eternity in a single moment of overwhelming passion that she never wants to end—she feels him gently release his grasp on her to the point that she, filled to the brim with blissful weakness, completely unable to command her body, draws away from him just enough to look into his eyes.

He is looking at her with tenderness and passion, such passion that her heart almost stops with excitement. And yet there is sadness beneath his passion, eternal sadness that she, in this moment of happiness, cannot understand.

"Hasan," she whispers, unable to hold back her overflowing wild hope. "Hasan, I wish for you to become a prince."

She is ready to close her eyes so that she can open them again to see Hasan in the place of Prince Amir—a splendid suitor, a noble prince. She is so close to him now that she can feel with her whole being his desire for her wish to come true—his wild desire, no less than hers. But his eyes answer her before words, as hope falls down like a stone and she tries in desperation to prolong, however little, this moment of enchantment, this beautiful moment that will never come again.

"Alas, princess." Hasan draws away from her. He lowers his head, having no strength to meet her desperate eyes. "At your will I can do anything. I am all-powerful. But that which I wish for most in the world, I cannot do, even for you, because, alas, it goes beyond my power. I cannot become a man. I have to forever remain a djinn and a slave."

As these cruel words sink slowly into her mind, losing the strength to resist a new overflow of weakness and ecstasy, she drops into his arms, clinging to him as if he were the only hope in this world. United in this embrace, they stand together in the dimness of the giant library—infinitely close, infinitely far—the princess and the djinn, the mistress and the slave. For this one time they give in to their desires, as they bid farewell to dreams that will never come true.

THE SEVEN STEPS

✤

*T*he night surrounds you. You are walking in the desert to a temple that you can never find in the dark. You don't really need to find it because you know: there is nothing for you in this temple. For the first time in your life you have to make your own choice. For the first time you have to question a decision that has been made for you. Sandy dunes roll and flare, pouring their countless grains on the scales of a balance. You have to walk the path chosen for you because you have already gone too far to turn back.

Poor is a traveler who walks most of his chosen way, then suddenly decides to turn off to explore some other unknown path. Such a traveler soon becomes a wanderer without a home or kin, dragging his miserable life before the mercy of people's kindness. And, to leave the comparisons alone, this desert isn't a dream anymore, is it?

You realize completely what is happening. On one side of the scale lies a respectable normal way. You were born a princess, a sultan's daughter, a rare beauty; you were brought up in decency, and your duty to your parents and your people lies in a proper marriage to a noble prince, a future monarch able to protect his subjects from misfortune. You were born to accept your lot, and your wishes have nothing to do with it. By the way, you were never against such a fate. What could be better than a decent marriage approved by your parents and blessed with children born to carry on in the same way?

What do you put on the other side of the balance? Summits and abysses, rising and falling, a chance to share your destiny with your loved one; but what would this destiny be? The burden of absolute knowledge, rebirth as a djinn, endless torture in a desert you know nothing about, serving Caliph Agabei or another unknown master—a chance to be slaves together at best? And, at worst, losing him forever to an unexpected turn of events or by the will of your cruel master? Alas, the answer seems obvious once you take everything into consideration. If you get married, if you walk the path chosen for you, if you do your duty, you will at least keep whatever you have now. After all, a little lie is a small price to pay for not having to make a terrible choice. Hasan will remain your carefree friend—your own personal djinn. True, you may see him less, but the alternative is intolerable. You cannot rush after Shogat and Agabei; you cannot accept the offer you have so proudly rejected before. You cannot, however much you may want it. You cannot regret what you did, either. There, in the glass desert, you made the right choice and Hasan approved of it. As for the madness that possessed the two of you in the library, *that* was never meant to be. Forget your childish fantasies, as Prince Amir properly says, and look reality in the face.

The palace plaza is flooded with people all the way up to the al-Gulsulim mosque. A special platform has been built in front of the palace balcony from where the princess chose her suitor only a few weeks before. Steps lead to the platform from the arched gateway of the palace. On this platform, in front of all the people of Dhagabad, the sultan himself will perform the wedding of his only daughter and her chosen groom, Prince Amir of Veridue.

The inhabitants of the palace are standing in groups at the base of the platform, separated from the crowd by a double row of guards. The nearest group consists of the sages and the members of the State Council; a little further back stands a group of free servants and all the way back, by the first step leading to the platform, crowd the slaves. Not a single woman can be found among them. All the slave women, nannies, wives and daughters of the courtiers, and even the sultaness herself, have stayed near the princess's chambers since early morning. Many are helping to dress the princess in her wedding gown; all of them, by tradition, are bidding farewell to their ward and mistress. Even though after the wedding she will not leave Dhagabad at once, she will already be considered the property of Veridue and her husband. When she walks out of the palace today, she will never return to it the same.

Tired of the seemingly endless preparations, the princess is standing in front of a huge mirror, allowing her nannies to clothe her with more and more pieces of her magnificent gown. She isn't tortured by doubts anymore, and this absence of doubt itself leaves a strange emptiness in her. Remembering the last days before the wedding, she cannot find anything worth thinking about: constant preparations and fittings; frequent talks with Prince Amir under the watchful eyes of the nannies; the inexhaustible eloquence of her future husband on the subjects of weather, military tournaments, and, naturally, the princess's numerous virtues—with no mention whatsoever of djinns or of their disagreements; attempts to convince herself that all this is exactly what she wants; and a total failure to imagine what her life will be like away from these walls, from the beloved faces, among new people and new duties.

During these days she has not seen Hasan alone and hasn't exchanged more than a couple of words with him. There is no place for a djinn in her new, splendid, and predestined life. Feeling very fatigued, the princess automatically answers the wives and daughters of the courtiers who are making polite conversation all around her.

"Prince Amir is so handsome," Alamid says beside her with a feeling going slightly beyond regular politeness. The princess gives her an absentminded smile.

"The princess is just afraid of getting married, your majesty,"

Nimeth whispers behind her. "Remember how restless you were yourself." Nimeth's slim hand gently pats the princess on the shoulder.

"All girls are sad before their wedding," old Nanny Zeinab agrees. "You just wait and see, your majesty. No later than tomorrow our beauty will see there is nothing to fear and will start singing like a sweet little bird again. Prince Amir is so gentle, he would never hurt her."

"It is very fortunate to have such a nice and kind groom, your highness," the wife of the grand vizier, a majestic woman in her forties with large features and a slight mustache, says to the princess. "Prince Amir will treat you well."

"Raise your arms, princess," says Zulbagad, the seamstress who has naturally designed and supervised the making of the princess's wedding outfit and is now personally overseeing the dressing of the princess.

A warm breath of the finest silk slides down her skin as the golden threads woven into the cloth make her shoulders tingle slightly. The princess glances at the mirror. Two slave girls are carefully covering her long hair with a delicate shiny net, the threads embellished with Veriduan pearls. This strange headgear lies unusually heavily on her back, crumpling the airy silk of her gown. Two other slave girls carry to the mirror a long translucent shawl as Zulbagad carefully straightens out the tiniest folds of the cloth.

"I think we can signal the beginning of the ceremony, your majesty," she says.

"Can I see Hasan, mother?" the princess asks.

"Hasan is already waiting for you outside, princess. As soon as you walk out of the palace, you will see him."

Sighing, the princess submits. Nothing can be changed, anyway. While Zulbagad herself places the shawl over her head, carefully tucking it under a shiny golden diadem, the slave girls bring in the veil that will cover her face—to be removed later by the hand of her new husband. The princess turns her thoughts to the palace plaza.

Fanfare is heard on the plaza and the herald announces:

"The great sultan Chamar Ali greets his subjects!"

The crowd cheers: "May he live forever!" as the sultan appears on the balcony, supported by the grand vizier on his right and the sage Haib al-Mutassim on his left. He steps over the low banister onto the platform, taking his appointed place for the ceremony. Two Ghullian slaves set a tall golden stand in front of the sultan, and two elder sages of the State Council bring out the Holy Book and pass it to the grand vizier. The vizier solemnly bows to the sultan and sets the book on the golden stand. The sages, bowing, take their places behind the sultan.

After the excitement of the sultan's appearance dies down, fanfare again is heard.

"Prince Amir of Veridue, the chosen groom of the princess of Dhagabad!"

Again the plaza is filled with cheers of greeting while Prince Amir, surrounded by his suite, appears on the balcony, easily steps over the banister onto the platform, bows to the sultan, and after exchanging some words with him takes his place to the right of the Holy Book.

Almost immediately, the sound of fanfare is heard a third time, and the gates under the palace arch swing open as the herald announces:

"The princess of Dhagabad!"

A dark-blue carpet with a golden pattern unrolls, leading the way from the palace gate to the steps up to the platform. Six slave girls, in time with the smooth rhythm of their walk, are throwing white jasmine petals on the carpet, spreading its sweet aroma all around.

Resembling a cloud in her white gown, the princess walks slowly from under the palace arch, as a long procession of women follows in her wake. All of the women's faces are covered, and even the sultaness walking beside the princess has a light white scarf lowered over her face.

As the women approach the platform, the slaves, standing at

the first step, bow their heads. The princess sees Hasan among them.

Her heart jumps out of her breast. How could they! How *dare* they put him down here when his place is at her side, first in the suite of the princess of Dhagabad! But another voice inside her softly whispers: *he is really a slave—where else to put him if not among the slaves?* The princess slows; Hasan raises his head and gives her a gentle, encouraging smile.

For the first time in days the princess feels something come alive inside her. She wants to stop, to say just a few words to him, but Hasan bows his head again and the sultaness gently pushes her forward with a firm hand.

The choice is made. The princess turns her back to the slaves and sets her foot on the first step leading up to the platform.

The cheers grow louder as the princess, walking to the foot of the stairs, becomes visible to the whole plaza. Seven steps separate her from the platform. The princess invests all her thoughts and feelings into the solemn ascent. Blood begins to pound in her temples to the torturing rhythm of her walk.

Step...

Why are you going there? You cannot betray these people: your mother and father, courtiers, slaves, citizens of Dhagabad who have worshipped you all your life as their mistress and prepared you for this day almost since your birth...

Step...

Time slows down as in a dream, her movements are smooth and unreal, noises move to the background giving way to the sound of the blood in her temples, to the waves of thoughts behind the veil...

Step...

Even if you turned back now, it wouldn't work. He does not need you—a naive, silly girl who doesn't know a thing about life. He needs a woman whose wisdom goes back countless centuries, a woman like Zobeide or Shogat, exquisite in her knowledge, capable of sharing her power with him. What can you possibly give him...?

Step…

The folds of your white gown rise and fall in a dreamlike motion, soft against your skin. You made this decision long ago, you know what you must do, and nothing can possibly change that…

Step…

There, ahead, destiny awaits in shining magnificence—Prince Amir, her chosen groom, her husband. She feels an aching desire to finally entrust herself to his reliable hands, to lay down her burden of doubt and choice. The decision is made.

Step…

There, behind her among the slaves, stands Hasan; and now, by taking just one step, she will lose him forever.

The princess stops.

A whisper passes through the crowd. The courtiers and the servants exchange glances as the sultaness hisses, pushing the princess forward.

Turning to the crowd, the princess raises her hand and tears the thin white veil from her face. Then, turning back, she collects her fluffy white gown around her and runs back down the wide stairs.

Scared to death, the slaves bow low before the princess. Only Hasan, held by her gaze, remains still.

"Hasan!" says the princess, and the ringing sound of her voice easily spreads over the motionless crowd. "Give me your bracelet!"

"I cannot take it off, princess," Hasan says, helplessly looking at his iron-clad wrists.

"You must do what I command, Hasan!"

The princess holds out her hand in an imperious gesture.

A sharp *crack!* is heard easily in the dead silence of the plaza. The band of iron on Hasan's right wrist cracks, and the bracelet slips into his open palm. Feeling completely lost, perhaps for the first time in a thousand years, Hasan gives her his bracelet. The princess, climbing back onto the stairs above the crowd, lifts up her hands.

"Listen, people of Dhagabad!" The motionless crowd catches her every word. "I am not your princess anymore! My name is Chamarat Gul' Agdar!

"I love my slave, Hasan, but I cannot free him from his slavery. Therefore I am becoming a slave myself!"

Holding her hands high above her head she slips the bracelet onto her wrist.

The palace, the mosque, the plaza, the crowd that was motionless only moments ago seethes forward shouting and presses against the ghostly chain of guards around you…. You see endless dunes, red fiery sun; you wait in terror for that moment when, pressed by the narrow walls of your prison, you will be pierced by a blast of sandy wind…. The horrible pain, asleep inside you for such a long time, echoes in shivers through your mighty, tortured body…. As you await your torturous fate, you feel that something inside you has changed, or maybe it is the desert that has changed around you, and you will never be able to submit to your destiny as before. The contours of your imprisonment are now broken at the will of she who is most dear to you and yet unattainable. She, knowing nothing about absolute power or eternity, with a holy recklessness wishes to share your destiny, accepting upon herself your curse. And you, forgetting the pain of the intolerable heat, the deadly sands, and eternal imprisonment, are ready to face any curse, any torture to save her—so beautiful and defenseless—from the same destiny. You throw yourself toward the fiery beams, the merciless needles of sand, and with all the force of a powerful blast, hit the invisible wall.

The metal bracelet on your other wrist shatters with a sound like breaking glass and falls into a thousand pieces—falls like rain on the ground all around you—joining with the remains of the other bracelet which fell off and broke, being much too big for her slender wrist.... Then you turn your head and meet her eyes, feeling a great power flow into you, a power you have never felt before, as you gradually come to realize that the ancient curse has blown away like a cloud of smoke and that never again will you be a djinn and a slave. You bow before her power—a force that tore through your ancient irons like a knife through silk thread. Now you smile, looking into her sapphire-blue eyes.

✿

"Are you free, Hasan?" the princess asks softly.

"I am free, princess," Hasan answers. "But I will forever belong to you."

The sultaness hurries down the stairs toward them, fighting her way through the chaos.

"What have you done, princess?" she demands.

"Can't you see—Hasan is free, mother!" The princess is smiling and tears tremble on her eyelashes. "And I will *never* part with him. Can you become a prince now, Hasan?"

Hasan turns to the sultaness. His eyes shine with such happiness that she feels her heart stand still. And, wiping away her tears with the end of her white scarf, she embraces the princess, holding her close.

"You will answer for this insult!" Prince Amir suddenly appears before them. His eyes are wild with anger, as his suite unceremoniously clears a space around him with their sheathed sabers. "You are not even worthy to be a slave girl in the Veriduan palace, princess! You will never, I repeat, never receive the forgiveness of Prince Amir!"

"Prince—" the sultaness begins.

"Don't interrupt me, your majesty! If you think I'll marry your stubborn daughter after what happened today, you are mistaken! Today she has dishonored Dhagabad itself!" Turning sharply away, he pushes his way through the rapidly parting crowd as his white and gold cloak flaps on his shoulders.

The roar of the crowd gradually shapes itself into a ceremonial greeting:

"Hail, Hasan, the chosen groom of Chamarat Gul' Agdar, the princess of Dhagabad!"

The princess and Hasan do not hear these words. Holding hands on the palace plaza, the noise, the shouting, and the arms of friends and servants embracing them cannot reach them.

You walk together in the desert, away from the temple that holds nothing for you. You tread lightly on the sand as the secret garden gradually reveals all of its beauty to your eyes. Never again will the fiery beams, the piercing sands, and merciless wind be able to harm you, Hasan. Never again, princess, will you rush about in despair at the base of the temple, unable to enter. From this day forth this desert will be a garden to you because together you are stronger than any force....

Acknowledgments

I would like to thank Poul and Karen Anderson for their support and help. I am also grateful to Fran Collin who spent time working with me and to Sarah Piel of Arthur Pine Associates for her encouragement and advice. I would like to thank Gary Konas for his help on earlier versions of this book. I am thankful to my friends for their advice and supportive comments that helped me through my most difficult times, especially to Roald Hoffmann and Dana Rashid. I am very grateful to my family for being there for me, and for both encouraging and challenging me to go on. I would also like to thank my publisher and editor Paul Williams of Herodias for putting his time and faith into my book and for all his wonderful work that made this publication possible.

A Note on the Type

The text was set in 12 point Adobe Caslon with a leading of 14 points space. The italic text has a leading of 16 points. William Caslon released his first typefaces in 1722. Caslon's types were based on seventeenth-century Dutch old style designs, which were then used extensively in England. Because of their incredible practicality Caslon's designs met with instant succes. Caslon's types became popular throughout Europe and the American colonies; printer Benjamin Franklin hardly used any other typeface. The first printings of the American Declaration of Independence and the Constitution were set in Caslon. For her Adobe Caslon, designer Carol Twombly studied specimen pages printed by William Caslon between 1734 and 1770.

The text and jacket display font is AT Pelican. Pelican was designed by Arthur Baker and released by Agfa Compugraphic in 1989. Pelican is a calligraphic typeface that is distinguished by the irregular shapes of the lowercase letters. The rough-edged quality of Pelican gives it an exotic flavor and makes it a good choice for informal display work. Pelican is a trademark of AlphaOmega Typography.

Composed by Patty Harris
New York, New York

Printed and bound by
Haddon Craftsmen